She looked up as Cooper approached her. . . .

"Cold?" he said, handing her a glass of white wine, then sitting down next to her on the bearskin rug.

"A little. This is better," she said, indicating the fire. "And now you're here."

She saw a quick little light of pleasure flare in those blue eyes. Keeping her gaze on him, she raised her glass of wine into the air. She might not be able to tell him this was her first time, but she wanted to toast tonight. She knew what she was giving up, and she was doing this of her own free will. She'd waited long enough, and somehow this just felt right.

Right time, right moment—and the right man.

Alyssa didn't want to live in her little ivory tower anymore. . . . Something had happened tonight when she'd danced, and she found she wanted to experience a lot more of life than she had thus far.

"To tonight," she whispered to Cooper. "To a night that, hopefully, will exceed both our wildest expectations."

He touched the rim of his glass against hers. "I'm sure it will."

# The Dare

## Elda Minger

BERKLEY SENSATION, NEW YORK

This is a work of fiction. Names, characters, places, and incidents either are the product of the author's imagination or are used fictitiously, and any resemblance to actual persons, living or dead, business establishments, events, or locales is entirely coincidental.

THE DARE

A Berkley Sensation Book / published by arrangement with the author

PRINTING HISTORY
Berkley Sensation edition / October 2003

Copyright © 2003 by Elda Minger
Cover design by George Long
Text design by Julie Rogers

ISBN: 0-425-19276-8

A BERKLEY SENSATION™ BOOK
Berkley Sensation Books are published by The Berkley Publishing Group,
a division of Penguin Group (USA) Inc.,
375 Hudson Street, New York, New York 10014.
BERKLEY SENSATION and the "B" design
are trademarks belonging to Penguin Group (USA) Inc.

PRINTED IN THE UNITED STATES OF AMERICA

10  9  8  7  6  5  4  3  2

*To my dear friend and spiritual sister, Terri Far-rell. You make me laugh harder than anyone else I know, and bring joy wherever you go. You're also a brilliant person to brainstorm a plot with; your feedback is emotionally sound and often hilarious! Thank you for giving my hero his distinctive tattoo and his parrot a voice.*

*Terri, I am blessed to have you in my life.*

# Chapter One

"You've got to be out of your mind!" Alyssa Preston stared at her best friend, Mindy, and wondered if the crazy scheme she'd just heard had really come out of her best friend's mouth, or if she'd simply hallucinated the words.

"Please, Lys, please! You're the only person I could ask to do this—"

"Wait a minute." Alyssa stood up, then paced the confines of her friend's large, feminine bedroom. "It's the night before your wedding to Tom, and you want me to go to his bachelor party, crash it—*inconspicuously,* of course—and make sure he's not making whoopee with one of the strippers?"

Mindy nodded her head, her chin-length brunette hair swinging gently against her delicate jaw. "That about covers it."

"This is insane! What this really means is that you're

actually considering marrying a man tomorrow afternoon who you don't trust!"

"No," Mindy said, sitting back on her bed, propped up with a profusion of ruffled, shell-pink pillows. "What it means is that I know Tom's a man."

"Oh, what's that supposed to mean?"

"You know that old joke, the one about the brain and the penis sharing one single blood supply—"

Alyssa had to laugh. "Right! And when the blood goes to the little head—"

"The big head can't think straight."

Alyssa walked to the window and stared outside. Oak trees devoid of their leaves this mid-December evening adorned the suburban streets of Wilmette, Illinois, outside Chicago. Multicolored Christmas lights twinkled on the two-story house across the street. She'd flown in late from San Francisco, just missing the rehearsal dinner earlier this evening, but in plenty of time to be in the actual wedding. Tomorrow was the big day, at precisely one in the afternoon. And she was maid of honor.

Alyssa had attended boarding school in Switzerland with Mindy, and Mindy had been as shy and terrified as Alyssa had been outgoing and adventurous. As roommates, they'd navigated their years away from home and become fast friends in the process. Now, on the evening that should've been one of the happiest moments in Mindy's life, she was terrified her husband-to-be would be tempted to cheat on her.

Alyssa sat down in the window seat and massaged her temples with her fingertips. She was starting to get a headache, and that was a bad sign. She hated conflict.

"Run this whole thing by me again," she said.

Mindy sat up straighter. "Okay. Tom knows you're

going to be in the wedding tomorrow, but he's never met you, so he won't recognize you. We can also fix you up some kind of disguise, a wig or something, you know? I found out where the party is tonight. It's only a few blocks from here, at Cooper's house. He's Tom's best man. You could run over there and come right back as soon as you were sure—"

"That no hanky-panky's going on."

"Right." Mindy took a deep breath. "You're a dancer, so if you had to get up on a table or something and pretend you were a—"

"Stripper," Alyssa finished for her.

"A . . . a dancer, you could pull the deception off."

Silence filled the bedroom. Alyssa couldn't believe she was actually considering doing this, but Mindy had pulled out all the stops, including crying, and she couldn't stand to see her best friend cry. It was tantamount to shooting Bambi at point-blank range with an assault weapon.

"And," Mindy said, "you wrote me about that dance recital where your whole troupe wore nothing but electric-blue body paint, so it isn't as if—"

"I'm overly modest," Alyssa finished for her. She got up and approached the canopy-covered bed, then sat down next to her dearest friend in the world. "But you realize what you're asking me to do, don't you?"

"What?" Mindy's clear gray eyes were totally serious.

"If I find Tom having . . . making . . . making whoopee with one of the girls, do you want me to tell you? And if I tell you, are you going to call off the entire wedding?"

No expense had been spared in putting together the elaborate wedding. Mindy's father and mother could afford it, and Alyssa knew that five hundred guests were set to arrive at church tomorrow to see the youngest child—

and only girl—in the Bickham family tie the knot just before Christmas.

The elegant flowers, the designer wedding dress, the sit-down dinner afterward, the enormous cake, the country club reception—when she thought about the planning and expense that had gone into this wedding, it boggled the mind.

"Well?" Alyssa pressed. "Would you call it off?"

"Yes. Yes, I would! I would call it off! Because if I couldn't trust Tom this evening, how could I build a marriage on such a fragile foundation?"

"Good point. I suppose it's different for a bachelor—"

"Well, sure! But anyone who's already committed and goes off with the . . . with the . . . *entertainment,* that's just too low for words!"

Alyssa could feel herself weakening. "I'm gong to regret this." She took a deep breath. "Oh, let me see Tom's picture again."

Mindy threw her arms around her. "I *knew* I could count on you!"

Late that evening, Alyssa walked briskly along the suburban sidewalk, hoping she wasn't drawing that many stares. She wore thigh-high black boots, borrowed from Mindy, along with a black trench coat and a black scarf over her head. On that head, she wore a black wig, the style short and bobbed, courtesy again of Mindy. It was the total opposite of her wavy, below-the-shoulder-length blonde hair. The last thing Alyssa wanted was for Tom to recognize her as he was standing at the altar tomorrow afternoon with his bride.

It wasn't every day that your maid of honor was also a spy.

She'd put on a little more makeup than usual, sultry black kohl eyeliner and shiny red lipstick. "I'm going for that Cleopatra thing and hoping I don't end up looking like Morticia Addams," she'd told Mindy. Her friend had helped her get ready and then sneak out onto the roof and down the trellis on the side of the house, a route she and her four brothers had taken many times in their childhood.

Simply waltzing out the front door was out of the question, because the house had been filled with relatives and friends from out of town, talking and laughing and toasting the event to come the following day. But as Alyssa had left the brightly lit house, lights shining from every window, laughter in every room, she wondered if what she was about to do was going to finish off this celebration once and for all.

Yet she could see Mindy's point. Why marry a man who was going to be unfaithful to you the night before your wedding? Why marry a man who didn't love you and want you enough to be satisfied by only you?

Tough questions, and now she was going to get her friend some tough answers.

It wasn't all that cold for a December night in the Midwest, very unusual weather for this time of year. There wasn't even any snow on the ground. Mindy had told her they were between storms. The ground looked dull and brown, the trees naked, their branches stark and black.

Alyssa pulled the scrap of paper out of the pocket of her black trench coat and studied the hastily scrawled map that Mindy had drawn her. She took a deep breath, squared her shoulders, and started north, toward Cooper Sinclair's house, or "Coop's Den of Iniquity," as the invite had stated.

\* \* \*

It wasn't that hard to find Cooper's house.

The first tip-off was all the cars parked in the circular drive.

The second indication was the sensual music floating out into the night, with a strong, sexy beat. That, and the sound of masculine laughter.

And the third, and final tip-off was the small group of women huddled to the side of the house, furiously arguing.

Alyssa decided to jump right in.

"Hey, you guys here for the party?"

The three women turned and stared at her. They seemed uncertain, almost afraid.

"What's wrong?" Alyssa said, moving closer.

A beautiful blonde with long, thick hair and a stunning figure that couldn't be disguised by the winter coat she was wearing said, "One of our girls couldn't make it. She got food poisoning from a taco. Tony's Taco Joint. I told Bambi not to stop, but oh no, she had to have a taco."

"With extra hot sauce," said another girl, a brunette.

A redhead chimed in. "Yeah, and we think the guy who hired us is going to mind. He insisted on four girls."

"What do you have to do?" Alyssa said, thinking that she might as well be aware of what she was getting into. She wanted to know just how far these girls were willing to go.

"Oh, it's simple. We just strip down to our underwear, keep it as tame as a Victoria's Secret catalog. All fantasy stuff, you know? But classy. Then we fuss over the groom a little bit, but nothing too raunchy, just a few kisses. But the guy who hired us wanted some really sexy dancing. And I guess you could call it a striptease, but the old-fashioned kind."

"Hmmm." Alyssa considered this. "Nothing kinky, like two girls going at it?"

"Nope. The guy who hired us was real clear that the groom really loves his bride. As he said, nothing too raunchy."

"Hmmm." For a moment, Alyssa considered just walking on home, but she knew Mindy would still be unsure.

"I can help you guys out," she finally said.

"What?" said the redhead. She had soft, auburn curls and a very sweet face.

"What was your friend's name again?" Alyssa said. "The one who couldn't make it."

"Bambi," said the blonde.

Alyssa held out her hand. "My name's Alyssa, but just call me Bambi."

"What?" The third girl, with her dark brown hair and dramatic eye makeup, stared at her. "What are you talking about?"

"Hey, you need a fourth girl, you need Bambi, and I need to get in there and party with those guys."

"Why?" The blonde stared at her suspiciously. "What the hell are you up to?"

Briefly, Alyssa explained her relationship to the bride and what Mindy had asked her to do.

"Really?" said the blonde, who had introduced herself as Kiki. "You think this Tom guy thinks we're going to do that kind of stuff? You know, we're from Rico's Fantasy Dancers, and we have a reputation to uphold!"

"I don't think Tom does," said Alyssa, deciding to omit the fact that she'd never even met the groom. "To tell you the truth, I think my friend is just a tad paranoid. Her first fiancé cheated on her right after he proposed. She found him at his apartment in bed with an old girlfriend, the headboard banging away, the whole thing."

"Bastard," Kiki muttered.

"Jerk," said Brooke, the redhead.

"She's better off without him," said the brunette, who introduced herself as Nina.

"My thoughts exactly," said Alyssa. "I'm really just doing this to humor her, you know? But I've got to get inside."

"You dance?" Kiki said.

"I do it all—classical, ballet, tap—I have a dance troupe in San Francisco called Emotion in Motion. We've even performed in nothing but blue body paint."

"Artsy stuff?" said Brooke, clearly suspicious.

"Any sexy stuff?" said Kiki hopefully.

Deciding to go for broke, Alyssa swept her trench coat off, snapped her fingers, then began to sway to the beat coming from Cooper's house behind them.

"Wow, those are great moves," Nina said. She glanced at Kiki. "C'mon Kiki, this would save our butts. You know it."

"I say we let her come with us," said Brooke. "Rico never has to know."

"Fine with me," Kiki said. She eyed Alyssa one last time. "Just stick close to me, and let me know if any of those guys tries anything funny."

It was so much easier than she'd expected.

She slipped right in the door behind Kiki, Brooke, and Nina. Tom was easy to spot, in the main chair in the family room. She also noticed that an enormous, heavy square coffee table in the midst of comfortable chairs and a sofa, had been cleared of everything and gleamed like a little ministage.

Alyssa followed Kiki's lead and flung her black trench coat over the side of the couch along with the other girls' winter garments.

*My first bachelor party. This should be interesting.*

She'd thought they would start dancing right away, but instead they were offered drinks and given introductions, but everyone offered first names only. Again, she followed Kiki's lead and introduced herself as Bambi. And she asked for a soda as opposed to anything alcoholic.

They were also offered beautiful, glittery domino masks with feathery plumes, and Alyssa realized this bachelor party actually had a theme: Mardi Gras. Gold coins and colorful plastic beads were scattered around the room between bowls of chips and dip and trays of sandwiches. The large sheet cake decorated with an edible cookie tombstone and the words "R.I.P. Tom" and "Another Man Bites the Dust" written in icing sparkled with colored sugar in golds, greens, and purples.

Alyssa took her mask and put it on. And in the strangest way, it made her feel almost invisible; as if she could watch everything without being seen.

There were about twenty-five men there, all in their early to mid-thirties. Alyssa could almost feel the testosterone sizzling through the family room.

"I don't see the guy who hired us," Kiki whispered to Nina, as Alyssa stayed close and merely listened.

"Maybe he decided not to come," Nina whispered back.

"Hmmm." Kiki considered this, then said, "Why don't you two get up on the coffee table and get the dancing started?"

As if on cue, the stereo system began to thump out the opening bars to The Rolling Stones' classic song, "Brown Sugar." Keith Richards's nasty guitar licks filled the room. If there was ever a song that seemed to be created especially for some dirty dancing, this one was it.

"Great," Alyssa said, and she and Nina made their way through the sea of male bodies and admiring eyes toward that large, gleaming coffee table. Alyssa had been keeping her eye on Tom, and she had a feeling he'd already had quite a bit to drink.

He wouldn't be doing anything amorous tonight.

One of the men offered her a hand up onto the coffee table, and she took it, gracing him with her sweetest smile. Then she began to sway to the music, her eyes closed, the smile on her lips in response to what Kiki had done, having two girls dance at once. Though she and Nina wouldn't be interacting, the suggestion would be there, and that would be enough for these guys.

Briefly, as she began to dance, she wondered what kind of money these girls took home. Though her family had money, her fledgling dance company always seemed to be in the red. And the troupe always refused her offers of a loan, telling her that they couldn't possibly take her money.

The music revved up, someone turned the sound up louder, and Alyssa opened her eyes, realizing that Nina had already tossed her skirt behind the couch, to the delighted cheers of the men.

*Whoops. Got to catch up. . . .*

She worked the zipper down on her black leather miniskirt, laughing as it snagged on her black satin panties. This was actually fun! She almost couldn't believe she was here, when just a few hours ago she'd been circling O'Hare Airport in a plane, the only thought in her mind a hot shower and something good to eat.

Off came the skirt, only when she threw it, it landed on a guy's head. That got delighted roars from the crowd as he pawed it off his face and flung it behind him, grinning. Nina winked at her as if to say, *Nice move.*

Alyssa matched her moves to Nina's, and at the end of the song, she still had her tight black top on. Another song, Billy Idol's "White Wedding," started, and Brooke, the redhead, joined them on the large table. The three of them danced, and by the end of the second song, they were down to their bras and panties.

It was exactly as Kiki had explained. Alyssa knew she wasn't showing this crowd anything more than she would've on a beach, but they were loving it. From the expression on all the delighted masculine faces staring at them, Christmas had definitely come early this year.

Then Nina surprised her.

They were in the middle of their third song, "You Can't Hurry Love" by the Dixie Chicks, when Nina opened the front clasp of her scarlet lace bra and flashed the crowd, grinning. Then she swiftly refastened her bra.

The roars of approval and spontaneous applause were deafening.

Brooke flashed them, her green eyes alight with laughter, then fastened her dark green bra again.

And Alyssa found every male eye in the place on her.

Unfortunately, she and Kiki were the women who would've been considered more amply endowed. And even more unfortunately, her bra fastened in back.

*What to do?*

She continued dancing around on the low coffee table, and realized that both Nina and Brooke had stepped down and she was alone on the table. And she could feel it, that every male in that room wanted to know what was beneath that black satin pushup bra.

She'd never been that self-conscious about her body. Part of it was growing up in San Francisco and attending boarding school in Europe. Summers in France and Italy, she'd regularly sunbathed topless. And she was a dancer and was at home with her body.

*Ah, what the heck . . .*

She was alone on the table, barely winded, as a familiar song began, and the masculine crowd roared encouragement. "Baby Did A Bad Bad Thing" by Chris Isaak filled the room, and Alyssa realized every eye in the place was on her.

Smiling a private, dreamy smile designed to drive a man crazy, she began to sway to the seductive music. And she reached for the hooks at the back of her bra.

Cooper Sinclair sat at his massive oak desk, on the phone, trying not to listen to the sounds of the party drifting beneath the door.

One of the trade-offs of being highly successful was that sometimes your working day just didn't stop at five.

And he was successful beyond his wildest dreams. He and his business partner, Jake McConahay, had designed a compact data storage device that had swept the computer industry and received rave reviews. They'd made millions with it when their company had gone public, and achieved instant fame within the industry. They also managed to have an awful lot of fun in the process.

Cooper frowned. At least Jake had managed the fun part. His partner routinely nagged him to loosen up and live a little, but he was a rather cautious man by nature.

That was why he and Jake complemented each other in business.

Cooper listened carefully, and as the conversation wound down, Jake said, "Wasn't there some sort of party you were supposed to go to tonight?"

"Yeah." He rubbed his fingers along his temples, a headache beginning. Not a good sign. He'd worked straight through lunch and needed something to eat. Well, he could wander down the hall and get a piece of cake and a glass of punch.

"Well, get going. And don't do anything I wouldn't do."

"Which means open season."

"You said it, not me," said Jake, sounding amused. "All I know, Coop, is that all work and no play makes for a life that sucks."

"You've got a point there," Cooper said, glancing at his watch. "How's Riley doing?" he said, referring to his four-year-old golden retriever. He'd asked Jake to baby-sit his dog this evening, as Riley didn't really like huge crowds in his home.

"Riley's under my desk as we speak, chewing on that blue plastic ball—oops, he just heard his name and he's looking at me with that expression that says, 'Let's play.' So we will."

"Thanks for keeping him overnight. Parties make him too nervous."

"He's fine. Don't even worry about him."

Cooper took a deep breath. "Okay, I'll call you tomorrow—"

"You won't, because Tom's getting married. Jesus, Coop, give it a rest."

"Yeah, you're right. Okay, I'll call you in the next few

days." Cooper hung up the phone, then stood, stretching. He cocked his head, listening to roars and enthusiastic masculine shouts coming from the family room down the hall.

What the hell was going on?

He started toward the door of the den, opened it, and headed toward the family room.

She teased, tormented, and tortured them. And where she got the desire to do so, Alyssa didn't have a clue. It was as if a natural talent she'd always kept carefully at bay had suddenly blasted out, taking her over. It helped that she had the black wig on and a mask that easily covered one-third of her face. In the sexy black underwear and with shiny red lipstick on her mouth, she felt like another woman. A sexy, experienced woman. A woman who could lead a man down all sorts of erotic roads.

She'd reached for the back fastening of her bra, then hesitated, her hands coming to her front, then drifting back, and the third time, still teasing, she'd finally unfastened her bra in back. Alyssa was a believer that a real striptease was a work of art, a celebration of the feminine form. She'd never had a chance to do one, she probably never would again, and she intended to make the most of this moment.

They were mesmerized, every man in the room riveted on her hands, waiting for her to slip the sexy garment down lower, lower, and finally completely off. . . .

But she didn't. She made them wait.

Alyssa slid the back fastenings apart, let the lacy bra straps slide down her shoulders, then moved her hands so she was cupping the bra in front of her breasts.

"Take it off, baby!" a male voice yelled.

She had the presence of mind to glance over at Tom, wondering how the husband-to-be was doing.

Sound asleep.

She smiled, almost laughed, and continued to dance, her hips swaying in time to the music, her hands on black satin. Then she flashed the garment up, revealing her naked breasts, and swiftly covered them again.

The crowd roared. Someone pounded on a table. Someone else threw their drink on some of the other men in the crowd, but they barely noticed.

Alyssa laughed. She lifted her bra again, allowing them only a slightly longer look. Totally teasing.

The roars were deafening, the appreciation immense.

She slipped the bra down her arms, then began to twirl the black satin garment over her head as she turned and turned and turned, moving, swaying seductively to the music.

Then she threw the bra into the crowd, straight toward a dark-haired man who was coming toward her with an expression on his handsome face that was not at all amused.

# *Chapter Two*

Cooper had come down the few steps into the large family room just in time to see the black-haired dancer flash her breasts to the crowd of frenzied men. And his first thought was, *When the hell did I ever see this in the Victoria's Secret catalog?*

His friend Tom was terrified enough of getting married in the morning. He didn't need anything like this to get him into trouble or help him along the path toward doing something profoundly stupid. Mindy would be brokenhearted if she thought he'd even considered cheating on her.

As the crowd parted to let his determined body through, the dancer turned, stopped, faced him, and threw her bra into the crowd.

He reached up, caught it, headed straight over to the coffee table, and took the half-naked woman into his arms, heaved her up over his shoulders, and stalked out of the family room, down the hall, and toward his den.

* * *

"Hey!" Alyssa said, wriggling in his grasp. "Let me down, you . . . you . . . caveman!"

He set her down in the den, and she promptly turned and ran outside the room, down the hall, and back toward the party.

He set off in hot pursuit.

When he found her, she was drinking a glass of punch that the bartender had handed her, and her bra was somehow miraculously back in place, covering those breasts. Just when had she gotten her bra away from him?

His eyes narrowed as he studied her. As annoyed as he was at her actions, he had to admit she had pretty magnificent breasts.

"Just what do you think you were doing up there?" he said, his tone low and even, his temper firmly under control.

"She was dancing, man," said the young blond bartender, a look of absolute worship in his hazel eyes. "And doing a damn fine job of it, too, if I might say so."

"Where's Tom?" Cooper said.

"He's asleep in the La-Z-Boy chair," the dancer said, and he glanced at her. He liked her voice, even though he didn't want to. Low and soft and sexy.

"How do you know Tom?" he asked her.

Alyssa hesitated. She had a feeling that if she didn't think fast, her cover was about to be blown. And so would the wedding, because no man would marry a woman who would stoop to spying on him!

"I was introduced to him when we first arrived," she said, thankful that she'd been able to come up with an excuse that fast. "I thought you wanted us to have a little harmless fun with him later, but he looks pretty wasted."

"He's terrified of getting married tomorrow," Cooper said through clenched teeth, "and he doesn't need to be pushed over the edge with a little number like the one you were doing up on that coffee table."

"Wow," Alyssa said. "Sorry." She might have sounded quite sincere, and the matter totally laid to rest, but some little demon forced her to add, "I just don't know what happened, they just sort of—jumped out. A will of their own, you know."

The bartender laughed, a snorting sound, as he turned away. Several of the men around them grinned, and Cooper reached for her arm.

"Ah, ah, ah! You can look, but you can't touch."

He stepped back. "I hired all of you with the stipulation that this party remain—"

"Tame?" Alyssa supplied the word for him, a little devil driving her. How dare this stuffed shirt ruin one of the most fun nights of her life! He was taking something that had been adventurous and exciting and turning it into something sordid.

He hesitated.

"Boring?" she added, then took a sip of punch.

"You," he said, "have quite an attitude."

"Do you boss everyone else around like this, or is it just me?" She couldn't believe the words coming out of her glossy red lips, but there was something about this man that made her want to goad him.

"At the moment," he said, his voice sounding even quieter if that was possible, "it seems to be just you."

"Hmmm," she said, considering this as she took another swig of her drink.

"Hey," he said, taking the plastic glass out of her hand. "Go easy on the booze."

She laughed. "There isn't any booze in that drink."

"Well, yes there is," said the bartender, his voice apologetic. "Vodka."

"Amazing," she said, staring at him. "It didn't seem like it; it tasted just like Hawaiian Punch." She squinted her eyes at the bartender. "Which one of you added the booze?"

Cooper sighed, took her arm, then swung her up over his shoulder.

Back in the den, he set her down on the leather sofa.

"Maybe you can sleep it off back here, while the other three girls do the dancing."

She pressed a hand to her forehead. "I am kind of dizzy."

"Were you drunk when you were dancing?"

She glared at him. "No. Not that it's any of your business."

"Oh, but it is. I arranged this party."

*Whoops.* The one thing she didn't want to do was get Kiki, Brooke, and Nina in trouble. If those were even their real names.

"I'm sorry," she said, trying to inject the proper amount of contrition into her voice.

"Somehow I doubt that."

"Oh, come on, how am I supposed to apologize to you if all you do is make everything I say sound like a lie?"

"You're doing a great job of that yourself."

She glared at him, then took off her mask and set it down on the coffee table. She lay down on the leather sofa and closed her eyes. "I'm just going to pretend that you're not here," she whispered.

"The feeling's mutual."

She hadn't been on the couch for three minutes when the phone rang. He answered it, and she heard the short, brusque side of his conversation. And it comforted her that at least it wasn't her. He seemed to be this goal-oriented with everyone, even this Jake guy on the phone.

He strode out of the room, the phone still off the hook, and Alyssa eyed the receiver. Acting on impulse, she got up and approached the massive desk, then picked it up.

"Jake?" she said.

"Hey, who's this?" came a very interested masculine voice.

She decided to get straight to the point. "Is he always this bad?"

"Coop? Bad? Nah, he's usually much worse."

She laughed.

"So he's refusing to have fun again, huh?"

*You could say that.* She decided to throw caution to the wind. Impulsively, she explained what had happened.

"Let me get this straight. You danced topless, and Coop objected?"

"Yep."

"He *has* been working too hard. How old are you?"

"Sixteen."

"Funny. Really, how old?"

"Twenty-four."

Jake sighed. "He's losing his mind."

"How can I get him to loosen up and have fun?" she said, amazed at the way the liquor was making her thoughts just pop out of her mouth.

Jake was silent for a moment, then said, "That's a great idea, and I have just the plan."

"What?"

"Coop can't refuse a dare. It must be something genetic, 'cause his old man is exactly the same way. Just dare him to do something, and he'll be putty in your hands."

"Hmmm." She hiccuped gently. "That sounds intriguing."

"Just be sure you really want him to do what you dare him to do, 'cause once you get him started, he won't back down."

"Got it."

"You got a name?"

She hiccuped again. "Alyssa. Oops, I mean, Bambi."

Jake laughed. "This just gets better and better. Well, I'm going to wish you luck, Alyssa Bambi, and we'd better get off the phone before Coop realizes I've been giving out state secrets."

"Okay. Thanks, Jake."

"My pleasure, only I think it's going to be Coop's."

She laughed, set down the receiver, and ran unsteadily back to the couch, where she lay down and closed her eyes. She'd pretend to sleep, then gather her thoughts, muster her forces, and figure out what to do next.

She was asleep before Coop came back into the room.

He sent the other three dancers home with hefty tips and his total appreciation.

Most of the guests had either retired to bedrooms in the massive house, or, like Tom, were passed out in the family room.

So Coop went back to the den and watched Bambi

sleep. And he got her some covering, a down-filled duvet, and threw it over her so she wouldn't get cold. Then he studied her face as she slept.

*She really is a stunner,* Coop thought. He wasn't the type who frequented strip clubs. That was more Tom's thing. But there had been a moment, that moment when he'd come striding through the crowd and she'd slipped off her bra and tossed it toward him . . . Well, he wouldn't have been a man if he hadn't appreciated that incredibly feminine body. Those curves, that sense of aliveness, that total feeling of being in the moment.

For the briefest second, he'd felt so alive. *Really* alive. And that moment had made him realize how seldom he'd felt that way over the last few years. All he'd really been focused on, for as long as he could remember, was building his business.

Cooper considered all this as he watched her sleep and thought about the wedding that would take place in the morning.

There was a part of him that had resented having to be responsible for Tom. Even though he was a close friend, he'd wondered why Tom was so afraid of marrying Mindy and was so nervous about giving up his bachelor status. Cooper had always assumed that when you knew it was right, when you knew you were finally with the right woman, things just sort of flowed from there. Fell into place.

Cooper sighed. Life could be complicated. Looking on the bright side, now he didn't have to be responsible for his friend anymore, because Tom had puked his guts out and was asleep on the floor of the family room. He lay sprawled beneath the pool table, on the carpet, totally passed out. As best man, Coop knew he'd get his friend to the church on time and see him married tomorrow afternoon.

Bambi groaned, then stretched, causing the duvet to fall to the floor by the couch. Her heavily mascaraed lashes fluttered open, and she glanced over at him.

"What time is it?" she whispered.

"Right around two in the morning," he whispered back.

She tried to sit up, then lay back down on the couch. "Whoa."

"You need something to eat," he said and handed her a piece of cake.

"Fantastic!" she said. "I'm starving!" He noticed she didn't use the white plastic fork he'd provided but picked up the slice of cake with her hands and took a bite. She finished it in record time, and he watched, fascinated, as she licked frosting off her fingers, then smeared some of the thick frosting off the paper plate and onto her finger, then licked that finger slowly, clearly enjoying the taste.

The unconsciously sensual movement, the pure enjoyment she radiated turned him on incredibly. She was just so *alive*. He couldn't believe the extremely sexual thoughts he was having. How could he be so attracted to a woman he'd been so annoyed with earlier?

"Do you have a way home?" he said, watching her, watching the way her eyes moved to the side, the way she couldn't quite meet his gaze.

"Sure."

"You're such a liar," he whispered.

"Oh, yeah?" She finished the cake, licked the last smear of frosting off the paper plate, and set it down on the coffee table to the side of the leather couch. "What makes you the expert?"

He didn't say anything, wondering why he had the urge to be so rude with her, to get her going. And he found that he liked arguing with her.

"How about a little game?" she said.

He liked the way her eyes were sparkling. This woman radiated fun. "What kind of a game?" The images in his head were totally X-rated.

"Truth or dare. I get to go first."

"Fine." He'd never been one to turn down a dare.

"Were you pissed off, having to baby-sit Tom?"

He hesitated. The quiet honor between friends warred with the truth.

"Truth," she said softly.

"Yeah. I was."

"Good."

He stared at her. "Are you some kind of exotic dancer?"

"You could say that."

"Yes or no. Truth."

"Yes." She smiled up at him, and he watched as she moistened her lips with her tongue. Those thoughts of his, definitely X-rated.

"Are you attracted to me?" she said, her voice barely a whisper.

He didn't even hesitate. "Yes."

"Do you want to kiss me?" she said.

He hesitated.

"Truth," she said.

"Yeah," he said.

The silence stretched between them until she said, "Well, we've done the truth, so how about the dare part?"

"What do you mean?" he said. His heart was pounding

heavily, slowly speeding up. This woman was absolutely incredible. A fantasy come true.

No, make that *his* fantasy come true.

"I dare you," she said, her eyes never leaving his.

"Dare me what?" he said.

"I dare you," she said, "to kiss me."

It was a dare he didn't even try to resist.

"You got it," he said softly and was pleased at her reaction. Those incredible hazel eyes widened slightly, and his entire body hummed with sexual anticipation as he watched her tongue come out and nervously lick those glossy red lips.

"Truth," he said. "Are you scared?"

"Of you?" she replied. "Of course not!"

"Good," he said, and he got up from the leather chair he'd been sitting in and approached the couch she was lying on. As he came around the large coffee table, he caught sight of the expression in her eyes and realized she was as excited as he was.

He knew it was going to be good with her, as he lowered his body down on to the couch. He sat down by her side, then leaned over.

He decided to go for broke and kicked off his shoes and slid over her, so his body was pressed along every single inch of hers. Their faces were close, but he still hadn't kissed her.

"Ah . . . ahem," she said, then started to laugh. Nerves. So she wasn't as confident as she made out to be.

"Truth. Do you want me to stop?" he said.

She smiled up at him. That mouth! Then she whispered, "Is that a gun in your pocket or are you really that happy to see me?"

He almost laughed. "I'm . . . just . . ." He moved his mouth closer to hers, quarter inch by quarter inch. "Really . . . happy . . . to . . ." His mouth hovered right above hers, so close he could feel her breath on his face. "See . . . you." He sighed, then lowered his lips to hers and took her mouth.

It tasted just as sweet as it looked, and the gloss had some kind of cinnamon flavoring to it. Hot and spicy. Sticky and sweet. He kissed her, and the added sensation of her body pressed against his fired him up so that he couldn't think straight.

She kissed him back with such feeling, moving her body in a slow, sensuous way against his. He remembered she was a dancer, and dancers knew how to move.

He broke the first kiss and didn't even give her a chance to breathe before going directly to the next. His hands started to roam, and he found that he had to touch her breasts. Those breasts had been tormenting him since he'd first seen them, since she'd flashed him while she was dancing. He'd thought of those breasts, how it would feel to touch them, to taste them.

As he continued to kiss her, his hand slid to the fastening in the back of her bra, and within seconds it was open. Then he slid his fingers around to her front and slid them up and under the black satin bra.

She whimpered beneath his mouth, made a small, strangled sound as he cupped her breast, then teased the erect nipple with his thumb and forefinger. He broke their kiss and slid down her body, taking that taut nipple into his mouth and pulling on it strongly.

\*　　\*　　\*

When he took her nipple into his mouth, Alyssa almost shot up off the couch.

She was in big trouble. This man could get more mileage out of a kiss than most men could out of an entire night. Those first two long, slow kisses had almost rendered her totally immobile. Soft. Pliable. Willing. *Wanting*.

Now she groaned deep in her throat and found herself moving against his mouth, wanting more, not quite sure what she was asking for, though she had a general idea of what happened next.

She tensed, a little anxious.

He stopped kissing and caressing her breasts, then whispered, "What is it?"

She realized her body had gone completely still. Searching for a reason he'd find acceptable, she whispered, "The door. Anyone could walk right in."

"Oh. Sorry." He seemed slightly ashamed he hadn't thought to lock it or at least close it. She watched Cooper as he got up off the couch so gracefully, and she liked the way he moved as he walked to the den door, shut it, locked it, then turned back toward her.

"How about a fire?"

She blinked, then said, "I think we've already got one going."

He laughed, then went to the large fireplace on the far wall and knelt down, moved the fire screen away, and proceeded to build a fire swiftly and efficiently.

Once that was accomplished, he came back to the sofa.

"Wine?" he whispered.

Maybe a glass of wine would make the whole thing a little easier. It was her first time at doing this sort of thing, and she'd waited what seemed like forever for it to seem right. For just a moment she wanted to tell him tonight would be a first for her, that she'd never been with a man before, but she knew that might blow her cover. He wouldn't get it, that she could dance half-naked in front of a group of men, yet she'd never been in bed with one, one-on-one.

"Why not?" she said, lying back on the couch and shrugging off her bra.

She was going for broke.

*God, she's glorious.*

Cooper had spent his entire adult male life surrounded by women who played games, who seemed sophisticated and sultry until that moment arrived when they really had to act on that image. Then they became all coy and even indignant. So Bambi was a totally refreshing change for him. He loved the way she just shrugged out of that black satin bra and lay back on the couch in just a pair of black panties and those thigh-high boots.

*If this is a sexual fantasy, don't wake me up!*

Cooper entered the large bathroom off his den. He'd installed a small, bar-sized refrigerator so he could grab sodas and snacks and keep right on working at his desk, and now he was thankful he'd stocked it with a bottle of white wine earlier. Locked away in his spacious den, they were in their own little world.

Thinking of Bambi, practically naked out there on the leather couch, he grabbed a corkscrew and opened the wine bottle, then filled two regular highball glasses all the way to the top.

He stared at them for a moment and frowned.

*Too obvious.*

But he wasn't trying to get her drunk; he just didn't

want to have to refill their glasses when they were in the middle of something far more interesting.

He felt like he was seventeen years old again, with the very first woman he'd ever made love with. She stirred him up, no doubt about it. She got him in touch with feelings he hadn't felt in years. He felt young and alive and so ready to just be in the moment, to enjoy sex in a way he hadn't in a long time.

*To hell with obvious. I want her.* Picking up both glasses of wine, he headed toward the den. And as he entered the room, he realized she'd moved from the couch and was sitting on the fake bearskin rug by the fire. It had been a gag gift from Jake, but it was extremely comfortable to sit on. Coop had thrown it by the fire for laughs, but now he was glad he had.

The firelight outlined her profile, that classic little face, that slender body, those magnificent breasts. He stopped, studying her, felt his body tighten with intense desire, and started toward her.

She looked up as Cooper approached her. The leather had been a little cold against her bare skin, so she'd moved toward the warmth of the fire.

"Cold?" he said, handing her a huge glass of cold white wine, then sitting down next to her on the bearskin rug.

"A little. This is better," she said, indicating the fire. "And now you're here."

She saw a quick little light of pleasure flare in those blue eyes. Keeping her gaze on him, she raised her glass of wine into the air. She might not be able to tell him this was her first time, but she wanted to toast tonight. She knew what she was giving up, and she was doing this of her own free will. She'd waited long enough, and somehow this just felt right.

Right time, right moment—and the right man.

Alyssa didn't want to live in her little ivory tower anymore. And no one back home was willing to give her any assistance in this. Lord knows, she'd tried. But more than that, something had happened tonight when she'd danced, and she found she wanted to experience a lot more of life than she had thus far.

"To tonight," she whispered to Cooper. "To a night that, hopefully, will exceed both of our wildest expectations."

He touched the rim of his glass against hers. "I'm sure it will."

She closed her eyes and took a long swallow of the chilled wine, then set it aside. "Well, let's get down to it," she said brightly.

He seemed to choke on a little wine as he swallowed; it almost spewed out his nose. He coughed, then set his glass of wine down on the floor. "Just like that?"

"Don't you want to?"

"Of course I do." He seemed puzzled. "I thought women liked to talk a little first." He glanced at her, his expression sheepish. "And I didn't want you to think, you know, just because you're a dancer—"

"That you wanted me for a night of intense, no-strings-attached, hot sex?"

She'd rendered him speechless.

"Isn't that what you wanted?" she whispered, picking up her glass and taking another sip of her wine. It really was quite good.

"That doesn't upset you?" he said, sounding incredulous.

"Cooper," she said, wondering if every girl had to work as hard at losing her virginity. "Do other women put all these demands on you?"

"Well . . . yeah."

She was flying back to San Francisco after the weekend, and she wanted to take some sexual memories with her. A night of great sex, an out-of-town affair, was exactly what she needed, because she wanted to feel like she was actually participating in the sensual side of her life.

"Well," she said, setting down her glass and slowly lying down, arching her back slightly as she did so, "not this girl." She gave him what she hoped was a sultry smile as she rested her head on the stuffed bear's head that was at one end of the faux bear rug.

"Danger," she whispered, "is my middle name." She'd heard that line in *The Lion King*, and it had always made her laugh. And she'd always wanted to be in a situation where she could use it.

And twenty-four was just too damn old to still be a virgin.

It was time to start really living.

He hesitated, and she decided to go all out. A faint heart never won anything and certainly didn't have any fun.

She lifted up her hips slightly. "Could you help me take these off?" she said, indicating her black satin panties. "I find that they just get in the way."

That did it. He grabbed for the bottom of his sweater with both hands, then pulled it over his head. His shirt came next, buttons flying. She was so excited, her stomach so jumpy that she couldn't have had any more wine if her life had depended on it.

Next, the pants, and she was sure Cooper set a new

land and speed record as far as unbuckling his belt and sliding his pants down off his lean, muscular legs. He managed to get his socks off at the same time, and he threw his clothing to the side with a reckless abandon that fired up her blood.

She couldn't wait until she felt his naked body against hers.

Only one small detail; as she looked at his aroused body, his magnificent, totally male, incredibly aroused body, she caught her breath at the sight of *it*.

She'd taken art in college. They'd drawn nude bodies, and she'd seen plenty of impressive men—or so she'd thought. She'd spent plenty of time on nude beaches, but she'd never, ever seen anything so . . . threatening.

He must have registered the expression on her face.

"What's wrong?"

She swallowed, then decided she could answer him honestly. "It's just . . . I've never seen one . . . quite so . . . *big*." That was the truth, at least.

He smiled then, and she got her first taste of true male ego.

"You aren't scared, are you?" he said.

*Of that? You bet.* "Me, oh, no, it's just—"

"Bambi, I promise you I won't do anything to you unless you tell me you want it. You're in charge tonight."

"Promise?" she whispered. Their gazes locked.

"I promise."

*Danger is my middle name. Hah!* She was either the stupidest, most naive woman in the world, or her intuition was working overtime, because she had this weird feeling she could actually trust him.

And it wasn't as if she didn't know anything at all about Cooper Sinclair. Mindy had told her an awful lot about Tom's closest friend, so she almost felt as if she knew him—a little.

"Okay," she said.

"Good," he said, and she watched as he came over to her and hooked two of his fingers underneath one side of her panties.

"Ah, can I leave those on for just a while, say, fifteen minutes?" Now that the moment of truth was upon her, she found she needed just a little more time. Just a little.

He smiled. "Sure." He lay down next to her, then eased just his chest over hers, taking his weight on his elbows. "You have the most gorgeous mouth," he whispered, looking into her eyes.

"Hmmm," she said, just before he kissed her.

This time it was different, with the warmth from the fire on their bodies. And, of course, he was naked. He'd turned out all the lights as he'd brought her the glass of white wine, so the only illumination in the den was the light from the fire as it hissed and snapped. The faux fur rug felt so sensuous beneath her body; his chest felt so hard and muscular.

She sighed with pure feminine delight as he kissed her again, then kissed her neck, then slowly began to work his way down her body until he was kissing and caressing her breasts.

She pressed her thighs together, trying to ease the wet, tingling, almost burning sensation between her legs. Her fingers tangled in his dark hair, she pressed his face more closely against her breasts and let out a long, breathy sigh.

"Good?" he whispered.

"Oh, yeah," she said softly, then slid her legs apart as she felt one of his hands sliding up her inner thigh, then his fingers easing beneath the elastic of her panties. Then his fingers were there, right there where she burned the most. He'd unerringly found her most sensitive spot, and he gently rubbed and pressed until she arched her hips and moaned softly.

"God," he whispered, "you're so *hot!*"

She didn't care what he thought, and no part of his body seemed that threatening anymore. She simply moved against that hand, that knowing hand, that wicked hand, that sure and steady hand that was taking her to places she'd never dreamed existed.

Of course she'd done a little fooling around with herself, but there was no contest; it was so much more exciting when a man touched her. It was so sensual, so sexy, so . . . *unpredictable.*

"That's it," he whispered as she pressed up against his hand. "That's it."

Then it happened. She climaxed and cried out, grabbing his arm as her breath caught sharply. She closed her eyes and her mouth opened in a silent *oh.* He held her tightly, laughing softly, a satisfied and very pleasurable masculine laugh.

"You are *so* beautiful," he whispered, kissing one breast. "Especially now."

She couldn't seem to think; she could only look at him through heavy-lidded eyes. Thank God he wasn't a hair-puller. She didn't know how she would have explained it if her wig had come off. Of course, she'd anchored it with enough hairpins to sink a battleship.

"You can do it to me now," she said, stretching her arms above her head and arching her back. She started to laugh. "You can do anything you *want* to me now!"

He laughed, then she watched him as he picked up her glass of wine. She thought he was going to offer her a sip, and was surprised when he took a mouthful and held it in his mouth.

"What are you up to?" she whispered, then she found out as he slid down her body, her legs still wide open, and settled his head between her thighs. With one hand, he pulled her panties to the side and found her with his lips and tongue.

"Oh . . . my . . . *God!*" she cried out, and climaxed again within minutes.

He was enough of a gentleman to let her recover.

The minute she was capable of coherent thought, she decided she wanted to go all out. If this was the first and last sex she might be having for a long time, she wanted all her questions answered.

"I want to see you," she whispered.

"Oh, be my guest," he breathed, as she scooted down the fur rug and took her first really good look at him.

He was impressive. *Extremely* impressive. She circled the base of his erection with her hand, amazed that her fingers didn't touch.

Impressive was the word, that was for sure.

She didn't want to give away any inexperience to him, so she said, "I know all men are different, so could you show me what you like?"

For a minute she thought she'd done something wrong, because he started to laugh, his flat stomach moving. This guy had beautifully defined muscles, even a six-pack.

"What?" she said.

"I think I've died and gone to heaven." He put his hand over hers and showed her what he liked.

"Thanks, I can take it from here."

"I'm sure you can," he said, his voice tight.

She'd snuck some videos into the house in the past, so

she wasn't totally ignorant. It was just the first time she'd had a real live man to practice on, a full-size action figure, as it were. And as she was never going to see this guy again, why not go all the way?

Slowly, so carefully, she lowered her mouth to the tip of his erection and eased him in. And almost laughed when she heard his strangled moan. She experimented, pleasing herself and satisfying her own curiosity about men almost as much as she focused on pleasuring him.

When he stopped her, she was confused.

"You didn't like it?"

"Oh, no. You might say I liked it way too much. If you'd done what you were doing much longer, well . . ."

"Oh." Her face flamed as she suddenly understood what he was getting at. Thank God he couldn't possibly know how ignorant she was about all this.

"Come here," he said, drawing her into his arms as he sat up on the rug. He kissed her, long and hard, cupping her face in his hands. "You're the best thing that's happened to me in . . . forever."

"You, too," she said, and meant it.

"Let's take those off, okay?" he said, hooking his fingers into the sides of her black satin panties.

The moment of truth had arrived, and Alyssa found that she wanted to know. She'd come this far and enjoyed herself immensely, so now she wanted to know all of it.

"Okay," she whispered; then bit her lip to stop its trembling.

"Hey," he said, and traced that lip with his finger. "Are you okay?"

She nodded her head. "I'm just . . . I'm just really excited."

"Me, too," he whispered.

Then she rose up on her knees, and he slipped her panties down her thighs. She sat back down, her bare bottom against the fake fur, and he slid her panties down past her ankles, then helped her take off her boots—and she was totally naked.

"What's that?" he said, his eye caught by something.

"What?"

"On your butt."

"Oh. It's a rose." She'd gotten the tattoo on her twenty-first birthday, on a dare. A small red rose with a green stem and two leaves. It was so much a part of her, there were times she forgot she even had it.

"Turn over," he said, and she obediently lay on her stomach while he studied it.

"It's very pretty."

"I like it."

"You're very pretty."

She smiled. "I like you."

"Hang on a minute; this floor is getting hard." He got up and walked over to the couch, where he grabbed the duvet that had fallen on the floor. Folding it in half, he brought it back over and, motioning for her to scoot back, he lay it on top of the rug.

"Better," he said, then took her hand and pulled her toward him.

And kissed her. And kissed her again, harder. More insistently.

And she knew it was going to happen.

He kissed her eyelids, her nose, her mouth. Her neck, her chest, and her breasts. He kissed her nipples, rolled them around on his tongue, teased them gently with his teeth until she was whimpering with need. He kissed his way down her belly, he kissed her inner thighs, he kissed her *there,* whispering, "You're pretty all over," and then he slid up her body and braced himself over her, and she looked up at him and knew that this was it.

He slid into her with an unchecked masculine force that rocked her back hard against the floor. At the sharp, quick pain, tears gathered in her eyes, but she closed them because she didn't want him to see them, didn't want him to know.

But that pain, that peculiar burning, stretching sensation, was so quickly replaced by intense pleasure that she found herself grabbing his shoulders, rearing up off the folded quilt, then grasping his buttocks so he had to move against her just *so.*

And then it happened again, another climax, and she thought he would finish, but he kept moving right through it, thrusting into her again and again, the intensely sexual rhythm increasing, the strength of it, the speed.

He was pounding into her, his body moving as if it was out of his conscious control. Then she felt him stop, tense, and felt those masculine contractions. He groaned, buried his face against her shoulder, then gasped for air as if he'd been running for miles.

She could feel his heartbeat racing against her chest. When it finally slowed, he raised his head and found her lips with his. He kissed her, then slowly slid to the side, keeping their bodies joined.

She couldn't keep her eyes open. Her eyelids drifted shut, and the only thought on her mind was that it had certainly been worth the wait.

She didn't know how much time had passed when she woke, but she knew the quilt had slipped off her shoulders, and she was cold. The fire had burned down to embers, and the den was almost totally dark.

She pulled at the quilt, managed to get a little more out from under Cooper's prone body, then started when she heard his voice.

"You awake?"

She hesitated. "Yeah."

He rolled over and moved his body so that they could cover themselves with the duvet while lying on the fake fur rug.

"You okay?" he asked, and she heard the hesitation in his voice.

"I'm great. How about you?"

In answer, an arm came around her waist and pulled her tightly against him.

"What do you think?" he whispered, and she realized he was aroused again, hard and ready.

She searched for his face in the dark, kissed him. He responded, and she found it took a lot less foreplay to get both of them ready, because they had been so primed for it before. And even though she was sore, when he reached between her legs and started to caress her, she knew she would let him inside her again.

But she was surprised when he rolled onto his back, the quilt still over them, and positioned her over his hard arousal. She slid down onto him, and this time it was easier; there was no pain as he entered her, then filled her so completely. Only pleasure, waves of it, immense pleasure as he began to move beneath her and she matched his rhythm.

She could barely see his face in the darkness, and she found she didn't need to. She would never forget Cooper and what he had given her tonight. He didn't know who she was and hadn't treated her like some breakable little china doll that should be stored away in a closet. He'd treated her—was treating her—like a woman, and she'd needed this for so long and it felt so right.

She moved against him with absolutely no inhibitions. Being a dancer, she was at home in her body, but this man matched her move for move; he was a fantastic sexual partner. His hands moved to her waist, his fingers biting into the sides of her body; then they moved lower, so both his thumbs grazed lower and then were touching her at that most sensitive spot.

"Come for me," he whispered, and his words fired her up even more.

"Come for me. I want to see you come."

He pressed harder, seeming to know what she wanted and needed even before she did. And when she did come, she threw back her head and cried out, *"Yes!"*

He rolled her over on her back after that, and pumped into her, seeking his own release. She wrapped her legs around his waist and hung on. She didn't think he could go in any deeper, but he moved back and hooked her legs over his shoulders, then started moving again, and she knew she was taking him deeper, and it felt incredible.

Then he found his release, and she went with him, right at the same time. And she didn't even feel him crushing down on her after it was all over, because she had her arms tightly around his neck and had decided that she couldn't possibly leave something this good.

She'd tell Cooper the truth in the morning.

He moved off her, and she snuggled up against his big, warm body. The man seemed to radiate heat. And as his muscular arm came around her waist and beneath her breasts, as he tucked himself in behind her like they were two little spoons in a kitchen drawer, Alyssa fell asleep with an incredibly satisfied smile on her face.

She'd tell him. She'd be a fool not to, after a night like this.

## Chapter Three

When Alyssa woke the following morning, it took her a few seconds to figure out where she was.

Her eyelids didn't seem to want to work properly, as her lashes were stuck together with heavy mascara. She rubbed them with her fingers, then blinked them open, her vision blurring as a speck of mascara flaked into one eye. It watered, she blinked, and the first thing she focused on, in the early morning winter sunlight streaming in the den window, was the glittery purple domino mask on the coffee table by the leather couch.

*A mask . . .*

The events of the previous night didn't come back to her until she glanced over and saw Coop asleep, his forearm thrown over his eyes, his chest impressively bare and hard muscled, sprinkled with dark hair. The puffy down quilt that had been over both of them had migrated down to where it barely covered his hips.

Alyssa blinked, stared at Coop, and remembered . . . all of it. In excruciating detail.

*Yikes!*

She blinked again.

*The wedding. Today. Oh my God.*

She had to get away. She had to get out of this house before Coop woke up and started asking all sorts of questions that she had no answers for.

Like the million-dollar one: What had she been thinking?

She wasn't the sort of girl who threw caution to the winds—at least not sexually. And Alyssa had the feeling that Coop was not the sort of man whose normal companions were as totally inexperienced as she was.

Well, as she'd *been*. Before last night. Before Coop had come into her life.

She glanced around, found her black satin underpants and reached for them. As she slipped into them and found her bra, Alyssa knew she couldn't blame Coop for what had happened between them. He'd been a gentleman, and she'd been the one who had dared him, then later that night double-dared him, and then . . .

She bit her lip against the groan that threatened to escape, fastened her bra, and reached for her boots.

*Oh, and one other little detail. Where are my clothes?*

*Out in the family room, with the rest of the guys.*

She could only hope they were all passed out.

She had her second boot zipped up and was about to stand, when Coop stretched, mumbled something, then turned toward her and gently grasped her upper arm with his hand.

"Bambi . . ." he muttered.

*He doesn't even know my real name.*

For some reason, this bothered her. Oh, she was never going to see this man again once Mindy's wedding was over, and Alyssa knew she'd never let on that she'd had wild sex with him. But it bothered her that she'd never hear that sexy, smoky voice say her real name. For just a moment she felt incredible guilt over her deception.

"Hey, Coop," she whispered. She leaned down and, on a sudden impulse, kissed his cheek, then those lips, those lips that had done such wild, sexy things to her last night.

He smiled, such a sweetly satisfied, masculine smile that her heart threatened to turn over in her chest.

"Bambi," he whispered again. "Dance for me. . . ."

And then he drifted off to sleep.

Well. This chapter of her life was over. The wedding, the reception, then a quick hop, skip, and a jump to O'Hare Airport, and she'd never see Coop again.

Alyssa hesitated, finding that leaving this man was harder than she'd thought. The truth, she was discovering, was that she was just plain lousy at one-night stands. She didn't like the morning after. They'd been so close, and now she had to leave him.

Then sanity returned in the next heartbeat.

*He thinks you're a stripper. You were a classic one-night stand, for God's sake. It's not as if Coop is offering you the little house with the white picket fence, two-car garage, and a golden retriever and two point five children, though I've never understood that point five when it came to a child. . . .*

She bit her lip as she stared at him, committing that body, that hair, that face, to memory.

*Those hands . . .*

She couldn't believe how shaken up she was.

*That voice . . .*

That voice in the dark had been magic.

She glanced at the dark hair on his chest and how it narrowed down his muscular stomach, below the quilt to where . . .

Ah, the man had been impressive in every single respect.

She couldn't seem to move.

*Get going!* the voice of sanity in her head screamed.

*But we had something special here,* another voice, slightly fainter and less sure of itself, argued.

*Maybe he doesn't think so,* the first voice insisted. *And a guy who made love to you the way this one did last night has had plenty of practice. Think about that.*

*Yeah, there's that. And, the fact that I've never done anything this crazy before.*

*Right. So get out!*

*But . . . but . . .*

For some crazy reason, she was about to touch Coop's shoulder, shake him awake, when she remembered Mindy.

*Best friend. Wedding day. You were spying on her husband-to-be. And if the truth comes out, there will be no wedding.*

Mindy would be the big loser here. And she couldn't do that to her best friend in the world, not when her entire future and all her happiness were at stake.

Thoughts of Mindy galvanized Alyssa into action. She got to her feet as quietly as possible, then tiptoed out of the den, took one long, last look at Coop, shut the door quietly behind her, and ran down the hallway in her black satin underwear and thigh-high boots.

It was a cinch finding the rest of her clothing and her black trench coat, though she had to pry her short leather skirt away from a sleeping reveler who was using it as a pillow. Tom, the groom, lay on the carpeted floor in a contented heap, the side of his face smooshed against the rug. Alyssa stopped and studied the man as she swiftly fastened the belt on her trench coat.

Then she kicked his butt.

He grunted, then continued to snore.

"This is all *your* fault," she whispered, allowing herself one small, satisfying moment of pettiness. Total immaturity.

It helped. A little.

She let herself out the front door and into the early morning light. Glancing up, as she shut the door, Alyssa realized it was snowing. Light, lacy flakes floated down out of the leaden sky. The bare branches of the trees in front of Coop's house were already frosted with white.

Judging from the look of the sky, it had to be somewhere in the vicinity of six in the morning. For one wild moment, Alyssa wished she had a car and could go get a cup of hot coffee and a freshly glazed Krispy Kreme doughnut. And perhaps drive all the way back home to San Francisco, right now.

Instead, she started to jog, her breath coming out in white puffs of air in front of her as snowflakes swirled to the ground. She ran swiftly in her high-heeled boots, carefully avoiding patches of ice, her hands tucked into the pockets of her trench coat, her head down. She didn't stop running until she was face-to-face with the trellis on the side of Mindy's house and started the short climb up to her friend's bedroom window.

Once inside that window, she hightailed it into the bathroom and locked the door. Only then did Alyssa let herself believe that she was actually going to get away with what she'd done.

Dressed as a stripper.

Crashed a bachelor party.

Spied on Tom.

Slept with Coop—*ooops! Not part of the plan.* And Alyssa resolved, as she took the short black wig off her head and set it on the bathroom counter, that this was one part of her evening that Mindy would never know about. It would upset her friend, and you couldn't upset the bride on her wedding day. It just wasn't done.

Alyssa took a deep breath and stared at her face in the mirror. Black mascaraed raccoon eyes stared back at her, the lashes crusted with makeup, the Cleopatra-like eyeliner and shadow smeared. Her glossy red lipstick was all gone, thoroughly kissed away. Her below-the-shoulder-length, wavy blonde hair, unpinned and full of static from the dry winter weather, flew every which way.

She looked like a wild woman—but a *satisfied* wild woman.

There was that darn twinkle in her eyes. The high color on her cheekbones. The slightly swollen lips that curved into a self-satisfied smile.

*Don't go there!*

Determined to forget, Alyssa took off the trench coat, stripped off her top and skirt, and then slipped off her underwear and turned on the shower.

But she couldn't stop remembering how exciting it had been to dance, how wild she'd been behind the safety and anonymity of that mask, how Coop had looked when he'd first stormed into the room and she'd thrown her black bra at him.

*No. You have to stop thinking about him. You mean*

*nothing to him; just a stripper on the road of life, two ships that met in the night.*

She was going to wash that man right out of her hair, off her body, get his scent off her, forget the feel of his hands, those lips, that voice, his—

*Forget it ever happened.*

She stepped beneath the hot shower spray and reached for the soap. As soon as she finished, she'd give Mindy a full report—leaving out the more intimate details, of course—and then her job was done.

Coop groaned and rolled over, taking the down quilt with him and tangling his legs in it. He grunted, then slowly came awake. He smiled as he took in a deep breath of her scent, and remembered. . . .

*Bambi . . .*

He reached for her, his body already primed, thinking ahead to the intense pleasure of an instant replay of last night and found—nothing.

He opened his eyes.

Bambi was gone.

Coop frowned, then slowly sat up and ran his fingers through his hair. *Odd.* He hadn't even paid her. Not for the sex, but for the dancing. She'd come to the house to do a job, and she'd done it well, whipping the guests up into a frenzy before he'd brought her back to his den. And he could honestly say that when he'd brought her back here, he'd had no intention of having sex with her.

He hadn't even known that sex like they'd had existed.

Coop glanced over at the coffee table and caught sight of the mask. And remembered that face, that short black bobbed hair, those sexy, glossy red lips forming the words that had done him in.

*I dare you to kiss me. . . .*

Once he'd kissed her, he hadn't wanted to stop. Neither had she.

He'd had a lot of sexual experience in his thirty-two years, but last night had been the single best night of his life.

Coop frowned.

*Then why had she left?*

A sudden thought chilled him. *Maybe she's married.*

*No.* He couldn't believe that. Didn't want to.

*Why had she left?*

He'd known, even as he'd drifted off to sleep last night, his arm firmly around her slender body, that he'd wanted to explore this relationship further. Jake had been right; he'd been living an all-work-and-no-play life for so long that when Bambi had burst into his life and dared him to play, all of what he'd spent months holding down had come rushing to the surface.

They'd played, all right.

But it was more than playing. He wanted her again; he was absolutely sure of that. He'd come awake wanting her, he'd reached for her and wanted to start up that incredible sexual heat all over again. If he hadn't had the damn wedding to get ready for, he'd have made sure they spent the entire day in bed.

*Wedding.*

Coop glanced at the clock. Eight forty-five in the morning.

Tom. The wedding.

He stood up, pulled on his pants, then started down the hallway as he buckled his belt. When he reached the family room, he saw Tom sleeping on the floor, oblivious.

Time to get moving. Get this show on the road.

"Tom," he said, shaking his buddy's shoulder lightly. Tom continued sleeping.

"Tom!" He shook harder.

"No," Tom mumbled. "Stop kicking me, okay?"

Coop stepped back, considering this. Mindy, kick Tom? This was interesting.

"Damn it, Tom, get up! You're getting married today!"

Tom opened a bleary eye and stared up at his friend.

"Don't shout, okay?" he said, his voice a whisper. "My head hurts."

"I'll make you some coffee while you get in a hot shower. We have to be at the church by noon."

"Yeah. Yeah, I know."

"Then let's get moving. You've got to look a lot better than you do now."

Tom slowly rose to his feet, and Coop took pity on him and pointed him in the direction of the downstairs bathroom. As soon as he heard the shower start, he headed toward the kitchen. But before he started the coffee, he grabbed a copy of the Yellow Pages and sat down at the small table in the breakfast nook.

Thumbing through the thick phone book, he found what he was looking for: Rico's Fantasy Dancers.

Coop grabbed a piece of paper and wrote down the number, then the name "Bambi" next to it.

How simple could it be? He'd simply hire Bambi again and tell her that he—

That he what? That he wanted to have sex with her again? That would be tantamount to hiring a prostitute. And he couldn't do that to her.

That he wanted a date? They couldn't exactly go out on a date without both of them thinking about the hot night they'd spent together. And he knew she'd found as much pleasure in it as he had, because no woman could have faked those sounds, those moans and sighs, that sharp cry when she'd reached her first climax.

He shook his head, trying to clear it of those erotic memories.

Maybe he'd just tell her that he wanted a private dance, one-on-one, in the privacy of his own home. But then she'd know exactly what he really wanted.

No fool, his Bambi. He found himself missing her sharp retorts.

This was getting complicated. And all Coop could remember was how uncomplicated it had been last night.

He closed his eyes, remembering, and could feel his body start to respond to the memory. Even in memory, Bambi was a total turn-on.

But more than that, he *liked* her. Really liked her. She made him laugh. Got him going. And he wanted to know more about her.

He glanced at the clock; a few minutes to nine. Swiftly and efficiently he made a large pot of coffee, remembering the other partygoers who were sprawled out in the living room. They'd all need coffee if they were going to make it to the church on time.

At nine on the dot, he called Rico's.

"Rico's Fantasy Dancers, whatever you can fantasize, we can bring to life," Rico said, picking up on the first ring. He sounded as if he were doing a bad impression of Dan Ackroyd from the early years of *Saturday Night Live*.

"Rico?"

"Yeah, that's me."

"Cooper Sinclair."

"Yeah, right. The bachelor party in Wilmette. How did my girls do?"

"They were fantastic." Coop hesitated. "We had a great time."

"Good. Those are words I like to hear. I'll let the girls know how happy you were with them."

"There's just one thing."

"There always is," Rico said. He sounded both resigned and amused. This guy had probably heard it all before.

"One of the girls—"

"Nina? Did she get a little too wild?"

"No, no, Nina was fine. It was Bambi I was thinking about."

"Bambi."

"Yeah, Bambi. I'd like to—" He couldn't believe he was hesitating. Coop could handle himself at a business meeting, and could be totally ruthless with negotiations, and now he was faltering because he wanted to hire a woman to dance for him?

"What I'd like to do is—"

"Hire her for a private party," Rico finished for him.

Coop felt embarrassed, could feel intense heat flame up in his face. He had the uneasy feeling the man could read his mind and knew exactly what he wanted. But it wasn't just sex. If he was honest with himself, Bambi totally fascinated him. She'd brought out a side of him he'd barely realized existed.

"Yeah." Coop sighed. "That's about it."

"Not a problem. When would you like her to come over?"

"Ah . . . tonight?"

"Sounds good. I'll give her a call and see if she can make it. Will you be home in the next hour or so?"

"Sure."

"I'll get back to you, Mr. Sinclair."

"Thanks." Coop hung up the phone, feeling strangely ashamed of himself. For just an instant, he wished that he and Bambi could have met in a more normal way.

*No. Not possible. Because how could you have met her at a party? You never go to parties. You threw this party for Tom, not for you. And if she'd walked down the street and you'd seen her, your mind would have been on other things. Business.*

He smiled, remembering. Remembering the moment when he'd walked into the family room and she'd flung her bra at him, and he'd gotten a look at her bare breasts.

She'd caught his eye, all right, in a way no other woman ever had before. And then she'd argued with him, challenged him, and he'd found that he liked it. Women usually became sweetly submissive around him. Bambi had been so different. *Challenge* could have been her middle name.

He couldn't stop thinking about the previous night, remembering the way she'd dared him to kiss her. Some dare. The moment his lips had come down over hers, he'd been lost.

Coop poured himself a cup of coffee—black—and leaned against the kitchen counter. He took a sip, his mind working, plotting. In the next hour, he'd get his guests up and out of the house, get Tom ready for his wedding to Mindy, and take the call from Rico that was going to change his life for the better.

He took another sip of coffee. He'd see Bambi tonight, and it couldn't be too soon.


"Lys?"

Alyssa turned at the sound of her friend's voice and

stopped drying her wet hair with a towel. She'd already dressed, pulling on a pair of blue gray sweatpants and a sweatshirt. Halfway through her shower, she'd realized she wasn't going to get any sleep.

Mindy sat up in her bed amid a profusion of pink pillows, and Alyssa could see that she'd had a restless night.

*Not as restless as mine, but then again, whose was?*

"Hey, how are you feeling?" Alyssa said.

Mindy patted the side of the bed. "Come here."

Alyssa sat on the side of the double bed.

"I waited up. What happened?" her friend said. "The truth."

For one awful moment, Alyssa was tempted to come clean, to admit that she'd really overstepped all bounds and had a wild night with Coop. She desperately wanted to pump Mindy for all the information she could give her on Coop. But one look at her best friend's hopeful face, and she knew she could never tell her.

She'd have to take this little escapade to her grave.

"Tom was a perfect angel. And I stayed really late to make absolutely sure."

Mindy frowned. "Oh, come on. With naked dancers in the room?"

"No, I swear! The guy who arranged the party—"

"Cooper. He's Tom's best friend."

*Cooper.* Even hearing his name gave her a little thrill.

"Cooper, yeah that's right. He told us that all he wanted was something like an ad in a Victoria's Secret catalog, nothing too raunchy. Sexy, but in a fun kind of way."

"Really?" said Mindy, and Alyssa could hear the faint skepticism in her voice.

"Well—"

"I knew it! What happened?"

"Two of the girls took off their tops, then I did, but Cooper put a stop to it."

"Wow. You took off your top?"

Alyssa shrugged. "When in Rome."

Mindy laughed, then sobered. "But did Tom seem interested in these girls?"

"Nah. He was drinking beer and having a good time. If anything, he seemed nervous and drank a little too much. That isn't a problem for him, is it?"

"No, but I could see him doing it if he got nervous."

"Then that's what it was. But I'm sure his friend—"

"Cooper."

"Yeah, Cooper." She moistened her lips nervously. "I'm sure Cooper will get Tom to the church on time."

Mindy's eyes filled. "You are the *best* friend anyone could ever have." She threw her arms around Alyssa and hugged her tightly.

"Hey, don't mention it." Alyssa hugged her friend back. She really wanted Mindy to be happy, and if Tom was the man who could make her happy, then that was that.

"Lys?" Mindy whispered.

"What?"

"I'm getting *married!*" She let go of her friend and stood up, then twirled around and ran to her closet, throwing open the door and staring at the white fantasy of a dress that hung there.

"Yeah, you are." On a whim, Alyssa jumped up on the double bed and began to bounce up and down. Mindy laughed, then jumped up on the bed, and the two of them bounced up and down, laughing and laughing, until Mindy's mother came in and asked them what they were doing.

"Getting ready for a wedding," Mindy answered, her face glowing.

"And blowing off some nervous energy," Alyssa said.

Blythe, Mindy's mother, tried to look stern, but her gentle face broke into a smile.

"I know the kind of mischief you two can get into. Now Mindy, you've got to eat something, and then we'll start getting you ready. Alyssa, you come with me, too."

"Pancakes?" Alyssa said hopefully. She'd always loved meals with Mindy's large, boisterous family, so different from her own.

"I think that can be arranged."

While Mindy followed her mother down the stairs, the two of them arm in arm, Alyssa went back into the bathroom and hung up the damp towel she'd been drying her hair with. Her gaze fell on the dark wig, the black boots, and the rest of the outfit she'd worn the night before. The clothing had been flung in the corner of the spacious bathroom, while she'd placed the wig on the pale pink, tiled counter.

With quick, economical movements, she put all the clothing back in Mindy's large, walk-in closet, after stashing the underwear in her duffel bag. She hung up the leather skirt she'd borrowed from her friend and tossed the top into the clothes hamper. She secured the black wig onto a wig stand in the closet, then took one last look at what had been the crucial element in her disguise. Except for the Mardi Gras mask she'd left in Cooper's den, of course.

"So long, Bambi," she whispered. "You were a total blast."

# *Chapter Four*

Riding in the limousine on the way to the church, Alyssa stared out the tinted window and thought of Cooper Sinclair.

He'd undoubtedly be at the wedding. As Tom's best man, he'd be up in the front of the church, by the groom's side, responsible for Tom and Mindy's wedding rings. But he couldn't possibly recognize her. The short black bobbed wig was no longer on her head. Her below-the-shoulder-length, wavy blonde hair had been styled in an elegant twist, with tiny, pale pink rosebuds twined in her hair. Her makeup was totally different, fresh and light, in keeping with what a maid of honor should look like; no Cleopatra kohl-lined eyes for her, no sir. And the bright, shiny red lipstick had been replaced by a deep pink gloss.

Her bridesmaid's dress couldn't have been more different from what she'd worn last night. No more short black leather skirts, thigh-high boots, and tight, clingy tops. The dress that Mindy had selected for her was a gorgeous silvery blue silk that set off her blonde hair and just happened to be one of Mindy's favorite colors. The Empire style suited Alyssa's slender body; she felt like a heroine in a Regency romance novel.

Mindy looked like a princess, the full, white skirt of her wedding dress billowing out around her legs. She'd chosen a gorgeous dress, with a halter-style, beaded bodice and a multilayered ivory tulle skirt. And she'd wanted to wear the same veil her mother had worn when she'd walked down the aisle since she was a little girl, so Blythe had carefully preserved her original veil for her daughter's wedding day. A sparkling tiara in Mindy's dark hair completed the fairy-tale look.

Her mother had also provided the something blue, by giving Mindy a pair of spectacular sapphire earrings. The something new, Mindy had decided, was the tiara she adored. The something old, her brothers had teased them all, was that their father, Howard, was walking her down the aisle. But Mindy also had chosen to wear a delicate bracelet that had belonged to her great-grandmother. And her mother's veil was the something borrowed.

So everything was covered.

Alyssa found herself totally happy for her friend. This was turning out to be an incredible weekend. After all, it wasn't every day that you were part of your best friend's wedding and lost your virginity, all in a matter of twenty-four hours.

The limousine turned a corner, and Alyssa clasped her hands tightly together. Tom and his family had gone on ahead, of course, as everyone knew it was bad luck for the groom to see his bride before the wedding. Alyssa was in the limousine with Mindy, her mother and father, and

Mindy's five-year-old niece, Stephanie, who was going to be the flower girl.

Alyssa tried to keep her attention on the upcoming wedding, not Coop.

They'd rehearsed without her, as she'd flown into town late and arrived right after the rehearsal dinner. But Mindy and her mother had explained the layout of the church to her, and she was confident that she could do a good job and make her friend happy.

Mindy, holding on to her father's arm, was absolutely radiant. Happiness seemed to shine off her, and in that instant Alyssa was glad she'd gone to the bachelor party.

But another, disquieting thought had entered her head.

It had been an amazingly spectacular, sensual night for her. If a girl ever had fantasies about how she wanted to lose her virginity, then Cooper Sinclair would be at the top of that particular wish list. It had been perfect. Not in the sense of a trail of rose petals across a huge bed or masses of lit white candles flickering in a bedroom, not the way it was usually portrayed in bridal magazines, romantic movies, or girlish daydreams. There hadn't been any string music swelling up in the background, and they certainly hadn't popped a bottle of champagne.

But it had been *perfect*.

She and Cooper had just . . . fit. Clicked. Chemistry, destiny, whatever you wanted to call it. There hadn't been any awkward moments, absolutely no hesitations. It had just . . . flowed. Beautifully. Incredible, considering it had been her first time. She wasn't naive enough to think that every woman's first time was even close to as good as hers had been.

Cooper had made it wonderful for her. But now, the morning after all that spectacular lovemaking, doubts began to creep in. And Alyssa wondered if he had that kind of chemistry with every single member of the opposite sex. Was Cooper Sinclair so incredibly sexual with every woman? Was what they'd shared last night something special and unique, or was it sensual business as usual for him?

She didn't have a clue.

He'd certainly seemed to know what he was doing in the den that night. Once he'd kissed her, the attraction had been so strong between them that she hadn't cared about any of the consequences, hadn't thought further ahead than spending an incredible evening with him. And she'd wanted him; she'd wanted him so badly that she'd simply gone with the moment.

Alyssa bit the inside of her lip and wondered if he'd had any idea how inexperienced she was. The den had been fairly dark, she'd been self-conscious about the noises she'd been making until Coop had laughed softly and told her to make all the noise she wanted; the door was locked, and he loved hearing her.

She'd never had many hang-ups about her body, but she certainly hadn't planned on losing her virginity last night. She'd wanted to hold out for a very special man.

*Coop was special,* a tiny voice nagged.

She couldn't deny that.

*Or was he?* That other, doubtful little voice returned with a vengeance.

The limousine turned into the church parking lot, and Alyssa was jarred out of her thoughts when Mindy's mother spoke to her daughter. Alyssa took a quick glance outside the tinted window, looking for Coop.

Nothing. He was probably already inside.

Well, no matter where he was, there was no way he'd

be able to recognize her. She looked so completely different, and most men weren't really all that observant, were they?

For just an instant, she remembered the intensity of his face as he'd looked down at her, the way he'd studied her, as if trying to see inside her head. The look he'd given her out of those dark blue eyes, just before he'd kissed her—

"Alyssa? We're here."

She started, then turned toward Mindy's father, Howard.

"Oh. Yes." And then she gathered up her skirt, wrapped her dark blue, hooded velvet cloak more tightly around her against the chill wind and the light snow that had started up again, and stepped out of the limousine and into the church parking lot.

Coop studied his friend as they stood up at the church's altar. Tom looked pretty darn good, all things considered.

After that hot shower, he'd made him down a few cups of coffee, then forced him to eat some dry toast. Then a brisk jog around the block—twice—in the crisp, cold air, then back to the house to get ready for the big day.

Coop patted his tuxedo pocket, confident that the rings were there. As best man, he had his responsibilities. But his mind wasn't really on the wedding. His mind was on this evening. He'd arranged for Bambi to come by his house at ten, confident that by that time he'd have been able to gracefully leave the reception.

She'd made him feel so *alive*. More so than he'd felt in years. He'd taken a lot of ribbing from Jake over the last few years, but he had never really understood what his friend was driving at until last night—until Bambi had rocked his world. Now he had absolutely no desire to show up at the office, let alone work.

The only thing on his mind was finding Bambi again.

He wouldn't rush her. He didn't even plan on asking her to do an erotic dance. He had a bottle of very good wine chilling in the fridge, and all he really wanted to do was sit in the family room and talk with her. Try to make sense of what had happened between them last night. Find out who she was and what she wanted out of life.

Oh, he was such a *liar.*

He wanted to hit the sheets with her again with a ferocity he couldn't believe. He wanted to get her naked and flat on her back in mere seconds and have a repeat of the night before. But even more than that, he wanted to make sure that he would see her again, so he would do anything she wanted in order not to scare her off.

She utterly fascinated him. And all the cards were in her hands.

The crazy thing was, he didn't even mind. And for a control freak like himself, that astounded him.

Coop came back to the present with a blink. Organ music played softly in the background as various family members and friends were taken to seats in pews by the ushers. Several of Mindy's nephews were escorting last-minute guests to their seats, and the young men looked proud and nervous in their dress suits, their hair carefully styled.

Coop had to grin. Normally he was rather uncomfortable at weddings, but this one was . . . special. He hadn't been in such a good mood in months.

"How're you holding up?" he whispered to Tom.

"Fine." Tom tugged at the neck of his shirt. "I just wish

this whole thing would get started. Let's get this show on the road."

*Do I know that feeling.* Coop grinned, then straightened up imperceptibly as the organist, an elderly woman from the church, began a rousing rendition of "The Wedding March."

By tonight, he'd be with Bambi again. Or he'd know why not.

"You look gorgeous," Alyssa whispered to Mindy, her eyes starting to fill. They were all crowded behind the closed, double doors leading into the main room of the old church. She and Mindy, Mindy's dad, Howard, Mindy's three bridesmaids, and little Steffie with her basket of rose petals. Mindy's mother had already gone inside and taken her seat.

"No crying," Mindy whispered back. "You'll wreck your mascara."

Alyssa couldn't believe how cool and composed her friend was, now that the moment was here. She supposed part of it was the absolute confidence Mindy had in her husband-to-be after Alyssa had given her that blow-by-blow account of the bachelor party.

Well, not quite all of it.

"All right, Steffie," Alyssa whispered to Mindy's five-year-old niece. "It's time to strut your stuff!"

The little girl smiled up at her, absolutely adorable in a silvery blue pinafore-style dress. Two of the bridesmaids eased the double doors open, and Steffie started down the runner covering the center aisle of the church. The little girl walked carefully in time to the music, her small hand reaching into the basket as she started to carefully scatter the red rose petals, just as she'd rehearsed the night before.

She had a ringlet of pink rosebuds on her small head, and Alyssa's throat tightened as she watched the little girl start down the aisle.

Mindy's three bridesmaids, also dressed in silvery blue silk, got into line and each slowly began their measured walk down that long aisle as Alyssa made some last-minute adjustments to Mindy's tulle bridal skirt.

"You look so incredible," she whispered to her friend.

"Off you go," said Howard, Mindy's father, as he touched Alyssa's arm. "You look beautiful, Alyssa."

"So do you," she whispered back to the elderly man, so filled with happiness and totally in the moment. The music swelled, she put one foot in front of the other, and started down the aisle with measured steps.

Mindy's wedding had officially begun.

Cooper, keeping an eye on Tom, had to grin when he saw Steffie coming down the aisle so carefully, a solemn look on her small face as she carefully scattered the rose petals on the church runner. The kid was absolutely adorable.

Then the first bridesmaid, and a second, and he wondered what it was that made bridesmaids' dresses so incredibly unattractive on most women. This particular style was totally unforgiving and had little room for hiding figure flaws, as the sensuous silk clung lovingly to every curve.

The third bridesmaid came into view, and Coop glanced back at Tom, who, though pale and nervous, seemed to be holding up remarkably well.

And then . . . and then . . . an incredibly beautiful woman swathed in silk, walking with measured steps. She had so much vibrant energy that it seemed to Coop she was lit up like a Christmas tree. Her blue eyes sparkled with energy and intense happiness.

Strangely enough, even after the wild and totally satisfying night he'd shared with Bambi, he felt himself attracted to her. And Coop decided that he really had been working way too hard, if this was the way he felt when he finally allowed himself to relax and have a good time.

He couldn't seem to take his eyes off her. God, she was a stunner!

But more than that, something about her seemed vaguely familiar.

Alyssa was two-thirds of the way to the altar when she glanced up and saw Tom and was amazed that he looked even vaguely human.

*Not bad, considering how ghastly he looked this morning. And that was quite a kick I gave him.*

Then she glanced to his side and saw Coop. Her heart sped up. He was standing next to the groom, resplendent in a tuxedo, absolutely gorgeous . . . and looking at her with a puzzled expression on his face, as if trying to place her.

*Uh-oh.*

Could he possibly know who she was? That expression on his face unnerved her, and all of a sudden she felt totally exposed, as if Cooper somehow had a sort of X-ray vision and could see beneath her blonde hair and sheer makeup to the woman with the short black wig and black eyeliner. To the woman with the mask who had danced and danced and danced, and had smart-mouthed him at every turn.

Now she knew exactly how superheroes felt, trying to hide their secret identities.

For one awful moment, Alyssa was sure she was going to ruin her best friend's wedding, the culmination of all her hopes and dreams for her future.

She caught Cooper's eye, smiled tremulously, *tried* to look innocent, and was rewarded by a look of complete and utter puzzlement on his handsome face.

*Gotcha.*

Still, it took every ounce of control she had to keep her face serene and composed, to look at him as if she'd never seen him before in her life, when in reality he'd been as close to her as was humanly possible last night.

Then she kept her attention off him as she reached the altar and positioned herself to the side of where the bride would stand. Mindy came down the aisle on her father's arm, glowing with love and basking in the attention of close friends and family, and thankfully, for the moment, all eyes including Cooper's were focused on the bride.

When Mindy reached Tom's side, she turned to Alyssa, handed her the bridal bouquet, and moved closer to Tom, her face filled with the absolute love and trust she had in him.

Alyssa's eyes filled; her heart felt as if it were going to choke her, the emotion filling her was so intense. Mindy was truly a gentle soul, and if ever a woman had been meant for marriage and a family, to be cared for and looked after, it was her friend. She so deserved it, and Alyssa found herself deeply happy for her friend. She looked like an ethereal fairy princess in her wedding finery, that exquisite veil covering her face.

Alyssa could sense someone's eyes on her, and glancing over in the direction of the groom, she saw Coop still looking at her intently. Like Lois Lane snooping around after Clark Kent.

She'd fix him. Nothing was going to ruin this day.

Alyssa gave him a watery, teary, emotional smile, as any good bridesmaid might do, then glanced down. Shy. *Demure*. That was the image to go for, the total opposite of last night.

The ceremony began, as the minister said the age-old words that would bind this man and woman together.

And like a little silvery blue moth to a huge, white-hot, deadly flame, Alyssa couldn't resist sneaking glances at Coop.

He was gorgeous.

Life was so unfair. If life were fair, Coop would have been sitting down in one of the pews, where she couldn't see him. Or he would have caught a cold and stayed home. Or pulled a muscle from all that strenuous activity they'd engaged in last night. Or at least sported a zit on that perfect face.

But no. Gorgeous. In her face. Right in front of her.

Her knees turned to water at the thought that the two of them would be walking down the aisle together, in reverse, of course. How strangely appropriate. But the thought of him touching her again . . .

*You can do this, you can do this.*

She kept repeating the tiny mantra to herself as she watched the wedding, trying to keep her eyes off Coop. Impossible. He was deadly, he was yummy, she kept remembering all the things they'd done, those talented lips, those sure hands, that—

She couldn't believe she was having a Technicolor sex fantasy in the middle of her best friend's wedding!

Then the organ music jarred her out of her thoughts,

and Alyssa realized Mindy was kissing Tom, her veil had been lifted off her face, and everyone in the church was looking at the newly married couple.

Except Cooper Sinclair, of course, whose attention was focused directly on *her.* Alyssa tried not to squirm, but his gaze felt like one of those red laser dots on someone's forehead in an action adventure movie right before a high-powered assault weapon blew them away.

*What's wrong with the man?* She looked nothing like Bambi; blonde versus black hair, demure versus blatant sexuality. How could the man have mixed up the two of them? He had to have some sort of personal radar where she was concerned.

*Damn Cooper Sinclair!*

Though she really liked the fact that he was no dummy, this whole deception was going to be trickier than she'd thought.

As Tom and Mindy started down the aisle to joyous music and the murmurings of family and friends, Coop realized that he was about to get up close and personal with the maid of honor as they walked down the aisle. What had Tom said her name was?

Alyssa something or other, from San Francisco.

She looked familiar, but he just couldn't place her. He dug his nails into his palms in an effort to regain some sort of mental clarity, to banish any of the slight sleepiness he'd felt during the latter part of the ceremony. After his all-night marathon with Bambi last night—

*Bambi? No. Impossible. And yet—something about her eyes. That damn twinkle.*

Then he was standing next to her, offering her his arm,

noticing the way the slightest of pink blushes rose up from her bodice into her neck.

This woman was a total innocent, not an exotic dancer. *And yet . . .*

"Great wedding," he murmured, for her ears alone.

"Yes," she whispered, and Coop had the oddest feeling. He suddenly flashed back to his den, the dimly lit room, as he reached for Bambi beneath the down comforter, pulling her up on top of him so he could see her as she straddled him. He'd placed his hands firmly around her slender waist, then moved his thumbs so they could both slide down and caress that most sensitive part of her.

"Yes!" she'd whispered. *"Yes!"*

He decided he was going insane, seeing Bambi in every woman he met. Because this woman couldn't be further in looks and temperament from the mystery woman of the night before. Pale blonde, while Bambi had black hair; fragile and shy, while Bambi had been brazen and sexually adventurous, utterly fearless.

Then they were caught up in a whirl of people in the church's vestibule, and she excused herself. He watched her move through the crowd, then decided he needed to see Bambi again. Bad.

Because he was seeing her in every woman he met.

*That was too close. Way too close.*

Alyssa deliberately stayed far away from Coop, talking with one of Mindy's aunts. Aunt Virginia was telling her all about how she'd used homeopathic medicine to cure her cat of a digestive disorder, and Alyssa was actually quite interested. Her grandfather was fascinated with alternative medicine, and one of his Pekingese dogs sometimes had trouble with his food.

*Anything to keep my mind off Coop.*

She hadn't been able to stay away from him during the photographs. Tom and Mindy had hired an extremely competent photographer, and another man was in charge of a video camera. He'd been taping the vows, but directly after the ceremony, the other photographer had insisted that they pose for a number of formal portraits.

Mindy had also hired a makeup artist, so that everyone would look great in the pictures years later. Alyssa had stood patiently while the young woman powdered her nose, then tried not to flinch when someone suggested, "We really should get a picture of the best man and the maid of honor together! Wouldn't that be *cute*?"

Alyssa had smiled and smiled and smiled through countless pictures until she'd thought her face was going to fall off, and then finally escaped and moved as far away from Cooper Sinclair as possible. Unobtrusively, of course.

But she couldn't stop looking at him. Then again, neither could most of the single women at this wedding. She knew from what Mindy had told her a long time ago that Tom's best friend had made a ton of money with some kind of company he'd started up.

Now, of course, she wished she'd been paying more attention back then when Mindy had told her all this. Brains, bucks, and great good looks: a lethal combination.

She furtively glanced over in his direction and noticed that two of Mindy's bridesmaids hovered around him. And Coop seemed gracious and charming with both of them. Alyssa felt her self-confidence drop several notches. It was true; he had this effect on all females, not just with her. They'd fit together so well, had such vibrant chemistry together, because Coop would have had intense chemistry with a tree stump.

She'd been nothing special to him, after all.

Feeling shaky, determined not to cry, she turned her attention back to Aunt Virginia.

Now he knew he had it bad, because none of these women could hold a candle to Bambi. It wasn't that they were boring, it wasn't that there was anything wrong with them.

They just weren't Bambi.

He glanced over toward Alyssa. It was the damnedest thing; one minute, as she'd been walking down the aisle, she'd seemed to light up like a Christmas tree. Yet here she was, after the ceremony, flickering out like Tinkerbell in *Peter Pan*. She'd seemed so vibrant before, and now it seemed as if some inner light had gone out.

And why was he even concerned when he had Bambi coming to his place tonight?

Well, he'd have to be a real cad not to notice Alyssa whats-her-name's change of emotion. Women were completely a mystery to Coop, and he liked them that way. But he tried to pay attention, tried to keep up with the program. He tried to notice the little details, and the details surrounding Alyssa were that the woman seemed exhausted.

She'd flown in the night before, after the rehearsal dinner. Mindy had mentioned something about a performance she had to do, and as she lived somewhere in California, Cooper wondered if she were some sort of actress. And, of course, flying during the holidays was the absolute worst. On top of that, she'd lost time flying east, and changing time zones could be exhausting.

But it seemed like more than that.

Maybe she was upset that her best friend had married and she was still single. Now, that sounded like the way a woman might be feeling at a wedding. Maybe it had all hit her during the final moments of the wedding ceremony. Coop studied her, the bright blonde hair, the slender body. She didn't have to worry. She was sparkly enough and pretty enough that she wouldn't be single for long. Or if she was, it would be her choice.

Alyssa decided to make a conscious choice.

Okay, so Coop had chemistry with every single female he came across. Fine. But she'd *chosen* to throw caution to the wind and have wild sex with him. She'd consciously made that decision. So starting right now, she was not going to regret that decision or beat herself up for it. She was going to accept it, realize that she'd had a night of lovemaking that most women spent their entire lives fantasizing about, even *praying* for—and move on.

*Move on. Yeah, right. That was the hard part.*

*You can get through the rest of this wedding. You are calm, collected, you know what you are capable of.*

Blythe, Mindy's mother, came up behind her and put a supportive hand on her back.

"Alyssa, we thought you and Cooper could ride over to the country club in the first limousine with Mindy and Tom. Would that be all right?"

*In a limo. With Coop. That close. Sure.*

She nodded her head. "Should we leave now?"

Blythe smiled. "I think the photographer's gotten all the pictures he wants. But they still want to take candids at the reception. And there's the video, of course. Remind Mindy to powder her nose, would you?"

\*     \*     \*

Mindy sat in Tom's lap the entire way over, both of them kissing each other, all over each other like two dogs that had just discovered rare prime rib. And Alyssa could sympathize, because Mindy had decided to wait until her wedding night to have sex.

"Are you all right?" Coop asked her.

His concern touched her.

"Just a little tired. I flew in yesterday and didn't get a lot of sleep last night."

"I know what you mean. Neither did I."

Her mind went into overdrive, her imagination going down a darkly sexual path.

She pulled it up short.

"How do you like Wilmette?" he said, and she could tell he was trying to make polite conversation as neither of them wanted to look at Tom and Mindy.

"I've visited Mindy and her family before," she said. "It's a lovely area."

*Lovely. God, do I sound boring.*

She decided to tweak him a little, mad at him that he should have such a powerful chemistry with the entire female population. She wanted it to be just between the two of them.

"How was the big bachelor party?"

He stared at her for a long moment, and for one awful instant, she thought she'd given herself away.

"It was actually quite wonderful," he said softly, and the tone of his voice seemed filled with awe. Coop hesitated, then said, "I'm still kind of getting over it. It was one of the—no, it was the most wonderful night of my life."

Her throat started to close.

"How so?" she managed to croak out.

He seemed suddenly surprised that he'd revealed so much to her, as if he hadn't meant to say what he'd said.

"You're a very easy woman to talk to."

"I've been told I'm a good listener."

"Hmmm." He stared out the window for a second, then glanced back at her.

"Maybe I could use a woman's opinion. Would you mind?"

Did she really have a choice? "Not at all."

"I met this dancer. She intrigued me. We ended up—" He seemed to catch himself as he looked down at her. He stopped.

"Go on."

"We—" He stopped. "No, I can't tell you this. I'm sorry—"

"You did the horizontal lambada."

"How did you know?"

"Some stories are obvious."

"Hmmm." He considered this. "I've been working so hard, I kind of tend to keep my nose to the grindstone, and this girl, this woman, she . . . she seemed to set me free."

She swallowed against the nervous tightness in her throat. "And did you like feeling this way?"

"Yes."

"So call her up."

"I did."

*"What?"*

He glanced down at her. "Are you that surprised?"

"A little." She thought furiously for a way out of this one. "I mean, most women complain because guys say they'll call, and then they don't."

"If a man doesn't call," Coop said confidently, "it means he's just not interested."

"You should consider writing a newspaper column. The women of America would appreciate it."

He studied her for a moment, and it seemed to Alyssa that he wasn't quite sure whether she was making fun of him or not.

"I'm serious. You have no idea how many women wait by the phone and make up excuses for these guys in their heads." She thought fast. "So, did you get her number last night?"

"No, I called the company she dances for. They're sending her over tonight."

"They are?" She had to really fight to keep her voice sounding normal. Well, by the time the jig was up, she'd be on her way home.

"What time is she arriving?" Alyssa said, wanting to cover her butt.

"Right around ten."

"I see."

"I just—I want her to know that it was more than just—"

"The sex."

"Yes." He hesitated. "I'm not sure what it was, but it was more than just—that."

"But, excuse me for saying this, but you seem to be the sort of man who could have a great time with any number of women. You know . . . that chemistry thing."

He shook his head. "Not like this. It's never been like this."

She smiled and leaned toward him, touched his arm.

*Tell him, tell him who you are and then you can—then you can wreck Mindy's marriage, that's what you can do.*

How would she ever be able to explain to Coop what she'd been doing at the bachelor party he'd arranged for

Tom? There was no way for either of the men to view it as anything short of an enormous betrayal.

He grinned down at her. "So, any last words of advice for me?"

"Next time you host a bachelor party, consider something a little less dangerous, like bungee-jumping or sky-diving. Or maybe fire-walking."

He laughed.

# Chapter Five

The country club had been transformed completely, both for the Christmas holidays and for this particular wedding. If Mindy looked like a fairy princess in her bridal finery, then this was her kingdom.

As the four of them walked into the club, Alyssa glanced at the enormous floor-to-ceiling noble fir Christmas tree in the foyer, decorated with twinkling colored lights and dazzling, hand-blown glass ornaments. Farther inside, in the spacious ballroom, she would see what Mindy, her mother, and the wedding planner had been up to.

Right now, she was horribly conscious of Cooper, right next to her. Their arms were touching because he'd graciously offered her his arm as they'd left the limo, and she'd taken it, knowing that not to do so would probably arouse suspicion. Feeling the hard muscles in his arm beneath his suit jacket had been a strange sort of torture, as she'd remembered what those muscular arms had been capable of. But even beyond those thoughts, all she could really think about as she carefully maneuvered the snow-covered steps up to the front door, was what he'd revealed in the limo.

So it had been special, as special as she'd thought it had been. The thought thrilled her, until she realized she could never reveal the fact that *she* was Bambi, *she'd* danced on the family room table, *she'd* gone back to his den, dared him to kiss her, and ended up naked in his arms. She couldn't betray her best friend and start her wedding off on that kind of note.

But she kind of suspected Cooper would get the fact that something was off when he opened his door at ten tonight and there was the real Bambi. Alyssa wondered what this Bambi looked like. But Coop would know, for sure, that the dancer who'd had food poisoning wasn't the Bambi he'd spent the night with.

And then what?

Once inside, the four of them made their way down one of the long halls until they came to the main ballroom. As they entered, Alyssa's eyes widened. Mindy hadn't been kidding when she said her father and mother had gone all out to give her the wedding of her dreams. Her friend was the youngest of five children, and as she had four older brothers, this was the only wedding her parents would ever finance.

They'd definitely gone all out.

"The florist is going to use sixteen different kinds of roses to get the effect we want," Mindy had told Alyssa over the phone. "I can't wait to see it!"

*Spectacular* was the word that came to mind. Each of the round tables, which seated about twelve people, had an incredible floral centerpiece, along with several candles, already lit. The lights were low, and the ballroom looked like a fairy kingdom come to life.

Mindy had told her that the menu for dinner tonight was pepper-crusted lamb and lobster, but the pièce de résistance was the six-tier wedding cake, a vanilla-buttercream cake covered with thousands of sugar flowers. And Alyssa knew she would have enjoyed all of this immensely if she didn't have to worry about Cooper.

It wasn't that she thought he was going to do anything crazy. Strangely enough, Alyssa found herself veering back and forth between telling him and remaining silent. She wasn't even sure how mad he'd be at her, though she was sure he'd be at least slightly annoyed. There was even a chance he might really laugh at the entire incident.

Maybe.

It was just that it was so *hard* for her to walk away from him after the intimate night they'd shared. Yet there was another part of her, the chicken part when it came to relationships, that wanted to do exactly that. And if she was honest with herself, she had to admit that she didn't even know this man. And yet . . . she *did*.

She turned to Mindy. "Your mom wanted me to remind you to powder your nose before the photographers arrive."

Mindy was busily kissing Tom.

Alyssa cleared her throat, suddenly uncomfortable. She realized that a part of her wanted to haul off and kiss Cooper. He was simply temptation in a tux. Testosterone on the hoof. How ironic, that she had the man of her wildest sexual dreams right next to her, and she couldn't do a thing about it.

"Ah, young love," Cooper whispered next to her. Something in his tone made her look up at him sharply.

Maybe she didn't know him as well as she thought she did.

"You don't believe in love?" she said.

"Let's just say I have a healthy respect for its limitations."

*Limitations? Oh, great. Not only can I never blow my cover, I had to hook up with Mr. Cynic. Mr. Cynic with great moves, but a cynic nonetheless.*

"Cooper, I get the feeling that you were the sort of little boy who didn't believe in Santa Claus."

"Not for long. What's the point?"

She frowned. "When the time came to tell me, I was told that the spirit of Santa Claus was in everyone and everything, and Christmas was the time we keep it alive."

He considered this. "I guess that works."

"What do you mean, that works! It's true!"

He smiled down at her. "You're a dreamer."

She bristled beneath his gaze. "Is that so bad?"

"As long as you keep it on a realistic level."

She narrowed her eyes. He might be great in bed, but there were definitely some problems, his cynicism being number one on the list. But what did she care? If things went as she thought they would, she'd never see this man after tonight.

"What about that dancer?" Alyssa regretted the words the minute they left her mouth. She couldn't believe she'd said them.

"Bambi?"

"Yes," she said, and a part of her couldn't believe she was stubbornly continuing this train of thought. It was sheer suicide if he connected her to her role as Bambi the dancer. "What about Bambi? You said it was more than just sex."

He laughed. "Oh, no. Don't go trying to pretty this up and make it all romantic. I know what it was, and even knowing what it was, it was pretty incredible."

So Mr. Cynic didn't believe in love. Interesting. And Alyssa found she wanted to tweak him again. She just couldn't resist. Feeling as if she had one of those cartoon devils on her shoulder, while the cartoon angel on the other shoulder was making motions like *Cut! Finish! No more! Stop now!* Alyssa said, "And what exactly *was* it?"

"The single best physical experience with a woman I ever had in my entire life. Just incredible."

*Touché. Me, too. But then again, what do I have to compare it to?*

"Really." She considered this, and for some strange reason, she felt incredibly proud of herself. Even with all her inexperience, it had been that great. And even *she* wasn't naive enough to believe that she was in love with a total stranger she'd shared a night of hot sex with. But she could still believe that they had a special connection.

She glanced up at Cooper again, studying his face.

"But could . . . could the best sex of your life lead to something else?"

*You are playing with fire.*

He gazed down at her, a speculative gleam in his dark blue eyes.

"You want to think so, don't you?" She caught her breath as he took her chin in his hand, his touch so gentle. Studying her face, he said, "Alyssa, find yourself a good man. Someone who shares all your dreams. You need that sort of person, because the real world is a very tough place."

She could feel her jaw set. "The real world is incredibly beautiful, full of wonder, and there's usually a surprise around every corner."

He smiled, dropped his hand. "You believe that?"

"I *know* that. Look at what happened with Bambi." At this point, that angel on her shoulder had just given up and was sitting in a crumpled heap, weeping, while the little red devil on her other shoulder was jumping up and down and whispering, "You *go* girl!"

"Cooper, I believe it with all my heart." For some strange reason, she felt it was absolutely crucial that she get through to this man. Even more crucial than revealing who she really was and what they'd experienced together.

He was silent for a long moment, looking down at her. "Good for you," he said softly, with no trace of cynicism or mockery. And to Alyssa, he suddenly looked unbearably tired.

*He needs me.* The thought hit her hard, a gut feeling, a rush of intuition. She reached for his arm, words on the tip of a tongue ready to confess all, when Cooper turned to her and said, "I see guests starting to file in, we'd better help Tom and Mindy get that receiving line together."

The moment, the instant she would have confessed, was gone. Mutely, she nodded her head.

She'd tell him later.

Later, she lost her nerve.

She sat with Tom and Mindy and Cooper, up at the slightly raised, larger table in front of all the other guests. And after their first course was served, Alyssa found herself pushing her salad around her plate with the tines of her fork.

Ordinarily, she would have enjoyed taking in the intricate details and appreciated all the planning that Mindy and her mother had done. Like the plain red, green, or gold ornament balls at each place setting that had people's names written on them. They were original little place cards, and Mindy had told everyone that they could take their own ornament home with them tonight.

She stared at the elegant writing. "Alyssa" had been written in gold across a green glass ball, but she barely paid any attention.

This whole thing was getting extremely complicated.

What had she been thinking, jumping into bed with Coop? But she had to admit, it was just like her. She had the sort of personality that leapt before it looked, but the funny thing was, she had such a strong sense of faith in life that things usually turned out all right if not excellent.

"Don't like the salad?" Coop asked, and she noticed that most of the people at their table had already finished theirs.

"No, it's . . . tasty." Determined not to call attention to herself, she speared some of the mixed greens in raspberry vinaigrette and raised the fork to her lips.

*There's something about her. . . .*

Coop just couldn't place what it was.

The weirdest thing was, when he was with Alyssa, he didn't even think about Bambi. Which was strange, because he was seeing the dancer tonight, and this morning he had been feeling like he could hardly wait for Bambi to come back to his house.

But something about Alyssa *challenged* him.

He was pretty sure she had no idea who he was or what he did. That in itself was refreshing. He couldn't even begin to remember how many dates he'd endured where he knew the woman in question was only interested in his bank balance and how quickly she could get her hands on it.

Waiters appeared with their entrée, and Cooper watched as Alyssa pushed her salad away and began to play with her entrée in the same way.

Something was bothering her, and it was more than watching her best friend get married. Besides, she didn't seem like the type who rained on another's parade.

Knowing that he could toast the bride and groom at any point during dinner, Cooper stood, then picked up his champagne flute. His table quieted instantly, and the silence spread to all the other tables until all five hundred guests were silent and looking up at him expectantly.

"I've known Tom since we were at military school together," Coop began. "He's been a good and loyal friend to me for many years, and I think that I speak for all of us here in saying that we're so happy for your happiness, Tom."

Tom smiled, then reached over and kissed his bride on her cheek. Mindy positively glowed.

"I wish you both the best life has to offer," Coop continued; then he grinned. "And a very happy honeymoon in the Bahamas."

"Yeah!" yelled a male voice from the tables below.

"You tell him, Coop!"

"Great party, bud!"

People were laughing, in a partying mood. As Coop sat back down, he caught Alyssa's eye and winked.

*Oh my God, he knows. . . .*

*Stop being paranoid. He's merely letting you know that you might want to give a little toast or something.*

She stood up, her legs shaky. She'd had no idea how sitting next to Coop would affect her, but his mere presence seemed to . . . rile her up.

All eyes were turned on her as she raised her champagne flute.

"I love you, Mindy," she said simply, looking at her friend. Tears welled up in Mindy's eyes, and Alyssa had to fight her emotions to keep her own tears from spilling over. She glanced away from her friend and out over the sea of people seated at the round tables glowing with candlelight.

"We used to dream about our weddings all the time, and pin lace tablecloths to our heads and parade around. But I don't think either of us could have dreamed up anything as exquisite as today has been."

Murmurs of approval swept the large ballroom.

"You have a great man in Tom, Mindy," she said. "I know that." For an instant, the two women's eyes met, and the look that passed between them acknowledged what had transpired last night. "You're going to have a great marriage, and I want you to know that I'm so happy for you, and I'm sure everyone else in this room is, as well. To the bride and groom!"

"To the bride and groom!" echoed throughout the spacious ballroom, and Alyssa took a sip of her champagne, then sat down next to Coop.

"Very nice," he said.

"Yours, too," she replied. "Are you cynical about weddings, as well?"

"Not this one. Tom loves her, and she's perfect for him."

"Hmmm." Alyssa considered this.

"And before you ask, I'm not really the marrying kind."

She stared at him and felt her face flush.

"As if I were interested!"

"I didn't say you were."

"Then why bring it up?"

"Forget it." Coop turned his attention back to his lamb.

"How about a little game?" she said, remembering her phone conversation with Jake the other evening.

"What?"

"Truth or dare," she whispered.

That got his attention. Those dark blue eyes honed in on her like a tracking beam, and for a moment, just a moment, she thought she'd blown her cover. Then sanity returned. She looked nothing like the Bambi of last night. He'd never suspect.

"Truth," she said quietly.

He nodded his head.

"How do you *really* feel about Tom getting married?"

He hesitated.

"Truth," she said. "The truth."

"Strange," he finally admitted. "As if he's found something that . . . I don't think I'll find in this lifetime."

She knew enough not to push him further.

"Now you," he said, never taking his eyes off her.

"Fine."

"Dare."

"You got it," she said.

"Dance with me once the music starts."

"I have to; you're the best man, and I'm the maid of honor—"

"No, I mean a real dance. The first slow one. The entire dance."

That would be sheer, sensual torture, but he'd told her the truth, so she had to match him with a dare.

"Fine."

Dinner plates had been quietly taken away, and now the band was assembling itself on the area just off the large dance floor.

"Just remember that dance you promised me," Coop whispered to Alyssa.

He had to be going completely insane. She reminded him of Bambi.

Impossible. Because there was one quality that Alyssa almost radiated, and that was innocence. And Bambi had been far from innocent, with her sleek, bobbed hair, glossy red lips, and catlike eyeliner.

The two women were like night and day. And yet . . .

Alyssa's throat tightened as she watched Tom lead Mindy out onto the empty dance floor to the beginning strains of "Someone to Watch Over Me." They began their dance, all eyes on them.

She could sense Coop standing next to her.

"Please don't say anything to ruin the moment," she whispered.

"Me? Never."

She knew he was genuinely happy for his friend.

As Mindy left Tom's arms for her father's, and Tom danced with his mother, Alyssa walked toward the dance floor, her arm through Cooper's.

"Remember," he whispered as they stepped onto

the dance floor, "you've promised me an entire other dance."

"I know."

And then she felt his arms come around her, and they felt so *right*. She leaned against him and discovered that he was just as good at dancing as he was at other one-on-one activities. They moved to the music as if they'd been dancing together for years.

And she knew that this, this physical contact, this dancing, was what might give her away.

Before she could worry further, she felt a masculine tap on her shoulder. Turning, she recognized one of the men from the bachelor party the night before. He gave Coop a look that seemed to say, *May I?* and while Alyssa noticed with a thrill that Coop didn't seem happy relinquishing her, he let her go without a struggle.

She turned to her new partner and couldn't help noticing how his hands just didn't feel right, touching her.

"Hi," she said brightly. "I'm Alyssa."

Coop stood on the sidelines, watching Alyssa dance with his friend Dan.

Something was not right.

Something had happened when he'd put his arms around her. He'd never touched this woman in his entire life except to offer her his arm, yet when he'd put his arms around her and started to dance with her, he'd felt as if he were coming home.

Something was up. He sensed he didn't have all the facts. It was something he wasn't quite aware of, but that sixth sense that had served him so well in business was alerting him.

He stood to the side of the dance floor, watching her.

\* \* \*

Once the dance with Dan ended, Alyssa remembered another promise she'd made to Mindy, one she would have no trouble keeping.

Mindy's oldest brother, Ryan, had a son named Evan. And Evan considered himself something of an awkward dork. Alyssa remembered her own dorky days all too well, so when Mindy had asked her if she would mind singling him out and dancing with him, she'd been totally enthusiastic about the idea.

"Fine with me," she'd told her friend.

Mindy had pointed out tall, painfully skinny, and somewhat geeky seventeen-year-old Evan to her earlier during the dinner. She had no trouble locating him, standing with a group of his peers.

"Hi," she said, coming up to the young man. "Evan?"

He peered at her suspiciously, and she suddenly knew that this teenager had been made the butt of a joke more often than he would have liked.

"Yeah," he said cautiously, and she caught the glint of braces in his mouth.

"I'm your aunt Mindy's friend, Alyssa, from San Francisco." She held out her hand and he took it, cautiously.

Those glinting teeth broke into a slow smile. "My dad used to tell us about all the trouble you got Mindy into at school." She could see the awed respect in his quiet brown eyes.

"He only knows the half of it! Do you want to dance?"

She held her breath, waiting for his answer. He'd been standing in a group of young people, and she could only guess that they were brothers, sisters, cousins, and friends. But she could see that Evan's stock had just risen in their eyes, because an "older woman" had asked him to dance. And better yet, an older woman with a reputation!

"Yeah!" He looked like he couldn't believe she'd asked him.

"Fast or slow?"

He grinned down at her, and she saw the faint blush stain his cheekbones.

"Let's go for a fast one!"


*Very nice,* thought Coop as he watched Alyssa approach Evan. He knew the kid was painfully shy, and he grudgingly had to admire Alyssa for bringing him out.

The band broke into a rendition of "White Wedding," and he watched as Evan led Alyssa out onto the dance floor. They began to dance, and Coop had to admit that Evan wasn't bad.

But Alyssa was stunning.

She certainly knew her way around the dance floor. He watched her body move, sway to the music, her laughter and enjoyment contagious. A tendril of bright blonde hair had escaped her upswept hairstyle, and the slight messiness of it suited her. She laughed, her head going back, and one of the small rosebuds woven into her hair fell to the dance floor.

He narrowed his eyes.

Something seemed very familiar. He felt as if something were starting to click into place, just on the edge of his consciousness.

The floor around the two dancers started to clear as their moves became more elaborate and intricate and people stopped dancing to watch. Who would've thought that Evan loved to dance or was so good at it? As Coop got a much better view of the two of them, all the emotion inside him stilled.

*Alyssa . . . Bambi . . . Alyssa . . . Bambi . . .*

He didn't know how. He didn't know why. He only knew that the woman he had spent the night with and had the most incredible sex of his life with was the same woman who was out on that dance floor, having a wild time with Mindy's nephew.

Cooper suddenly knew that the woman Rico would be sending over would not be the same woman he'd been with last night.

He'd just found Bambi.

# *Chapter Six*

He let her dance three more dances with Evan, then the flushed and triumphant teenager went back to his group of cronies with Alyssa on his arm. And Coop had a feeling that Evan's stock had just risen.

*Good for Alyssa. And Bambi.*

As he'd watched them dance together, he'd thought furiously. What had Alyssa been doing at the bachelor party? If what Mindy had told Tom was true, and she'd only flown in that evening after the rehearsal party, what had she been up to while crashing the party?

And why had she taken the risk of spending the night with him?

It made no sense. The bridesmaid he was watching seemed so innocent, so *inexperienced,* for lack of a better word. The Bambi he'd known that evening had been sultry and sophisticated, and once they'd gotten naked . . .

Well. It was time he found out exactly what she was up to.

The sounds of a slow dance number filled the ballroom, and he went in search of Alyssa, Bambi, the dancer. Whatever she wanted to call herself, he had something to settle with her.

She was still talking with Evan and his group of friends when she felt a hand lightly touch her back. Alyssa didn't even need to turn around to know it was Cooper.

"Thanks for the dance!" Evan said, and she impulsively gave him a hug.

"You had some pretty great moves out on that dance floor yourself. Save another one for me before this party's over, okay?"

Evan grinned and nodded.

Then she turned to Coop. And instantly she didn't feel comfortable with the way he was studying her.

"You promised me a dance," he said, and though his tone was pleasant enough, there was something behind it.

*You're being paranoid.*

"So I did," she said brightly. "Let's get down to it!"

*Let's get down to it!*

Cooper remembered the last time she'd said those words to him, as she'd lounged back on the fake fur rug in his den. And he also remembered that incredible, incendiary chemistry that had flared between them. It was all he could do not to haul her off in his arms and kiss her senseless, right here on the dance floor.

And he was a man who had always prided himself on his control.

*What a total laugh.* His so-called control was going up in flames. How Jake would laugh if he had any idea of what was going on right now.

How could you desire a woman and be pissed off at her at the same time? What kind of game was she playing with him? Why did a part of him really want to laugh, and another part of him was annoyed? And how was he going to get her to admit that she was his Bambi, his dancer?

This was going to be a total challenge . . . and he found that he liked that idea. A lot.

He led her out onto the packed dance floor, the area filled with couples. With the slower music and more intimate dancing style, many of the older guests were now out on the dance floor with their partners. Alyssa eased herself into Cooper's arms and once again felt that strange feeling of coming home.

They danced in silence for a minute or so before she felt his hand smoothing its way down from her waist, over the slippery silk of her bridesmaid's dress, then resting intimately on her right buttock. Cupping her cheek. The dance floor was so crowded she doubted anyone even noticed. But she did.

And it felt wonderful.

Stepping slightly away from him, feigning surprise, she glanced up at his face.

"What do you think you're doing?"

He grinned down at her. "Just taking a stroll through your garden."

"What?"

He moved so that his lips brushed her ear. "Your *rose* garden. The tattoo. Remember? I do."

Before she could help herself, she flashed back to last night in the den, the flickering light from the fireplace, and the butterflies in her stomach as Coop's lips brushed against the tiny rose tattoo on her right buttock.

*He knows.*

She had no idea how he'd found out, but he knew who she was.

"I remember thinking you have the most perfect little butt," he whispered, for her ears alone. "Such a turn-on . . ."

Her body stiffened, but before she could pull away, he eased her closer.

"Hello, Bambi," he whispered into her ear. "Now, before you try to escape, I want to set a few ground rules."

She swallowed, then swiftly decided the only possible course of action was to totally bluff him out.

"What are you talking about, Cooper Sinclair? And here I thought you were a gentleman! Is this just some weird excuse on your part so that you can fondle my butt?"

She could feel his hesitation and knew she'd planted just a seed of doubt. She also knew she'd do anything not to wreck her best friend's wedding. Glancing up at him, she feigned being hurt, sticking out her lower lip in a sensuous pout.

"I thought your taste in women was more toward the exotic dancer type, not *moi*!"

He threw his head back and laughed at that, his eyes sparkling as they studied her with lively interest. "You are *such* a liar! I'll bet good money that there's a rose on your butt!"

"Bet all you want, because you're never going to *see* my butt, especially the way you're acting right now!" She put just the right amount of accusatory indignation into her voice, enough so that an elderly gentleman dancing with one of the bridesmaids gave Cooper a dirty look before he moved away from them on the dance floor.

"Alyssa, I'll bet you have a rose tattoo, a single red rose with a green stem and a few tasteful leaves, on your right buttock."

"This is an awfully personal conversation we're having, Coop."

"We got up close and personal last night, if you recall. For quite a few hours, as I remember it. And I had ample opportunity to study that rose."

She reached back and removed his hand from her buttock, prying his hand off with her fingers firmly around his. Then she placed his hand back around her waist. "It's only my long and close friendship with Mindy that's preventing me from hauling off and smacking you! I don't want to make a scene at her wedding."

"I'd smack him." This came from the elderly gentleman with the bridesmaid, who seemed to have danced up close to them to see what was going on. "Go ahead, honey, make a scene."

"Nope," Alyssa said to the man. "No can do."

"Well, I do see your point," said the man as he danced away.

"Listen, Bambi—"

*"Alyssa.* The name is Alyssa, *not* Bambi—"

"All right, Alyssa. You want to know when I knew?"

"Knew what?"

He sighed, and she sensed that he was starting to lose his patience. "When I knew who you were—"

"When you knew who you *thought* I was."

"All right, I'll play along with your little game. When I knew who I *think* you are."

"Thank you."

"When you danced. Your dancing gave you away. You

were using those same moves on the coffee table in my family room."

"Must have been one hell of a party," said the elderly man as he danced by.

"Would you *lower* your voice?" Alyssa whispered.

Coop only gave her a very intense, very knowing look. *Damn.* The man was good, she had to give him credit. She collected her thoughts swiftly.

"Coffee table? Whatever are you talking about?"

He sighed again. "Come on, Bambi, don't make me beg—"

"Alyssa!"

He was silent for a moment, and she had the funniest feeling he was silently counting to ten.

"Bambi or Alyssa," he said quietly. "Which is your real name? Or do you do all your exotic dancing under the name Bambi?"

"My name is Alyssa," she said, gritting her teeth for effect and practically spitting the words out. "A-L-Y-S-S-A. Got it?"

"Got it."

They stopped when the music stopped, both clapped for the band, then when she would have made a beeline off the dance floor, he grabbed her hand and stopped her.

"Okay. Just answer me this, and I'll leave you alone. What were you doing at the bachelor party?"

"I wasn't there."

"Yes, you were."

"No, I wasn't!"

"Were!"

"Wasn't!"

He swept her into his arms as the music started up again, another slow dance.

"We can dance," she whispered into his ear, "but if you put your hand on my butt one more time, I'm going to kick you where it hurts!"

"You liked my hand there last night," he whispered back.

*I did. . . .*

"Look, Coop, playing along with this ridiculous theory of yours, supposing I was at that bachelor party last night—"

"Ah, now we're finally getting somewhere! So you admit you were there!"

"Suppose I was? Can't you see how ludicrous it sounds? What would I be doing there?" Gaining both confidence and momentum, Alyssa decided to elaborate. "I'd just flown into Chicago, I was absolutely exhausted, I *hate* traveling over the holidays, so the first thing I'm going to do is sneak over to your house and go to Tom's bachelor party and rock out? I think not!"

"I think she was there," said the elderly man to the young woman he was dancing with. They were so close on the crowded dance floor that Alyssa could hear him quite clearly. "I'm going with that theory. What do you think?" His partner gave both Alyssa and Cooper a speculative glance.

Cooper laughed and pulled Alyssa close.

"Look at all the trouble you're causing!" Alyssa whispered into his ear. "I would never do something like—"

"You would if Mindy asked you to—"

"No, the first thing I'd want after a long plane trip is a hot shower and a—*what* did you say?"

"You would if *Mindy* asked you to. You'd do anything for her, that's just the kind of friend you are. The same way you danced with Evan."

One dance segued into the next, and they didn't even notice, they were so busy arguing.

"Coop, why—just for argument's sake in this stupid supposition—*why* would Mindy want me to do something like that?"

He tightened his grip on her waist. "Because she caught her last fiancé in bed with an old girlfriend and, oh, I don't know, maybe she just wanted to be absolutely sure she could trust Tom before she married him."

She swallowed. "Tom told you that?" She hated the fact that her voice seemed to come out in a squeak. Squeaking did not project confidence.

"He told me he was having a lot of trouble convincing Mindy he was a trustworthy man because of what that other jerk had done to her."

"Oh." She considered this. Coop was awfully good at putting all the pieces together. Her excuses were running out.

He pulled her closer against him. "Alyssa, I have a way we can solve all this, once and for all," he whispered in her ear.

"Good. I'd like that. I'd like you to put this ridiculous theory to rest, because I think you're just obsessed with this Bambi dancer, and you're seeing her in every single woman you meet, including me!"

He studied her. "You're quite good. I have to admire your nerve. I've caught you dead to rights, and you're not even nervous."

"I have nothing to be nervous about."

"That's what you think," he said. "Here's my plan. We go back to one of the bathrooms, perhaps one that isn't so crowded. You dance practically naked, so showing off your body is no hardship for you. We go into one of the stalls, and you lift up your dress and show me your right buttock. No rose, I lose. A rose on that cute little butt, I win. Deal?"

She stared up at him. Why hadn't she brought along any waterproof makeup, and why hadn't she thought to cover up her rose tattoo? Because she'd never met a man like Cooper Sinclair, and she suddenly realized he was not going to let the matter rest.

Well, the best offense was a good defense.

"I'm going to get into a bathroom stall with you, a total stranger—"

"Not so total after what we did last night—"

"And lift my skirt up? You've *got* to be kidding."

"Hah, I knew it! You're Bambi!"

*"You're* way out of line!" And with that, she wrenched herself out of his arms and marched off the dance floor.

Coop watched her go, then slowly grinned. He did so love a challenge.

"What a woman!"

They circled around each other like two big cats through more elaborate wedding photographs, and then when Mindy and Tom cut their wedding cake and fed each other pieces.

"Look," Alyssa whispered to Mindy after the cake cutting, searching for an excuse to leave and avoid Cooper, "I'm going to have to race out of here pretty soon, so have a wonderful honeymoon—"

"I saw you arguing with Cooper. Is everything okay?"

*Peachy.* "Sure. We were just having a spirited debate. He's got quite a few interesting theories."

"He's a neat guy. You know, he was the one who finally

convinced me I should take a chance on Tom and trust him."

*Mr. Cynic?* "He did?"

"He did. He told me that he'd never seen Tom so crazy about a woman as he was with me, and that I should marry him and put him out of his misery."

"Wow."

"You know," Mindy whispered, "it was kind of a fantasy of mine that you and Cooper would get together and—"

*If only you knew how together we got.* "Nope. Not my type."

"Oh." Mindy was clearly disappointed.

"Anyway, I've got to run, but I'll call you once you and Tom get back from the Bahamas and we'll talk."

"Okay."

Alyssa hugged and kissed her friend. "One last favor?"

"Anything," Mindy said.

"Just don't throw the bouquet anywhere near me, all right?"

Of course, Mindy threw the wedding bouquet toward her at the speed of sound, and Alyssa automatically reached up and caught it.

Reflex action. Nothing to get upset about. Until she glanced up and saw Coop smiling at her, then shaking his head. She promptly stuck out her tongue at him.

But she had the last laugh when he caught the bride's pink garter.

Mindy changed into her traveling outfit, and the happy couple headed toward the limousine that would take them to O'Hare Airport and their flight to the luxurious villa in the Bahamas. Everyone attending the wedding who had followed them outside lit sparklers and created a sparkling, fairy-tale send-off. The Bahamas had been Mindy's father's idea. Just as with the wedding, Mindy's parents had spared no expense on their honeymoon.

As Alyssa watched the sleek black limo turn out of the country club's parking lot and into traffic, she breathed a sigh of relief. Nothing had spoiled Mindy's perfect day.

And now it was time to get out of Dodge.

As she walked back into the country club to find her velvet cloak, she promptly bumped into Cooper Sinclair.

"Coop," she said, backing away from him.

"Time for you to run, huh?" He eyed the delicate blue paper goodie bag she had in her hand, with the wedding favors Mindy had given to all her guests, the strangest look in his eyes. Almost predatory.

And pretty damn exciting.

"Whatever do you mean?"

"You're going to run, the same way you ran this morning."

"I have no idea what you're talking about." As they walked along the length of the country club's hallway, she thought quickly. She'd have to call a cab, then double back to Mindy's house to get her bag.

"I can give you a ride back to Mindy's house. Dan brought my car over for me."

"I don't think so."

"Scared of me, Alyssa?"

"I'm scared of all your crackpot theories."

"I'm not." Once again he cupped her chin in his hand. "Look, I'm not really good at all this sort of stuff—"

"What stuff?" she said breathlessly.

"Romantic stuff. What women want to hear. But I've never promised a woman more than I can give her. All I know is that I took one look at your hazel eyes and . . . something happened. I don't know what."

"When?" she said, confused.

"When I walked into my family room, and you were dancing, and you looked up, and before you threw your bra at me, I looked straight into your eyes—"

She stepped back from him, breaking contact with his hand, her heart in her throat. "Oh, you *liar!* How could you know what color my eyes were! I was wearing a mask—"

She stopped, horrified.

*Jig's up.*

*Checkmate.*

*If I were on that* Survivor *show, this would be the moment I'd be voted off . . . my torch snuffed out . . . the tribe has spoken. . . .*

"A purple mask," he said softly. "A Mardi Gras mask. It brought out the green in those hazel eyes."

"Don't." She put up a hand as if to physically ward him off.

"You were the most beautiful thing I'd ever seen," he whispered. Taking her hand, he pulled her up against him. "Come home with me," he said, his lips close to her ear. "Come home with me tonight. *Please . . .*"

For one awful, wonderful moment, she considered it. Then her eyes closed, she remembered their conversation earlier, before all the guests had arrived.

*Don't go trying to pretty this up and make it all romantic. I know what it was, and even knowing what it was, it was pretty incredible. The best sex I ever had in my entire life.*

What was Coop going to do, hire her to come out to his house and dance for him? And then hire her for—

The thought of what that made her brought her up short.

She swallowed. Hard.

"Could you go get our coats? Mine's the blue velvet cape."

"I remember it." He lowered his head, and she knew just before he kissed her exactly what he was going to do. She gave herself over to the kiss, memories flooding her body as his lips covered and then expertly parted hers, as his tongue slid into her mouth and she shyly answered in kind, as that erotic action made her body go all soft and liquid, filled with feminine need.

The sheer intensity of his kiss and the fierce masculinity behind it caused her toes to curl inside her high heels. His arm came around her, steadying her, offering her support. And she was so close to his body that she had absolutely no doubts as to how much he wanted her. They were alone in the hallway, and she knew if he touched her breasts, she wouldn't be able to resist him.

Coop broke the kiss, then rested his forehead against hers for just an instant. "I'll be right back," he said, his voice not quite steady. "Wait here."

She waited, taking deep, steadying breaths, until he rounded the corner of the hallway before she raced out the front door. The evening air was absolutely freezing, though the snow had finally stopped. The frigid air jolted her silk-clad body out of its state of sexual arousal, as effective as a cold shower or a bathtub full of ice cubes. Alyssa took a deep breath, clearing her head, and looked around.

The country club's parking lot was jammed with cars, bumper to bumper, and she raced toward the street entrance. Perhaps she could get a cab.

In the midst of this melee, she saw Evan behind the wheel of a battered orange Volkswagen, right at the exit, just about to head into the street.

"Evan!" she yelled, and his head came around, his face breaking into a grin.

"Hey, Alyssa!"

She opened the passenger side door and flung herself inside. The heater, at full blast, felt heavenly against her chilled skin.

"Can you get me back to Mindy's in record time?"

"Sure thing!" He laughed as he put the car in gear and started out the driveway. "What kind of trouble are you in now?"

She glanced back, just in time to see Cooper standing at the country club's doorway, both their coats in hand.

"You don't want to know."

He saw the flash of silvery blue silk against the evening sky, then saw Alyssa hurl herself into the orange Volkswagen, her silken skirts frothing around her legs. Then whoever was driving the bug shot out into the street, into the light traffic, while he saw Dan and his car, backed up about fifteen cars from the exit.

*Damn it!* She'd bolted, just like this morning.

Well, there was nothing he could do about it right now. Shrugging into his winter coat and carrying her deep blue velvet cloak, Coop headed toward his car.

Evan got her to Mindy's in record time. Alyssa raced up the stairs to Mindy's bedroom, blessing the fact that she'd completely packed all her stuff into her duffel bag before she'd left for the wedding. Feeling like the hounds of hell were snapping at her heels and she had no time to change, she rummaged around inside her bag for a casual jacket to replace the velvet cloak, then zipped the duffel shut. She slung the strap over her shoulder, grabbed her purse, and headed back out the bedroom door.

And stopped. There on Mindy's bed was the blue paper bag that held her wedding favors, right where she'd set it down as she'd raced in the bedroom door. The Christmas ornament ball with her name on it that had been her place card for the wedding dinner. And a pair of exquisite, cream-colored candles. Each of them had gold scroll lettering on the side that said, "And they lived happily ever after. . . ."

But Alyssa knew how dangerously elusive that happily ever after was in real life.

Yet she couldn't just leave her wedding favor bag on her best friend's bed and reject her present, no matter how she knew things usually turned out in real life.

She struggled with her feelings for a tense moment, then grabbed the goodie bag and raced out of the bedroom, down the steps, and out the front door. Evan sat in his car, the motor still running.

"Are you sure I shouldn't take a cab?" she asked Mindy's nephew.

"Nah," he said with newfound confidence. "I can get you there in plenty of time for your flight."

He was as good as his word. She changed shoes while they drove to the airport, trading in her elegant heels for a pair of comfy running shoes, then gave Evan a kiss as he dropped her off. Running inside with her carry-on bag, Alyssa stood in the short line to the ticket counter, then basically begged the young man to give her the first flight to San Francisco that had an empty seat—no mean feat during the holidays. Her original flight didn't leave until later that night, and she couldn't take a chance that Cooper would come to O'Hare looking for her.

"There's a flight to the Bay Area in about forty-five minutes," the young man behind the airline counter said, "but it'll cost you a little extra—"

"Great." She whipped out her credit card and her original ticket. "Do it." Once she was past the security checkpoint, Coop wouldn't be able to follow her, and she'd be safe.

She didn't rest until she was on the plane. Alyssa was one of the last persons to run aboard, barely making the nonstop flight to San Francisco after racing madly through the airport, going through X rays, and praying that her duffel bag wouldn't be searched because of her strange outfit.

She'd run to the gate just in time to board the plane, holding the long skirts of her bridesmaid's dress in one hand, her carry-on duffel bag slung over her shoulder, clutching her small purse and goodie bag in her other hand.

"Must've been one hell of a wedding!" a guy called out as she passed him. His friends laughed.

Alyssa didn't even look back.

When she finally boarded the plane and practically fell down into her coach-class seat, it took her a moment to realize that all eyes were focused on her, including the flight attendant's.

In her bridesmaid's dress, rosebuds twined in her hair, with her casual jacket and running shoes, she had to look like something of a fashion disaster. Definitely a *don't*, according to that infamous *Glamour* magazine column.

"Don't ask," she said to one man in his thirties who

was staring, and another passenger, a woman in her late fifties, simply started to laugh.

At precisely ten that evening, Coop heard the doorbell ring. He walked slowly to the front door, then opened it. But he already knew the woman he wanted wouldn't be standing outside.

The woman who stood on the front step was very short. She had streaked blonde hair and a voluptuous figure, her breasts almost spilling out of the pink, bustier-type top she wore. And she was chewing an enormous wad of gum, snapping it as she chewed.

But she wasn't his Bambi. Not even close.

"Hi," she said brusquely. "Rico said you wanted a private dance."

"Come on in."

He guided her into the family room, poured her a glass of very good white wine, and settled them both by the comfortably crackling fire.

"Let's not waste any time," Coop said. "I'm trying to find a woman named Bambi, the Bambi that danced here the other night, and unfortunately, you're not her."

"But I *am* Bambi!"

"But did you dance at my bachelor party?"

She hesitated.

"The truth, please. I won't tell Rico or make any trouble for you."

"No, I didn't." She hesitated. "I ate a bad taco, and I couldn't make it."

Okay. Now things were beginning to make sense.

"Do you know the names of the other girls?"

"Kiki, Nina, and Brooke."

"So there were four of you, but you didn't make it."

"That's right."

"Of those three girls, who's the one who's the leader?"

Bambi considered this. "I'd say Kiki."

"Do you have her phone number?" He saw her doubtful expression and said, "I'm really not going to create trouble for any of you."

She sighed. "Sure. Right on my cell phone."

"Could you call her and ask if she'd be available for coffee tonight?"

She eyed him suspiciously. "Just coffee?"

"Just coffee. I give you my word."

"Okay." She rummaged around in her large purse, pulled out a cell phone, and punched in a number.

Keeping her brown eyes on him the entire time, Bambi said, "Kiki? Hey, it's me. Listen, I need a favor, real bad. Can you meet me for coffee in about—" She glanced at Cooper.

"Thirty minutes," he whispered.

"Thirty minutes? You know, that place by your apartment, with the great cheesecake? I'll meet you there. Oh, and there's going to be a guy with me, so don't get all freaked out, okay? Great. I'll see you soon."

She tossed the phone in her bag and glanced at Coop. "Are you sure I'm not in trouble? Rico won't be thrilled when he hears I bailed on your bachelor party."

"Rico never has to know. I just need some information about the girl who danced in your place."

"Huh." Bambi considered this. "Well, okay. We better get going if we're going to meet Kiki. Should we take separate cars?"

"Fine with me. Just give me the name and address of the place with the great cheesecake."

She scribbled it down for him. As she did, Coop

sighed, then pinched the bridge of his nose. He could feel a headache coming on. It was going to be a long night, but one way or another, he was going to get to the bottom of this whole mess.

And when he did, he'd figure out how to make sure Alyssa gave him another chance.

*Chapter Seven*

As the jumbo jet thundered through the night sky toward San Francisco, Alyssa had no idea that as she slept, emotionally exhausted, sprawled in her seat in her bridesmaid's dress, Cooper Sinclair was doing everything in his power to find out how she'd managed to infiltrate the bachelor party. And what city she'd escaped to.

He'd ordered both himself and the real Bambi espressos and chocolate-dipped biscotti, and paid for them, which seemed to have reassured the voluptuous dancer immensely. Cooper's first clue that things weren't quite on the up-and-up was when Kiki, a gorgeous blonde woman he definitely recognized from the party the night before, gave him an absolutely horrified look when she saw that he was sitting at the coffeehouse table with Bambi.

"No, it's okay!" Bambi called across the expanse of the coffeehouse, "he doesn't want a threesome or anything like that, he just wants to talk!"

Her announcement stopped all conversation in the coffeehouse dead. And Cooper had to laugh at the expressions on the men in the coffeehouse. Some date they thought *he* was having!

"Sorry about that," Bambi muttered. "But a girl has to be careful. Sometimes, the work we do, we come into contact with a kind of unsavory element, if you get my drift."

"I understand," Cooper said.

Cautiously, as if she were traversing a minefield, Kiki approached their table. Eyeing him warily, she eased herself into the seat across from him.

"Is this true?" she said.

"Cross my heart," Coop replied.

"I'd try for the threesome myself," said a thirty-something man at the table next to them. He had an unruly shock of bright auburn hair and was dressed in a brown handknit sweater and a pair of corduroys.

"Your mother would be ashamed of you!" said Kiki, but the young man only laughed. She turned back toward Coop. "I must be losing my touch. That line usually gets them."

"Mom and apple pie? I should think so. Do you want some coffee?"

"A latte would be nice. A grande."

"You got it. Biscotti?"

"I'd rather have a croissant. Chocolate if they have it."

Once they were all settled with their coffees and pastries, Coop got straight to the point.

"Who was the girl who called herself Bambi last night?" He glanced over at the real Bambi. "Because it sure wasn't her."

Bambi glared at Kiki. "I don't know, *I* wasn't there."

"Look," Kiki began, nervously stirring two packs of sugar into her latte with a wooden coffee stirrer. "Rico gets really pissed off if things don't go according to plan."

"Does he get abusive?" Coop asked, concerned.

"No, nothing like that. He's just a pain in the butt for weeks afterwards. He's one of those guys that never lets you forget a mistake. Know what I mean?"

Coop nodded.

"Anyway," said Kiki, "Bambi called me right before your party and told me she was dying because she had to have this taco—"

"Tony's Taco Joint," Bambi chimed in. "A great taco, but the aftermath wasn't worth it, let me tell you."

"All right," Coop interjected. "The real Bambi got a bad taco and couldn't make it. So where did the fake Bambi come in?"

"We met her just outside your house," said Kiki. "Me, Nina, and Brooke. She said she wanted to get inside your house and see what was really going to go on. You know, with the groom."

"Was it because of Mindy?" Coop said.

"How'd you know?" Kiki eyed him with new respect.

"I've just been trying to put the pieces together."

"Yeah, that was it. It seems this Mindy caught the last guy she was engaged to in the sack with an old girlfriend, and she was really insecure the night before her wedding, so this friend of hers—"

"What was her name?"

"Lisa something. Or Lissa."

"Alyssa?"

"That's it! So this friend of hers is a dancer anyway, and Mindy begged her to infiltrate the party and report back to her if her hubby-to-be sampled the goods, if you know what I mean."

"Okay. Go on."

"So we were all huddled outside wondering what to do because after all, you had hired four dancers, and we were one short, and, well . . ." She looked up at him beseechingly. "It just seemed like a good idea at the time."

Coop sat back in his chair and considered this. Just as he'd thought. Alyssa hadn't been able to resist Mindy's pleas.

"Are we in some kind of trouble?" Kiki asked quietly.

"No. I called Rico the morning after the party and told him you all did a terrific job."

"Like he mentioned anything about it to us," Bambi muttered.

"Then I asked him if I could see Bambi this evening—"

"And I," said Bambi to Kiki, "finally feeling better, went to his house, only I could tell I was the wrong girl from the look on his face when he opened the door."

"Do you know anything else about this woman?" Coop asked.

"She's kind of a free spirit," said Kiki.

*No kidding.*

"It was real sweet of her to help us out, don't you think?" Kiki said. Her eyes suddenly narrowed as she looked at Coop. "Why do you want to know?"

"I want to see her again, and I can't seem to locate her."

"She had to be at that wedding today," Bambi observed. "Did it go off as planned?"

"Beautifully," Coop said. "I recognized her too late, and she'd already left."

"Tough break." Kiki took a sip of her coffee. "I'm trying to remember—wait a minute, when we were talking outside your house, she said she had this dance troupe she was a part of—wait, wait, I'm trying to remember . . ."

Coop held his breath. Oh, he knew he could have called Mindy when she got home from her honeymoon, but he didn't want to wait ten days, and he certainly didn't want to bother the happy couple while they were at their villa in the Bahamas. And he couldn't quite picture asking Mindy's parents.

And he was sure Mindy or any of her family would call Alyssa and alert her to his nosing around, and that was the last thing he wanted. She hadn't been that happy with him when she'd skipped out of the wedding.

"Emotion in Motion! That was it! It's this sort of artsy dance troupe. She said they did one recital in nothing but blue body paint."

Remembering Alyssa's body, Coop wished he could have seen that one.

"You've been really helpful, both of you," he said.

"You're not so bad yourself," Bambi replied. "You know that thing I said about the threesome? Now I feel bad. I mean, you're a really good looking guy—"

"It's okay," said Coop, trying not to laugh out loud at the awed and slightly envious expression on the red-headed man's face at the table next to them. "I'm kind of in a hurry, but maybe some other time."

"Sure thing!" Bambi called after him as he got up from the table and headed toward his car. Kiki smiled and waved.

"Bye, Cooper! Thanks for the coffee!"

The captain's voice startled Alyssa awake.

"We'll be landing in San Francisco in about fifteen minutes. The weather there is fifty-eight degrees, with a bit of fog. If everyone could please fasten their seat belts and make sure their tray tables are in place . . ."

Groggily, she sat up, stretched as best she could, and brought her seat to an upright position.

"She is so!" she heard a childish voice whisper.

"Is not!" another voice whispered back.

It took her a few seconds before she realized that the two children, a boy and a girl, were talking about her.

"Is what?" she asked them. Both blond and blue-eyed, the brother and sister were sitting just across the aisle from her.

The little girl got straight to the point. "My stupid little brother thinks you're one of Santa's helpers."

This was interesting.

"Why do you think that?" she asked the boy.

"Because you're wearing such a pretty dress and you have those flowers in your hair."

Ah, yes. Her stunning travel outfit, courtesy of running out on Cooper Sinclair.

"Are you?" the girl insisted.

Alyssa studied her. She couldn't be more than eight years old. *So young to be so wary, so cynical.*

"Santa has helpers all over the place," Alyssa hedged. She noticed the children's mother sitting in the seat behind them, and the woman gave her a tired smile.

"So do you think that you can get *any* present you want?" the girl insisted, and Alyssa heard that same edge of upset cynicism in her young voice.

*Interesting.*

"If you've been good," Alyssa said.

"I've been very good!"

"Then I'm sure you'll get exactly what you want."

"Good! Because I want a pony!"

Alyssa turned toward the girl and noticed her mother just beyond the shining halo of blonde curls, slowly shaking her head *No*.

Alyssa leaned closer to the girl. "How long have you wanted a pony?"

"Forever and ever. Santa didn't give me one last year, 'cause my mom said that I'm too young."

Alyssa's gaze carefully took in the two children's outfits. Though they were clean, and they both looked well cared for, the little girl's navy and white sweater was slightly faded, and the ribbed cuffs were worn. The knees of her navy pants were shiny, and their mother's outfit had seen better days.

And something in the child touched her deeply. She saw herself at that age, full of dreams and wanting nothing but happiness, before she'd learned so abruptly that the world sometimes didn't give you what you wanted most.

She had a feeling that this child was in the midst of learning the same life lessons, and she was much too young to have to realize that.

She made her decision with lightning speed, and it made her happy. These were the moments when Alyssa was glad her family had a ton of money. She loved creating happiness.

"Where do you live? Could a pony live with you?"

The girl told her the suburb outside of San Francisco where she lived, and Alyssa knew there were several stables in the area.

"Well, we'll see what Santa can do, but if it doesn't happen this year, it won't be because you were bad."

"Then why not?" the girl insisted.

"Santa works in mysterious ways."

The plane touched down at San Francisco Airport, and Alyssa waited until everyone was waiting for their bags at the luggage area before she approached the children's mother. The woman's daughter was keeping an eye on her little brother, who was running around a short distance from them.

"I'm sorry if my children bothered you," the woman said. Standing this close to her, Alyssa saw just how tired the older woman was.

"Not at all. They're darling." She hesitated just a heartbeat before she said, "Is money the only obstacle?"

For a moment she thought the woman wasn't going to continue their conversation. And she had been asked a rather personal question. Alyssa realized this woman was sizing her up and must have seen something she liked, because she began to talk.

"Yes. My husband passed away unexpectedly almost two years ago, and things have been . . . difficult."

"Would your daughter be good with a pony?"

The woman smiled tiredly. "It's all she ever talks about."

"If I could get your daughter a pony, find a place to board it, arrange for riding lessons, and get her a scholarship to defray all the pony's expenses, would you want her to have this responsibility?"

"Would that be possible?" Alyssa loved the spark of hope she saw in this woman's calm gray eyes.

"Leave it to me. I just wanted to check and see if it was all right with you before I did anything." She hefted her duffel bag more firmly up on her shoulder, then said, "Can I reach you at work?" She glanced over toward the luggage carousel, and noticed that both children were approaching them. "That way we can talk freely."

"Here's my card." The woman rummaged in her purse and handed Alyssa a business card. "But, I don't understand. Who are you?"

Alyssa smiled. "Just call me Santa's little helper."

Cooper sat in his den, trying to keep his mind on the computer screen in front of him and not succumb to memories of what had happened in this very room less than twenty-four hours ago.

He found the search engine he wanted and carefully typed in the words, "Emotion in Motion." Then he hit Enter, and waited.

He didn't have long to wait. A page of various web sites came up, and he scanned them rapidly, grinning when he found a dance troupe in San Francisco well-known for its avant-garde entertainment.

He clicked on the web site, and his screen filled with a brilliant background that looked like bright splashes of vividly colored paint. There was a small picture in the corner, with instructions to click on it if you wanted to see a larger version.

He did, then, "Bingo," he said very softly.

In the middle of a group of people, all in various leotards and costumes, was Alyssa. He'd recognize that laughing grin anywhere, those vivid eyes. There was so much life to her, a vibrant energy that seemed to shimmer off her body.

He grabbed a pad of paper and a pen, then wrote down the address and phone number of the dance troupe. He was just shutting off the computer when the other line on his desk rang. His private line. It had to be Jake. For once, Coop found that his mind wasn't on business.

Coop picked up on the second ring.

"Hey, Coop, how'd the wedding go?"

"Great. Can you cover for me for a few days?"

"What's up?"

"I'm going to be flying to San Francisco."

"What?" His friend and business partner sounded amazed. "A quick getaway during one of our busiest times of the year?"

"It's important."

Jake was silent, then said, with total delight in his voice, "It's a woman, isn't it?"

"What makes you say that?"

"It's that Bambi Alyssa girl, isn't it? The dancer?"

Coop stared into the phone. How did everyone in the world seem to know all his business?

"How did you know her name?"

"We had a little chat on the phone last night."

"You did."

"Don't tell me you're jealous! Coop, I love this!"

He didn't know what to say.

"Look, she picked up the phone and asked me if you were always this bad."

"This . . . bad?"

"You know, Coop. All work and no play?"

"Yeah."

"Anyway, it was my impression that she really liked you."

"She doesn't like me at all," he said.

Jake laughed. "Give her a chance. I assume you're going out to San Francisco to meet her."

"In a way."

"This just gets better and better. Coop, take all the time you need. I'll be here running things, and Riley will be fine with me. If you have any worries about the company or this dancer, call me day or night."

Coop suddenly found himself very grateful that he had a partner like Jake. His business partner was both a friend and the brother he'd never had.

"Thanks, Jake. That means a lot."

"Hey, any time. I just want you to be happy, you know?"

"Yeah, I do."

Coop hung up the phone, then turned the computer back on, went on-line, and found several travel sites. After comparing prices for several flights, he picked one, charged it, and turned off the computer. Though he could have afforded a private jet if he'd wanted one, he was a frugal man by nature and saw no sense in spending money wildly. He'd invested carefully for the future and was perfectly content to fly on regular airlines.

He sat in his den, all alone, and it was as if Alyssa's spirit had possessed the place. He only had to close his eyes and he could see her dancing, her body swaying to the music, that glittering purple Mardi Gras mask on her face. He couldn't look at the crackling fire without seeing her lying in front of it on the fake fur rug, totally naked. He couldn't glance at the long leather couch without smiling, thinking of all those sharp, challenging retorts coming out of her glossy red mouth. And he hadn't even bothered to put the down comforter away; he'd merely thrown it up on top of the couch.

Well, he didn't leave for O'Hare Airport until morning, which gave him plenty of time to pack and do a little cleaning up. He'd vacuumed the family room before he and Tom had left for the wedding and also put the garbage out, the dark green trash bags filled with paper plates and plastic cups and forks. He'd fold up the down comforter and leave it here, then go upstairs and pack.

Coop got up from his desk chair and walked over to the sofa. He lifted the comforter off the leather couch, shook it out, and saw the small, dark stains against the cream-colored duvet cover.

Puzzled, he looked closer. It took him a moment before he realized he was looking at bloodstains.

*Bloodstains. Did she hurt herself, cut herself, did I hurt her in any way?*

When the obvious answer asserted itself in his mind, he went totally still. And remembered how right it had felt when their bodies had been joined together, and how very tight she'd felt, how exquisitely her body had sheathed him.

Alyssa had been a virgin.

She'd been totally inexperienced, and he'd treated her as if she'd known exactly what she was doing, as if she were a very experienced woman. He'd done nothing to reassure her, nothing to make her first time special.

He'd stayed away from virgins for this very reason, preferring women who knew the score and knew what they were doing. And what he was going to do to them.

*A virgin.*

He had to sit down; his legs were starting to wobble.

He sat, still staring at the duvet. After almost a full minute, he pushed it away from him, tossed it back on to the leather couch, and put his face in his hands.

This made things ever so much more complicated. Now he had two new reasons to go to San Francisco and find Alyssa Preston.

One, he had to apologize for treating her as if . . . as if

she were really Bambi. Basically, as if she'd had any idea at all of what she was doing.

And two, he hadn't bothered with any birth control, assuming that she'd taken care of the matter. Now Coop realized that he couldn't really assume anything. For all he knew, Alyssa might right now be pregnant with his child.

How right that funny little expression was, to never assume anything because all you do is make an *ass* out of *u* and *me*.

He'd treated her badly. As badly as a virgin could be treated. She'd been like Little Red Riding Hood to his Big Bad Wolf. Coop cringed as he remembered hauling her up over his shoulder and carrying her down to the den, and later locking the door so they could be alone together.

*Let's not get carried away here. You didn't lock her in. She was definitely a consenting party.*

But he should've known better. He was older than she was, more experienced, but he'd just let every shred of common sense fly right out the window.

*Right about the time you got a really good look at her breasts. And then of course there was that stellar moment on the dance floor when you grabbed her ass.*

It just got worse and worse. After a few moments, Coop stood up, grabbed the comforter, bundled it up, and headed upstairs to his bedroom to pack for his flight out to San Francisco.

It looked like he was going to have to eat crow, after all.

# Chapter Eight

Alyssa found herself relieved to be back in San Francisco, with its familiar cool and breezy seaside weather, the hills, the fog, and the smell of the ocean in the air. She loved looking up at clear blue skies with seagulls wheeling overhead. Though winter usually brought its fair share of rain, she came back to good weather.

She'd grown up in the city, always in the care of her maternal grandfather, Phillip Preston. After her mother had died, her grandparents had been the only constants in her life. They'd adopted her and she'd taken their name. Now, with only her grandfather left, she considered him both mother and father. She also considered San Francisco her home and hoped it always would be.

This morning, she found her grandfather in the sunny breakfast room of the large Nob Hill mansion they both lived in, an open copy of the *San Francisco Chronicle* shielding his face. His usual breakfast sat in front of him on the glass-topped table: strong tea, whole-grain rye toast with just a little butter, and an organic, free-range poached egg.

His three beloved Pekingese dogs sat at his feet, their small pink tongues hanging out of their mouths, their little wrinkly faces inquisitive, their black button eyes sparkling.

"Hello, Grandpapa," she said, bending to give him a quick kiss on his weathered cheek. How she loved this man. He'd been her rock when her world had caved in when her mother had died. He'd been there for her through some very hard times, and his love and devotion to her had never faltered. She adored him and had decided long ago if she could give him back even a tenth of the love and devotion he'd showered on her from the day she was born, she would be satisfied.

The rest of their large, extended family, none of whom she was close to, thought it rather odd that she still lived with him. Many times they'd remarked on the fact that she could certainly afford a place of her own. But she enjoyed her grandfather so much, and he'd never made her feel as if she had to justify her comings and goings. And now that he was older, she wanted to keep an eye on him, though she could never tell him that. He would have been highly offended, because Phillip Preston refused to think of himself as someone who needed to be taken care of.

Not in a physical sense, but in an emotional one. She hated the thought of his eating by himself and wandering through his spacious home alone. Alyssa had made the conscious choice that she wanted to spend time with her grandfather simply because being around him made her very happy.

In his seventies, her grandfather lived a very full life.

Healthy and fit, almost six feet tall with a full head of white hair, he took long walks with his dogs up and down the hills of his beloved city. He also ran several incredibly successful charities, had a mind sharper than almost anyone she'd ever met, and believed that people were meant to find their better halves and *marry*. He'd adored her grandmother; they'd had a long and very happy marriage.

And he wanted the same for his only granddaughter.

The only negative concerning her grandfather was that he tended to be a tad overprotective. He often despaired of the performances she and her dance troupe put on. But most of the time he found out about them after the fact, reading the reviews in the paper. She'd always listen to his gentle chiding, then acknowledge he had a right to be upset at the thought of her "prancing around a stage in nothing but blue body paint," but then she went right back to doing what her heart told her was correct.

"You are so like your mother," he often said.

"And that's why you worry," she often replied.

His clear hazel eyes, so like her own, would twinkle, but he watched her like a hawk.

And he didn't miss a trick.

*Overprotective, thy name is Phillip Preston.*

"Good morning, Alyssa," he said, setting down his cup of tea. "I trust Mindy's wedding went well?"

"It was absolutely beautiful."

"Hmmm. That's good to hear. And the young man she chose?"

"A very nice guy."

"Good. The selection of a life partner is crucial, you know—"

"Oh, yes," she said, cutting her grandfather off at the pass. He wanted her to get married, preferably to a man he approved of who would take care of her and perhaps curb her wilder ways. Protect her. Yes, Phillip Preston was something of a chauvinist, but in the nicest of ways. It was simply part of the thought process of his entire generation.

She'd always considered that sort of arrangement, married or not, as the kiss of death. And her grandfather had wasted no time in parading a whole host of eligible young men past her, at all sorts of social events, practically begging her to give one of them a chance. She hadn't really cared for any of them; none of them had elicited a response from her.

But now, as she sat at the breakfast table, she wondered what her grandfather would think of Cooper Sinclair. Strange as it seemed, she had an intuitive feeling that the two men would get along quite well.

Trying to think of a way to distract him, Alyssa jumped right back into the conversation.

"Which charity are you sponsoring right before Christmas?" she said, pouring herself a cup of coffee from the small pot on the table. She reached for the sugar, then the cream, fixed her coffee the way she liked it, and raised the rose-patterned china cup to her lips.

"Don't try to distract me, Alyssa!" Her grandfather's eyes twinkled as he set down his teacup. "Did you meet anyone nice at this wedding?"

She barely managed to escape blowing hot coffee out her nose. As it was, she almost swallowed some of it down the wrong pipe.

*Did I!*

She knew her grandfather could never, ever, *ever* in a million years find out about what had happened between her and Cooper Sinclair. She might think that the two men would get along if they ever met, which was highly unlikely, but she doubted her grandfather needed—or wanted—to know some of the intimate details of her life. He would not be amused.

Of all the crazy stunts she'd pulled over the years, sleeping with Coop after having known him—oh, about two hours—well, that was far worse than running around onstage in blue body paint, dancing and welcoming in the spring.

"Alyssa?" He was watching her carefully, and for a moment she felt like a tiny mouse, looking up and seeing a powerful hawk swooping down on her.

"Meet someone? Me?"

"Yes, you."

"I met a lot of nice people, including Mindy's nephew, Evan." She went on to describe Mindy's seventeen-year-old nephew and the dances they'd shared at the reception, trying to ignore the slight frown on her grandfather's concerned face.

"He was such a nice guy, he even drove me to the airport when the reception was over."

"No one closer to your own age was at that wedding?"

She thought frantically. "No. Most of them were paired off—"

*Oops!* She'd slipped up big time.

"I've been meaning to discuss something along those lines with you," her grandfather said, smoothly changing the subject. "You see, Alyssa, one of these days, between your dancing and your own charity work, you're going to wake up and realize that all of the really outstanding young men are already spoken for."

She hesitated, then said, "I suppose you're right."

He smiled at her, a smile so full of love that she couldn't be mad at him.

"Grandpapa, I know what you're getting at. But I want it to be exactly like you and Grandmother, where you took one look at each other and you *knew*—"

"And I want exactly the same for you."

"It's different these days. Men are different. There are no rules, not as much structure as in the old—as in the days when—"

Her grandfather leaned back in his chair. "As in the Stone Age. Oh, I know you consider me to be an opinionated old fart—"

"Not true!"

"But I want you to know that I'm concerned about what's going to happen to you when I'm no longer around."

This was a subject she absolutely hated to think about.

"Can we please not talk about—"

"My darling, we have to. When I pass away, you're going to be left an extremely wealthy woman, and there are many men out there who prey on wealthy women."

*Then maybe I could just never get married.*

Marriage was a hot button emotionally for Alyssa, because of all the stories she'd heard about her own mother. Elizabeth Preston had been a dancer as well, a classical ballerina with immense talent and potential, when she'd fallen madly in love and married Alyssa's father.

The marriage had been a disaster, and Elizabeth had come home to her parents' house one rainy winter night, a broken woman with an infant daughter in tow. And while Phillip and Amelia Preston had taken exquisite care of their granddaughter, Elizabeth had gone into a long decline from which she'd never really recovered.

That left Alyssa terrified of marriage. She didn't want

anyone holding her down, keeping her back, making her suitable, or deciding what was best for her.

Hence, her new idea of one-night stands.

*No,* she thought as she studied her grandfather, *that isn't really true.* She'd had no idea she was even capable of a one-night stand until many things had conspired that evening. Mindy's impassioned plea, the actual party, dancing on that table, wearing the mask and the wig and the makeup, throwing her bra out into the crowd—

*And Cooper Sinclair.*

"Alyssa?"

She blinked and stared at her grandfather.

"Where did you go just now? What were you thinking?" He seemed genuinely curious.

"I was just thinking, where do you think I could get a pony?"

He was so used to her lightning-fast changes of subject that he didn't even flinch.

"I would call Monty down at his stable by Carmel. If anyone knows where to get a good-minded pony, he's the man."

"Great idea!" Quickly, she told him about the woman and her two children on her flight back to San Francisco, and the little girl's dream of receiving a pony from Santa.

"You have a good heart, Alyssa."

"Thank you."

"You'd make an excellent mother."

Her smile faded. She remembered, not for the first time, that she and Cooper hadn't used any birth control during their night together. And though she was fairly sure she hadn't had unprotected sex during a crucial time in her cycle, it had still been a foolhardy thing to do. She hadn't been thinking clearly.

*The understatement of my entire life.*

That her grandfather should bring up the thought of any future children so close after an event that could make that thought into a potential reality . . . Sometimes he absolutely unnerved her. She had a feeling that he saw a lot more than he let on. Yet she knew he couldn't possibly know about her wild night with Cooper.

She forced a smile and said, "Thank you."

He eyed her for a moment, then picked up his paper and turned to the society pages.

"Well," she said brightly, finishing up the last of her coffee, "that's it for me."

"That's all you're going to eat?"

"I really stuffed myself at the wedding. Don't you worry about me, I'm not starving." She glanced at her watch. "I thought I'd go down to the theater and check out the class schedule, then call Monty and get the pony project going."

"Excellent. I'm going to be making some phone calls for that charity dinner and auction right before Christmas. The one that benefits my animal shelter."

Phillip had several charitable interests, one of the main ones being an animal shelter in North Beach that he sponsored. This particular dinner would be a gourmet's vegetarian delight, with the price per plate at one thousand dollars. All of the money would go toward the shelter to benefit any lost and injured animals in the city.

"What's the date on that again?"

"The twenty-second. Six o'clock on the dot."

"I'll be there," she promised.

"I thought that perhaps you could act as my hostess for the evening."

"I'd be honored," she said, then gave him a swift hug and a kiss before she headed out the door.

Cooper sat in his rental car, parked across from The Destiny Theater in San Francisco's Upper Mission District. The building was huge but kept up pretty decently, painted an amazing purple color. He'd done some reading about it in his guidebook and learned that it had once been a machine shop before being converted into a theater. It was here that Alyssa's dance troupe, Emotion in Motion, both practiced and performed.

He leaned back in the seat of his rental car, half asleep. He'd flown out to San Francisco with barely a plan formed, kind of winging it, as it were. He had no idea what he was going to say to her when he saw her, or if she'd even want to see him.

A flash of bright color caught his eye, and he turned in his seat, then sank down and pulled the bill of his black baseball cap farther over his face.

There she was, walking along the street—no, a gait like that could only be called *dancing*. She had on a bright pink dress, silver boots, and swung a large tote bag decorated with some ridiculous flowers. A turquoise sweater, a cute little number that barely made it to her waist and was knit out of some chunky yarn, completed her outfit.

She looked absolutely wonderful.

Her bright blonde hair was pulled back in a high ponytail, and he watched as a slender young man in his twenties came running up to her. They hugged each other, then fell into step, side by side, arms around each other and engaged in animated conversation.

And at that moment, Cooper found himself wanting to be a part of her world, no matter what it cost him. She simply lit up wherever she was, with her own glowing little spotlight.

They both entered the double theater doors, and Coop settled back in his rental car. He wasn't quite sure what he was going to do next, but he knew he had to find a way to locate where she lived and then call her and set up some sort of meeting.

If only to apologize.

The news was not good, Alyssa thought as she sat around the large circular table in one of the offices offstage and chewed on a fingernail.

The roof was leaking again. One of their dancers had fallen down at a party over the weekend and severely twisted her ankle. And they were behind where they should be in rehearsal for their dance recital that opened the last week in January.

"I'm going to suggest—" she began.

"No," several people said in unison. Alyssa bit her lip, then smiled wryly. The answer never changed, though she never stopped making the suggestion. Even though she had access to a veritable ton of money, no one in the dance troupe would let her use it to help finance their struggling group. They had long ago decided that they would make it on their own effort or not at all.

"Okay. Can Sonya take Anna's part?" she said, Anna being the dancer in question who had twisted her ankle.

"She'll pick it up quick," Barry said. He was her right-hand man, and had been waiting for her outside the theater.

"Sounds like a plan," said Walter in a slight monotone. He was a big, burly, bearded bear of a man, who usually dressed in flannel plaid shirts and overalls. Married with five children, Walter didn't dance, but his oldest daughter, Natalie, did. So he came down to the theater on a regular basis, helping by selling tickets before their performances, then punch and cookies at intermission. He did a ton of odd handyman jobs around the place.

Walter had a resigned, sorrowful outlook on life, as if he didn't expect much good to come of anything, and he reminded Alyssa of the donkey, Eeyore, in Winnie-the-Pooh.

But he was no match for a leaky roof.

The plan had been to take the monies received from the recital in January and use them to help fix the roof. But now with their main dancer out of the show—

"Okay!" Alyssa said, standing up. "Let's not worry too much; these problems have a way of working out. I say we go for a killer rehearsal."

Murmured approvals and nods met this suggestion.

"Let's get our blood going with some jazz," Alyssa suggested. "Walter, can you man the music and lights?"

"Sure thing," he said gloomily.

"Thanks!" She gave him a swift hug before heading for the dressing rooms they'd built in the drafty basement of the building.

He knew he was playing with fire, but Cooper found himself sneaking in the theater, then walking through the large lobby and into the back of the actual theater itself.

All the lights were focused onstage, on the dancers, and he found that he could hide in the shadows. Trying to draw as little attention to himself as possible, he quickly sat down in the very back row, in one of the side sections, and hunched down in the seat, pulling his baseball cap back down over his face.

The music was jazz, hot jazz, and the movement on-stage was thoroughly modern and lively. And very, very sexy.

It took him mere seconds to see Alyssa.

She was dressed in a black leotard with a shocking pink and orange filmy piece of material tied around her middle like a belt. Another scarf was tied around her head, tight, keeping her hair out of her eyes as she moved. And she was in front of all of them, leading both male and female dancers through an intricate jazz routine.

"And one and two and—that's it, that's it!"

He noticed that she seemed to be focused on one particular woman in the back, more a girl really, a chubby brunette in a red leotard who seemed to be having trouble keeping up with the routine. Cooper watched, fascinated, then frowned when in the middle of the dance number, the chubby girl stopped, a look of desperate resignation on her face.

She started toward the front of the stage, grabbed a large blue tote bag, slung it over her shoulder, and then raced down the side stage steps that led to the aisle that divided two sections of the audience's seats.

He crouched lower in his seat, and as she came closer, he scrambled down onto the cold, carpeted floor.

Cooper heard swift footsteps running up the aisle, then Alyssa's concerned voice.

"Natalie, wait!"

One set of footsteps stopped, only about three rows down from where he was hiding. And Cooper wondered what he would say if Alyssa found him in her theater, in her territory, groveling on the floor.

*Oh, hi, I just flew in all the way from Chicago to spy on you. By the way, you're an excellent dancer.*

This was not the way he'd planned their first meeting.

"Natalie." Alyssa's voice was gentle. "What's wrong?"

The girl's voice was thick with emotion. "I'm fat and I'm ugly and I'm never going to learn this stupid routine!"

"I don't think that's true."

"You're just saying that because my dad helps out!"

"Do you really believe that?"

Silence.

Cooper marveled at her, at the genuine concern and caring he heard in her voice. She was a woman unlike any other he'd met, and he was discovering that the more he found out about her, the more he really liked her.

"No." The one whispered word was said in a very grudging tone.

"Do you just need to take today off?"

Silence, then, "Yeah, I think I do."

"Could you sit in back here and watch the lesson? Then maybe afterward we could go out for coffee and talk. I'd really like that, Natalie."

"Okay." This word sounded as if the teenager was on the brink of tears.

"Oh, honey." Cooper heard the sound of Alyssa's arms enfolding the self-conscious teenager. "I can still remember," she whispered. "Being a teenager can be the pits!"

"Tell me about it," Natalie said. Then, about a minute later, Cooper heard the sound of the teen blowing her nose.

"Promise me you'll sit right here and wait for me to finish, okay Natalie?"

"Okay."

"I shouldn't be much longer than about another forty minutes, okay?"

"All right."

"And then we'll get that coffee. Maybe a vanilla latte."

"Yeah."

Cooper heard the sound of a theater seat opening, then Natalie sitting down. He heard Alyssa's light tread as she flew down the aisle of the theater. And he realized—

*Forty minutes!*

He'd have to remain on the floor for the next forty minutes—at least!—to escape detection.

Though the theater was heated, the carpeted floor was ice cold. Cooper was sure the dancers up onstage were warm, what with the hot lights and all that movement. But he only had on a thin windbreaker, jeans, a T-shirt, and running shoes. Oh yes, and his black baseball cap, which was a blessing, because he'd once read an article that said you could lose something like 80 percent of your body heat out the top of your head.

And he remembered a quote he'd once read, attributed to Mark Twain, that had gone something like, "The coldest winter I ever endured was the summer I spent in San Francisco."

Winters were milder, but still not that warm.

God, it was cold this close to the floor.

Wishing he could rub his hands together for a little warmth but not daring to make a sound or shift his position in any way, Cooper gritted his teeth and determined to wait it out.

"Okay, that's it for today! How about three o'clock tomorrow?"

Cooper opened his eyes at the sound of Alyssa's voice. His left leg had fallen asleep, and now his right hand was following suit. That, and spasms of muscle cramps had been going on for close to the last fifteen minutes.

"Why so late?" someone asked.

"I have to purchase a pony," Alyssa said.

Laughter followed this announcement.

"Playing Santa again?" Coop heard a man's voice, strangely monotone.

"Yep. All she wants for Christmas is a pony."

"Good for you. I'll be here at two and get the heater going, set things up."

"Thanks, Walter."

He heard her footsteps coming down the aisle. "Okay, Natalie, let's go."

"You know," said the teenager, sounding better than she had before, "it helped just sitting out here and watching the whole routine, over and over."

And Cooper had to grin at the smile he heard in Alyssa's voice. "Funny how that works, isn't it? Let's go get that coffee."

They headed up the aisle and out the back door into the lobby, and Cooper waited until he heard the rest of the dancers leave the stage. Feeling sore in every single muscle of his body, cold and stiff, he sat up, winced, then slowly made his way out into the lobby. He pushed open the large double doors and squinted up at the blinding, bright sunshine, feeling like a mole that had just been pushed up from underground.

Lying in the large bathroom in his hotel suite, the tub filled with blissfully hot water and whatever sort of bubble bath had been in the generously sized guest bottle on the sink, Cooper stared up at the ceiling and admitted defeat.

He didn't know how he was going to approach Alyssa. He didn't like following her around without her knowing about it. It smacked of stalking, and he certainly didn't want her to think of him in that way.

But he wanted to see her again; he was sure of that.

Cooper couldn't seem to stop remembering the night they'd spent together. His thoughts kept coming back to that moment in time. It had been the most sensually incredible night of his entire life, and he'd had plenty of nights of sensuous experiences.

If nothing else, he wanted to know why she'd done it, why she'd thrown caution to the wind and chosen to lose her virginity that particular way. And why with him?

*Not that I'm complaining.* No, that night with Alyssa held nothing but the happiest of memories for him. She'd shocked him out of his rut. Jake had been right; he'd been in a serious funk, all work and no play. And it had taken a free-spirited dancer in a Mardi Gras mask with a smart mouth and a sharp wit to knock him right out of it!

Now all he had to do was figure out a way to meet her. Legitimately, no more of this skulking around stuff. His body couldn't take much more of being contorted in the cold.

But it was more than that, more than any physical discomfort on his part. He'd told Alyssa at the wedding not to go and try to make the whole encounter with Bambi something it wasn't. The trouble was, at the time, Cooper knew he'd had no idea what had happened. Alyssa—as Bambi the dancer—had simply blown into his life that night and knocked him for a loop. She'd stunned him.

She was like no other woman he'd ever encountered. And the only thing he was sure of was that he really liked the man he was around her, the person he became. He loved the way she made him feel, and not just sexually. He felt more alive when he was around her.

He sighed, settled back more deeply into the hot water. It was simply time to regroup. He reached over to the room service tray and picked up another shrimp, dabbed it in cocktail sauce, and swiftly ate it. One thing you could count on in San Francisco: the seafood was always first class.

His cell phone rang, and he reached for it, right next to the tub where he'd placed it.

"Coop here."

"Coop!" Jake said. Just what he needed, a problem at work or at home.

"What's wrong? Is Riley okay?" He'd left his golden retriever, Riley, with Jake during the bachelor party at his house and had asked his friend to take care of his dog while he was out of town.

Jake laughed. "Nothing! Riley and I are fine. We took a long run by Lake Michigan the other day. Hey, can't I just call you to say hello and see how things are going?"

"I suppose you can."

Jake laughed again. "You don't sound too happy. What's going on?"

Coop thought for a minute, then said, "How much vacation time do I have coming?"

"Let's see—at four weeks per year, and six years without taking any vacation time at all, that comes out to your having six months of paid leave."

Cooper stared morosely at his plate of shrimp and cocktail sauce. "I may have to take it all."

"Does this have anything to do with that little dancer?"

Cooper found himself annoyed by the hint of laughter in his business partner's voice.

"Oh, never mind—"

"Listen Coop, the reason I called is that I was thinking

about what you were up to, and there's this woman I know—"

"No more of these women, Jake—"

"No, not that kind of woman, this woman is in her late sixties, she knows everyone in San Francisco, and—well, I asked her about a certain Alyssa Preston, and she claims to know quite a lot about her and the grandfather she lives with."

Coop sat up in the bathtub, sloshing bubbly water all over the white marble floor. He remembered some of the details he'd read about Alyssa on the dance troupe's web site, including her training and her grandfather.

"You've got my attention."

"Her name is Danielle Tallant, and she said you could call her and come over for dinner anytime, just give her chef a couple of hours' notice."

Sloshing out of the tub, slipping every which way, Cooper walked into the living area of his suite, holding the cell phone to his ear, and reached for one of the hotel pads of paper and a pen.

"Okay. I've got a pen."

Swiftly he wrote down the woman's name, address, and phone number.

"It's the only way it can work," Jake said emphatically. "With high society, you need a connection, and this woman is a great one."

"I owe you, buddy."

"Don't mention it. Just give Alyssa Bambi my best. Oh, and don't do anything I wouldn't do."

"Sure thing." Cooper hung up and set the phone down on the desk, then picked up the pad of paper carefully with his wet hand and studied the address, in a very exclusive area of the city.

No time like the present.

He dialed the number.

As soon as he stated who he was to the phone machine, the receiver on the other end picked up.

"Cooper Sinclair," the woman's voice on the other end of the line fairly purred, and he pictured a huge white Persian cat on the other end of the line. "I've been expecting your call. Your friend Jake is quite an entertaining man."

"Isn't he ever." Cooper felt his entire body tense, filled with impatience. "I'd like to take you out to dinner. Tonight."

"My, aren't we forceful. How about dinner at my place, say, about eight?"

"Sounds good. I'll be there."

"Anything you're allergic to or can't eat?"

"Nope."

"Any favorite foods?"

He smiled. "You pick for me."

He hung up the phone, then padded into the bathroom, got into the tub, lay back, and picked up another shrimp. Things were definitely looking up.

*"Don't do anything I wouldn't do,"* Jake had said.

"Which means," he whispered to the empty bathroom, "All's fair. . . ."

# Chapter Nine

Danielle Tallant did look like a big, pampered cat, with her rounded, voluptuous body, her thick, silvery hair in its soft, upswept style, and her bright blue eyes that tilted slightly up at the corners.

When Cooper rang the bell to her luxurious mansion in Nob Hill, her butler answered and escorted him into her front parlor, where she lay reclined on a red velvet chaise lounge. The rest of the place had been decorated in a style that Cooper would have assumed was called Early Bordello, circa San Francisco during its wild, Barbary Coast days.

This woman would have been right at home in the salons of eighteenth-century London and France, and for one wild moment Coop wondered what his friend Jake had gotten him into.

"So," she practically purred, "you're interested in Alyssa Preston?"

Nothing like a woman who got straight to the point.

He decided he had nothing to gain by hedging the question. "Yes."

"Well," she said, and she fell silent. Cooper felt the strangest sensation as she studied him, as if she were wondering if he were worthy of Alyssa and if he were up to the challenge.

He held her gaze calmly, refusing to back down or appear intimidated.

"Good," she murmured softly. "Would you care for a glass of wine?"

For one wild moment he thought she might be testing him to see if he was a drinker; then he threw caution to the wind and said, "Sure."

She rang for her butler, who returned shortly with two glasses of excellent Merlot.

"I do so love a good romantic intrigue," Danielle said, indicating that he should take a seat on the couch across from her. "And I have a rather proprietorial interest in Alyssa, as she and her grandfather are my next-door neighbors."

Cooper almost choked on his mouthful of wine.

"You didn't know?" Danielle took a small sip of her wine. "Better and better. So you honestly had no idea she comes from money?"

He shook his head.

"Her relatives made their money during the gold rush, then increased it through very canny investments. The Prestons are one of the oldest and wealthiest families in San Francisco. So you can see how Phillip—her grandfather—would be concerned."

Cooper nodded his head, feeling totally out of his league. He and Jake had made a ton of money with their computer company, but new money wasn't the same as old money, and both he and Danielle knew it.

"Her grandfather is concerned she'll never marry."

"And why is that?" New money or not, Cooper wasn't giving up.

Briefly, Danielle told him the Preston family story, all about Elizabeth Preston and her disastrous marriage, and the long decline that had followed.

"It affected her only child. How could it not? When Alyssa and her grandfather argue about it, she's told him she will never marry, and she seems to find flaws with every young man he brings to the house. Both of them are as stubborn as can be. And Phillip is worried about her, I know that. She's twenty-four—"

"That's young in this day and age, with people getting married for the first time in their forties."

"I know, Cooper, but you have to consider Phillip's point of view. He wants her to marry, and marry well. A man who will protect her and all that money." Danielle didn't impart these facts as a gossip might, or maliciously. She had a matter-of-fact manner that Cooper found extremely refreshing and very French.

The slight accent gave away Danielle's country of origin.

"I don't care about the money," he said softly.

"I believe you."

"I met Alyssa at her friend's wedding outside Chicago, and, well, we got off on the wrong foot."

"I see."

"I came out here to set things straight and to make her aware of my intentions."

"And those intentions are?"

For one crazy moment, Cooper felt as if he were in the

middle of a *Masterpiece Theater* special on PBS. All that was missing were the British accents.

Everything around him added to the effect. The immensity and timelessness of the mansions outside, the sense of history he had felt in the architecture in this section of the city. The rather ornate décor of this room, the formality, the butler, the glass of fine wine, the frank way he and Danielle were speaking.

The truth about what it was he wanted from a relationship with Alyssa hit him, broadsided him with the intensity of a sucker punch. And he thought back to Tom, and how nervous and unsure he'd been the night before his wedding. Cooper had believed, and still did, that when it was right, it was right. You knew. A man decided what it was that he wanted and went after it, no hesitations, no excuses.

This was it.

"I want to marry her."

Danielle smiled, those brilliant blue eyes sparkling, and Cooper knew she was satisfied with his answer.

He'd known the truth before the words were out of his mouth. Cooper knew there could be nothing else *but* marriage with a woman like Alyssa. He'd been her first lover, and he wanted to be her only lover, her last. He didn't want her to be with anyone else that way, share the intimacy they'd had together that night with any other man.

So he was politically incorrect and something of a Neanderthal in his thinking; or at least, that's what most contemporary women would think. He didn't care. This had more to do with feeling than thinking, anyway.

Alyssa was different from any woman he'd ever met. She made him feel differently about himself. And Cooper realized that the only reason she wasn't married was by her own choice. She was an independent woman and had experienced some harsh lessons in life. Together, that could be a deadly combination when it came to forming an emotional commitment.

His feelings had shocked him at first, but he couldn't ignore how right they felt. Cooper had always been a man who had shunned the idea of marriage, crept carefully around the whole concept. But now he realized that when you met the right woman, when it was right, there was really no choice involved at all. His entire life, what he wanted from it and how he wanted to live it, had changed the moment he'd met her. Changed forever.

The only thing he knew was that he wanted to be with her.

"But you realize what you're up against," Danielle said, eyeing him closely.

"Now I do, thanks to you." He took another sip of his wine, feeling more at ease with this woman. His instinct, instinct that had served him well in the business world, told him she had a good heart and could be trusted.

At that moment, a very fat, smoke-colored Persian cat with gold eyes sauntered into the parlor.

"Ah, you must meet Maurice."

The cat wandered nonchalantly over to Cooper, who petted the top of his head. Then as the massive cat leaned against his legs, Cooper scratched the feline beneath his chin. The sound of Maurice's loud purrs soon filled the silent room.

"That's something in your favor," Danielle said. "Because both Alyssa and her grandfather love animals. In fact, he's giving a charity ball on the twenty-second of this month to benefit his favorite animal shelter. I'm sure Alyssa will act as his hostess."

This was as good an opening as any. "Can I still get a ticket?"

"At a thousand dollars a plate, I'm sure there are still tickets available. I'll give you the number before you leave. Oh, it's a formal dinner. Did you bring a tuxedo?"

"No, but I can buy one tomorrow."

"Wonderful." She eyed him again, those catlike blue eyes alive with interest. "You'd look very good in Armani. Would you like the name of a good place to buy a designer suit? Roberto has wonderful tailors."

"Sure." Cooper grinned. Things were getting better and better. But there was one thing he had to know. "Jake called me at my hotel and told me about you. How did the two of you meet?"

A slight cloud seemed to hover over her open expression. "His mother was a friend of mine, and he came to my daughter's aid in the midst of a very messy situation. After it was all over, I told him I was forever in his debt. So when he called and told me all about Alyssa and how you wanted to see her again, I promised him I would do everything in my power to help you."

Cooper considered this, then remembered just how much Jake knew.

"What did Jake tell you about our meeting?" He might as well know the worst.

"Just that you met at a wedding and you were enchanted with her. But she left before you could let her know that."

*Basically the truth, with one or two crucial details omitted.*

He could live with that. Coop nodded his head.

"There's more?" she said, clearly curious.

He smiled. "Nothing I'm going to tell you."

She laughed, delighted. "Cooper, you're very entertaining company. Now, shall we go into the dining room and have dinner?"

Over dinner, Danielle explained how this benefit dinner of Phillip Preston's worked.

"It's a bit like the Fire and Ice Ball down in Los Angeles. Everyone has to come dressed in either black, or white, or both, so you'll be fine in a black tuxedo with a white shirt. The tables and a small stage for the auction after dinner are set up in an airline hangar by the airport for one crucial reason. Phillip allows people to bring their companion animals, and many do. The only rule is, you cannot bring an animal who might fight or hurt anyone at the ball."

Cooper considered this. "I don't have an animal with me. I left my dog at home with Jake." He thought of Riley, the golden retriever he'd found wandering the streets about four years ago and brought back home.

Danielle tapped a perfectly manicured fingernail on the table as she thought. "Phillip isn't the only one in this city who does animal rescue work. I think I have the perfect little friend for you, and he'll look stunning with your suit."

The following day, Alyssa drove down to Carmel and met up with her grandfather's friend Monty the horse trainer. She'd already explained to him over the phone that she needed his help in order to pick out a very gentle pony for a special little girl in time for a Christmas delivery.

"I think Cider here is the one you want to go with," Monty said, leading her inside a spacious stall. Alyssa had known Monty from childhood and had a soft spot for the former jockey with his bandy little legs and almost bald head.

The pony in question was a gorgeous Connemara, a reddish bay with black legs and a black mane and tail. A white blaze adorned his intelligent face, and one of his legs had a white sock.

"He's gorgeous," she said. "Thank you, Monty, I think he'll be quite perfect."

"He's twelve years old, and as solid and sound as they come. Thirteen hands high, so she won't outgrow him. And Connemaras are bred for their temperament, so this one's perfect for your little miss."

The Irish pony looked up with interest as they both approached him.

"So you're sure he'll be safe for an eight-year-old?" Alyssa said as she gently stroked the pony's brow.

"Alyssa," said Monty, "you could light a bomb beneath this one's arse, and he wouldn't kick her off."

"He sounds exactly like what we're looking for," she said as she studied the gelding, then smiled and gave him a final pat. "Gentle, smart, the perfect pony for her to learn on."

"A nice little man, Cider is, if I do say so myself. He's a sweetie, and loves people. I know his temperament because I trained him myself."

"That settles it," Alyssa said, reaching for her checkbook. She told him the name of the stable she'd reserved space at, then said, "Can he be delivered by Christmas morning?"

\*  \*  \*

Cooper bought a suit the very next day, and endured standing for his fitting. The tailor Roberto assigned to him was quick and efficient and promised him that the Armani tuxedo would be delivered to his hotel room within forty-eight hours. Even though the charity ball was still several days away, Cooper had the feeling that this would be the right moment for him to meet Alyssa again.

As he left the store that morning, he was feeling a lot more confident than he had less than twenty-four hours earlier, crawling out from beneath those theater seats. He had gone all out and purchased an entire round table of ten seats for The Animal Dance, as the event was called, and had phoned Jake to let him know that their company had found an entirely new charity to support.

"Ten grand for one party?" Jake had said. "Are you sure you know what you're doing?"

"I do, indeed," Cooper told him. "The woman on the phone assured me that by buying all the seats at one table, I could have one right up by the front, near the stage."

"But just you, at this one table?"

"Me and . . . a friend." Briefly he told her about his animal companion, loaned to him for the evening by Danielle herself.

Jake laughed so hard he dropped the phone.

"Oh, man," he finally said when he managed to pick the receiver back up, "I have to admit, I wish I could be there to see this! You'll have to tell me all the details—well, not all of them, depending on how lucky you get."

"Funny. Anyway, I didn't want you to be surprised by the ten thousand dollar donation."

Jake started to laugh again. "As long as I know it's for a good cause!"

\*　　\*　　\*

"You look wonderful, darling."

"Thank you, Grandpapa," Alyssa said as she continued down the circular staircase and stepped onto the black-and-white marble floor of the foyer. She'd dressed with care for The Animal Dance, as she knew she would be acting as her grandfather's hostess tonight.

She'd chosen black, and the short black slip of an evening gown, beaded lightly with jet-black bugle beads, caught the chandelier's light and shimmered. She'd worn her hair up again, this time in an intricately braided style, so it wouldn't get caught in the beading. Her small evening purse, a black shawl, and high, black heels completed her outfit.

And Coco, her grandfather's cream-colored Pekingese, rested securely in her arms.

The other two Pekes, Chang and Ming, trotted at her grandfather's heels as he gathered up the last of his notes for the auction. Phillip had originally wanted to name all his prize Pekes after different Chinese dynasties. While Ming, his brownish red Peke, and Chang, his black Peke, had responded to their names as puppies, Coco had steadfastly refused to answer to any of the other dynasties that were left.

One rainy and windy Saturday morning, while they had been watching television together, a commercial for Coco Puffs cereal had come on the screen, and the tiny cream-colored bundle of fur had started barking madly. Amused, her grandfather had tried out all the different words he could remember from the commercial, and Coco had stuck.

As her grandfather had said, it wasn't exactly a dynasty, but it would have to do.

Now Alyssa waited as their car, a Bentley, was brought

around front. She was thankful for the chance to remain busy. It kept her from thinking about Cooper too much.

*You really are lousy at this one-night-stand thing. You're supposed to love 'em and leave 'em, not love 'em and then not be able to stop thinking about them! You have got to get these memories under control.*

But it was hard, especially late at night. She'd toss and turn in her bed, remembering everything that they'd done together, getting herself into such a state that she'd actually gone into her bathroom and turned on the shower. A cold shower! Anything to dampen the memories she had of Coop.

The solution, she thought, is to keep busy.

And she'd certainly be busy tonight.

Alyssa loved helping her grandfather with his various charities, and it was from him that she'd learned the spirit of philanthropy. Giving always made the world a better place.

Cooper hummed as he adjusted his tuxedo jacket, then studied himself in the full-length mirror.

*Excellent.*

He glanced at his watch. Within the hour, he'd see Alyssa again.

Then he glanced at the hotel bed, where his animal companion for the evening snoozed, a furry heap by his pillow.

Danielle was right; the little guy matched his suit perfectly!

The airplane hangar out by San Francisco Airport was packed tightly with people, everyone milling around in their evening wear and greeting each other, dogs on leather leashes, cats with sparkly collars lounging around their owner's necks or in their arms. A few people had brought brightly colored parrots, and a little girl with her parents had brought her white bunny rabbit in a secure carrier.

Two or three monkeys chattered in the distance, and a potbellied pig walked by, snorting, as Alyssa busily trailed after her grandfather, a clipboard in hand and Coco following close at her heels. Phillip Preston was always nervous before his charity events started, but once they did, he calmed right down. Alyssa saw part of her job this evening as keeping him calm before the big event began.

"I can't see where there's anything left to do," she said to her grandfather. He was fluttering around like a demented hummingbird. Both Chang and Ming stayed right at his heels, like a pair of animated bunny slippers. "You've done an absolutely spectacular job of planning this, and really, you've thought of everything."

"There is one more little detail, darling."

"And what is that?"

"Well, there's this one young man. I got the impression from Marge, who talked with him on the phone when he purchased his tickets, that he's new in town. But he loves animals as much as we do, and he did the most incredible thing! He bought an entire table of tickets, and so we placed him toward the front, where he'll have an excellent view of the stage for the auction after dinner. But I just hate to think of him sitting at that table and eating all alone, so would you—"

She patted his arm, not even allowing him to finish the sentence. He was such a dear, but he really did get way too nervous.

"Of *course* I'll go sit at his table and have dinner with him. It's the least I can do. What did he pay for the table, ten thousand dollars?"

Her grandfather shook his head. "I still can't quite believe it. Generosity on that level renews my faith in my fellow man."

She gave him a quick kiss. "Not to worry. You point me in the direction of his table, and once the cocktail hour is over and we sit down to dinner, I'll be the hostess with the mostest!"

Cooper watched her work the crowd from a distance.

She petted potbellied pigs and gave a parrot a slice of apple. She took a very frightened bunny out of his cage and calmed him right down with a carrot. And she didn't even complain when a very messy Saint Bernard drooled all over the skirt of her evening dress.

He was liking her more and more.

Cocktails were from six to seven, and at seven the lights dimmed, candles were lit, and everyone was escorted to their tables. Cooper walked to his, toward the front of the immense hangar, and sat down in the one chair among the ten that directly faced the stage. His animal friend was slightly shy, and now he took the small creature out of his jacket where it had hidden, and settled it on the comfortable chair right next to him.

He'd heard there was going to be an auction afterward, and was glad he was offered such a clear view of whatever would be auctioned off. At least ten grand could still buy you an excellent view.

He glanced up in time to see Phillip Preston pointing Alyssa in the direction of his table.

*Excellent.*

He could figure out the older man's motive. Phillip probably wanted to ensure that he had a good time, because, after all, he'd purchased an entire table and still had no one to sit with. And as Alyssa was obviously the hostess at her grandfather's charity ball, she would be going out of her way to make sure that everyone had a great time, including a lonely man, a new man in town, who'd bought ten expensive dinners.

He'd asked Danielle to accompany him. She'd merely laughed.

"You flatter me, Cooper! I bought my ticket ages ago. I'll be sitting at the head table with Phillip himself. But I'll probably have a pretty good view of your table, because you know I don't want to miss a thing."

He watched, fascinated, as Alyssa made her way through the tables, a cream-colored, hairy little dog in her arms, her dress sparkling in the soft candlelight. She stopped to pet a Persian, stroke a Siberian husky, and cuddle a chinchilla.

Trying not to grin, he turned his head so that she could only see his tuxedo-clad back and lavished some attention on his companion animal for the evening. This particular animal was a true original; he hadn't seen another of its kind here tonight.

It was almost as if he had radar where she was concerned; he could literally feel her approach. Within minutes, he heard her say, "Hello, I'm so happy to meet you, Mr. . . ."

He turned, and Cooper could honestly say that her reaction was not quite what he'd hoped it would be. Those glorious hazel eyes widened, her face paled, and she almost dropped the little dog, who squirmed forward to plant a very wet doggy kiss on his cheek.

"*You!*" she whispered, her expression a picture of total shock.

# *Chapter Ten*

*Definitely* not the reaction he'd hoped for.

"Yes, me," he said brightly, standing up and pulling out a chair for her. She hesitated, then glanced back, and he saw her make eye contact with her grandfather. The silver-haired gentleman was smiling, fairly beaming. Though Coop hated for her to be so uncomfortable, he was glad she wasn't going to run away from him as she had at the end of Mindy's wedding.

"Sit down," he whispered. "Stay a spell."

She sat, and he followed suit.

She turned toward him, about to say something, when her eye caught the small furry animal sitting calmly in the chair next to him.

"*What,*" she said, pointing to the creature in question, "is *that!*"

"I should think the answer to that should be obvious,"

he said, picking up the small bundle of striking black-and-white fur and placing it in his lap.

"A *skunk?*"

"The one and only. I haven't seen another one here, and I really do think they should be represented at this extravaganza."

"Is he—"

"Fully de-scented. He's just a baby, but very well socialized. This little guy is not a bomb ready to blow."

She opened her mouth, seemed to consider the words that were about to burst out, and snapped it shut again.

He smiled. They were in sync again; it was as if he could tell what she'd been about to say.

"Thank you for not making the obvious smart remark."

That set her off. "You mean, a skunk for a skunk?"

He lowered his voice as he petted the small creature's head. "What exactly do you mean by that? I seem to remember that you were a pretty willing partner to everything we did that night. And remembering further, and in great detail, we did quite a lot—"

"Would you *please* lower your voice?" she hissed, glancing around at the nearby tables nervously. "You are *not* a gentleman!"

"And you're no lady, but that's a compliment, coming from me."

*"Ohhh!"* She turned in her seat just in time to see a waiter, clad in black pants and a white jacket, come up to their table and place two salads in front of them.

The skunk perked up at the sight and smell of food. The black-and-white animal had riveted Coco's attention since she'd first set eyes on him, and now she wriggled and wagged her plumed tail, wanting to get closer and check out this new and interesting friend.

"Could I get some avocado for my friend here?" Cooper said to the waiter. "I don't think he'll like it drenched in dressing."

Dead silence reigned as the waiter scurried away.

"Oh, come on, Alyssa, let's at least try to be civil to each other." He held the baby skunk a few inches off his lap and waved one of its tiny paws at her. "Mr. LePew, this is Alyssa Preston. Alyssa, meet—"

"You're not funny."

"I'm not trying to be. I'm trying to salvage what, up until now, has been a very pleasant evening."

"What are you doing here in San Francisco?"

"Business brought me here," he said, improvising madly. "Jake and I—you remember Jake, the guy you talked on the phone with that night—well, we're looking to open an office on the West Coast. We're getting awfully tired of all that cold weather outside Chicago."

"Just when did you decide this?"

He almost laughed out loud; those glorious hazel eyes were so darn suspicious. He couldn't get anything past her. And Cooper decided a little truth was in order.

"Oh, about five minutes after you ditched me at the wedding." He picked up his fork and speared a few of the baby greens on his plate. "By the way, I have a blue velvet wrap that I want to return to you."

"Throw it away."

"Alyssa." He set his fork down. "Can't we behave like normal adults? Must we keep going round and round like this?"

"You weren't supposed to come back into my life!" she said desperately. "You were supposed to be a moment out of time!" She lowered her voice and leaned toward him. "A one-night stand, a, a—a moment of total insanity."

He considered this. "I'm flattered. I think."

"But that was to be the end of it."

She started to rise, and he reacted on impulse, grabbing her wrist and making her sit back down. All around them, elegantly dressed people were eating, and here they were, fighting like two kids who each wanted the same toy in the communal sandbox.

"It can't be the end of it, Alyssa. You know it as well as I do. Not when I found out you were a virgin—"

He stopped talking when the waiter set down a small plate of avocado, the thin, perfectly cut slices fanned out in a stunning presentation.

"For your skunk, sir," he said, then glided away.

"Here you go, Pepe," Coop said, placing the plate on the chair next to him, and the baby skunk set to work on the food with gusto.

When he glanced back up at Alyssa, her face was flaming with embarrassment.

"If you were a gentleman, you wouldn't even be talking about such a subject—"

"If I were a gentleman, I'd be boring the pants off you, just like all those other suitable men your grandfather has been parading by you for the past five years."

"How did you find out about that?" Now she seemed truly shocked.

"I have my ways. Now, are we going to enjoy dinner together or not? Do we have to hold hands the entire evening to ensure that you'll stay right here with me? I want you to know that I'm fully prepared to eat my entire dinner with my left hand, or even my fingers if necessary. I'm ambidextrous, if you remember correctly."

She seemed to be counting to ten, ready to blow. Then

she hesitated, seemed to calm down. Her final answer surprised him.

"No. No, Mr. Sinclair, I'll have dinner with you and your Mr. LePew, but only because by doing so, I'll make my grandfather very happy." She glanced pointedly at his hand holding her wrist. "You can let go of me now."

"Very well."

Each of them picked up their forks and began to eat their salads. Cooper was impressed with this first course, a mix of baby greens, thinly sliced fennel bulb, white mushrooms, a few choice pieces of avocado, and some shaved Parmesan cheese, all lightly coated in a shallot vinaigrette.

Phillip Preston certainly knew his food.

After a few minutes he said, "Would it be too much to hope for a little dinner conversation?"

"I have an idea," she said, setting down her salad fork. "How about if we pretend we're total strangers and we've just met?"

He perked up at this. "You mean like that sexual fantasy where a husband and wife meet at a bar and—"

"Does everything have to ultimately be sexual with you?"

He sobered instantly. "Actually, no. Actually, Jake has no idea I'm considering opening a West Coast office, because I just thought of it today. And the only reason I'm out here is that I wanted to say I'm sorry for what happened, for the way I treated you. If I'd known you weren't that experienced—"

"No," she said quickly, interrupting him. "It was a—a change, a really refreshing change, from the way most of the men in my life treat me. It's like they put me up on this pedestal, and I can't quite breathe. . . ."

She seemed to remember exactly who she was talking to and fell silent, but Cooper filed this crucial bit of information away for future reference. He decided to make nice and not push her any further.

"Does your grandfather put on a show like this every year for the animals?" he said, reaching for his wineglass. Alyssa seemed to relax back into her chair, and that fuzzy, cream-colored dog in her lap started to nod off. Coop glanced over at Mr. LePew, who had just finished his avocado salad and was curled up in his chair, quite content.

"He loves it. He loves animals. It's a total joy to him, every single minute of this. Now all he has left to worry about is whether he'll raise enough money with the auction."

"What are they going to auction off?" Coop said, genuinely interested.

"Animals from the shelter."

That reassured him. As he was living in a hotel room and had no place to keep an animal, Coop knew he wouldn't even be tempted to bid for a pet, no matter how cute the puppy or kitten turned out to be. Nope, Mr. LePew was enough for him, and he'd return the baby skunk to Danielle in the morning, as planned.

Their waiter came and expertly removed their salad plates, while another young man placed their dinners in front of them. As Cooper didn't normally eat vegetarian cuisine, he asked the waiter for a quick clarification.

"That, sir, is an artichoke, celery root, and potato gratin, with a golden crust of bread crumbs."

"It looks fabulous," he said, picking up his dinner fork. The casserole was incredibly good.

"This is first class," he said, after his first mouthful.

"At a thousand dollars a plate, my grandfather believes

he has a certain responsibility to go all out. There are four courses to the dinner, including the salad. And he always lets me pick out the dessert."

"That I can't wait to see." He took another bite of the gratin, chewed, and swallowed. "So there's more after this?"

"One more main course. You'll like it."

Mr. LePew had woken out of his sound sleep and was eyeing Cooper's plate.

"It must be because he's French," Cooper teased Alyssa. "He must have smelled all the butter in the sauce."

He was rewarded by her laughter, then he took a tiny piece of the casserole and transferred it to the skunk's plate. Pepe happily gobbled it down.

"Only the finest cuisine for our French friend."

"It's also all organic," Alyssa said. "Absolutely everything on your plate tonight. That's part of why it tastes so good."

"Your grandfather's a pretty progressive guy."

"You don't know the half of it."

The next course arrived, portobello mushrooms with pappardelle pasta, and Cooper could smell the rich pasta sauce with its garlic, tomato paste, red wine, cream, and rosemary.

"Where did your grandfather get this food?" he said as he forked up another bite of pasta.

"He eats a largely vegetarian diet at his age. His doctor recommended it. So he knows a lot of the best vegetarian restaurants in the city. And this city is known for its food."

"I can see why." Cooper couldn't believe they were actually having a civilized conversation. And he began to hope. They could build on this; he wasn't that bad a guy, she could learn to like him.

He glanced over at her grandfather's table and saw Danielle studying the two of them. She gave him a wink, and he smiled at her before turning his attention back to Alyssa.

She truly looked stunning tonight. Very few women could wear black successfully, but it was the perfect way to set off that gleaming blonde hair. And that short skirt! Those dancer's legs! He consciously refused to go there, back to those memories of her legs and how they'd felt wrapped around him as he'd—

"I'm extremely impressed with this whole shindig," he said. "You and your grandfather really know how to throw a party." Cooper glanced down at the skunk. "None for you, stinky boy. I don't even know if skunks can handle mushrooms, and this cream sauce might be a little too rich for you."

"A wise move, Mr. Sinclair. You have no idea if it might upset his stomach or not."

"Please. Call me Cooper."

The look she gave him out of those hazel eyes dashed his hopes of having made any progress at all.

"I'm continuing to pretend that we've just met."

"I see." He set his fork down, finished with his pasta, and the unobtrusive waiter swept in and cleared away the plate. "Well, I can't force you, Alyssa, but I do want you to know that had I known you were as inexperienced as you were, I would have taken . . . a little more care."

He could tell he'd gotten to her by the expression on her face. Slightly softer, less wary. She wasn't on guard for just a moment, and he wondered what her life had to be like, a very wealthy and sheltered young woman, constantly on the lookout, feeling she had to be that vigilant in protecting her freedom.

"Thank you. I appreciate that."

"There's one more thing I have to know. And then if you absolutely insist, I'll leave you alone."

She sighed. "And what might that be?"

"That night before the wedding when we . . . got to know each other. Did you use any sort of protection?"

"Against what?"

"Possible pregnancy."

"Oh." She was silent as the waiter came to their table and placed their dessert dishes in front of them; a chocolate terrine, rich slices of decadence on a plate.

"Did you?" Cooper pressed. "Because I'm ashamed to admit, I certainly didn't."

He watched, fascinated, as a blush slowly rose from the swell of her breasts, up her neck, and into those cheekbones. He'd fantasized about that face, late at night, and now he found that blush rather charming.

"No," she said softly, as his gaze caught and held her own. "I wasn't—I didn't—I mean, I wasn't even thinking right about that time."

They stared at each other, both remembering that night and their response to each other, their chocolate desserts going untouched. Cooper leaned closer, close enough to see those distinct flecks of green and gold in her incredible eyes.

"Listen Alyssa, I have to tell you—"

"Ladies and gentlemen, The Dance for Animals official auction is about to begin!"

Cooper glanced up at the stage. Phillip Preston stood there, tall and proud behind the podium and microphone.

Disappointed that his moment with Alyssa had been interrupted, Cooper sat back in his chair and unobtrusively watched her. At least she hadn't bolted from his table as soon as dinner was over. But then again, that terrine would be eaten soon, and then she'd no longer have any excuse to stay.

If he was going to make his move, he'd have to move fast.

"We have one of San Francisco's finest auctioneers here tonight from Josephine's Antiques," said Phillip, "and to start things off with a bang, here's our first prize, a glorious parrot named Jean Lafitte. He's named after the famous buccaneer who terrorized the Gulf of Mexico during the early eighteen hundreds. Lafitte is an African gray, possibly the smartest bird around, and has a vocabulary of over two hundred words, many of them expressions that pirates themselves would have used on the high seas."

Phillip stepped back, the gray parrot perched happily on his shoulder. It squawked loudly in his ear, and the audience laughed.

"Let the bidding begin!" Phillip called out. "And remember, everyone, that every single penny raised here tonight will be used to benefit the Amelia Preston Animal Shelter in North Beach."

Cooper glanced at Alyssa and was surprised to see her hazel eyes bright with unshed tears. And he thought he knew the reason.

"Amelia?" he said.

"He named the shelter after my grandmother," she said softly.

"That's beautiful," he said, and meant it.

The bidding began, fast and furious. In no time at all, the bids had topped one thousand dollars, then two thousand, then swiftly escalated to three. Cooper sat back, amused, watching the richest people in San Francisco society, everyone dressed in elegant black-and-white clothing, fight for the right to take home this immensely intelligent bird.

Lafitte seemed to know he was on display. Phillip walked up and down the length of the stage with the parrot on his arm. The elegant bird fluttered his wings and shrieked, "Pieces of eight! Pieces of eight! *Arghhh,* matey! Avast ye scurvy bilge rats, fire that cannon!"

Amid the laughter, bids flew fast and furious.

And Cooper sensed Alyssa was ready to bolt out of his life.

He had to act now or lose her forever.

Taking a huge emotional chance, he placed a hand on her shoulder. She stiffened, then turned and looked at him, and all of a sudden he saw the hurt and loneliness in her eyes, the actual fear she had of getting close to anyone but her grandfather.

And he remembered how she'd lost her mother at such a young age and had never really known her father. He'd pretty much abandoned her. Oh, her grandfather had done what he could, but a kid never really got over the loss of a father.

Cooper knew he'd had his differences with his parents; they hadn't always approved of the direction he'd taken his life, but they'd always supported him emotionally. They'd always been there for him. He couldn't imagine how it would feel to have been abandoned, first by your father's callousness and then your mother's early death. Alyssa had been six years old and all alone in the world except for Phillip and Amelia Preston.

"Alyssa, listen to me for a moment—"

"*Four* thousand *five* hundred!" the auctioneer called

onstage, his diction rapid and flawless. "Ladies and gentlemen, do I hear *five*? Will we go to *five*?"

"Coop, no! Don't! I just can't—"

And every good intention he had of going slow, giving her time, flew out the window. What was it about this woman that made him lose all rational control, that made him want to push and push and simply make her his own? That ignited his emotions in a way no other woman in his life ever had?

He threw up his hands in disgust. "Damn it, Alyssa—"

"Sold!" The auctioneer pointed directly to him and his outstretched hand as the spotlight shone on their table, illuminating him and Alyssa. "For *five thousand dollars,* to the man with the *skunk!*" Cooper shielded his eyes as Mr. LePew, scared by all the commotion, crawled into his lap and attempted to hide beneath his tuxedo jacket.

"Sold?" he said, confused, then realized that when he'd thrown up his hands, the auctioneer had misunderstood and thought he was bidding for the bird.

"But I—but I didn't mean—"

Then he saw Phillip Preston's delighted face. The older man was coming down off the stage with the parrot on his arm, personally presenting him with his prize.

"Walk the plank! *Arghhh,* matey!" shrieked Lafitte.

"But—I—" Cooper stopped, recognizing defeat when it stared him in the face.

He was now the proud owner of a parrot.

# *Chapter Eleven*

Cooper turned to Alyssa, astonishment in his gaze. "Look what you made me do!"

"*I* made you do?" She started to laugh. Her grandfather had reached their table and made a great show of presenting Cooper with his parrot, letting the bird walk on to his arm. An assistant followed her grandfather, with a portable perch, and Lafitte hopped right up on it.

"Won't he fly away?" Cooper asked nervously, and Alyssa almost felt pity for him.

Almost.

Of course, there was a part of her that was really enjoying his predicament.

"No, no, my boy, his wings have been clipped," said Phillip. "Now, he also comes with a large cage, a cage cover, several toys, a six-month supply of food, and a free first visit to a vet who specializes in birds." He clapped Cooper soundly on the back. "Thank you, you've been most generous in getting our auction off to a rip-snorting start!"

As Phillip headed back toward the stage and grasped the leash of a harlequin-spotted Great Dane, Alyssa decided there was no time like the present to exit, stage right. But as she started to rise out of her chair, she felt Cooper's fingers close around her wrist.

"What about dessert?" he asked, his voice low. She sat back down.

*That voice.* It took her back to a moment in time in a darkened den, firelight flickering, his face so close to hers, his expression so intense . . .

*Don't go there!*

"Ah, I don't—"

"You like chocolate just fine. You told me your grandfather lets you pick out the dessert every year, so I'm assuming you're not self-sacrificing enough to choose something you don't like."

He had her there, dead to rights.

"Okay." She picked up her fork and cut off a small, smooth piece of the chocolate terrine. "You like chocolate, don't you?"

*"Chocolate!"* said Lafitte.

Cooper stared at the bird. The perch had been placed behind Mr. LePew's chair, and the parrot looked at the skunk with great interest, his bright eyes gleaming. Cooper had finally managed to persuade the baby skunk that there was indeed life outside his tuxedo jacket.

"That bird is frightening. Are all parrots such fast learners?"

"They say the African grays are the smartest; they pick up words after hearing them just a few times. Sometimes even only once." She smiled at him sweetly. "You'll have to watch your language."

"Maybe I can donate him to some charity," Cooper muttered, picking up his fork.

They ate their dessert in silence while the Great Dane, an Angora rabbit, and an iguana were all auctioned off. "Four thousand five hundred," muttered Lafitte, imitating the auctioneer. The parrot paced on his perch, spreading his wings and cocking his feathered head. "No, five thousand, five thousand it is!"

"Cheer up," Alyssa said. "You could have walked away with the iguana!"

"Iguana!" Lafitte agreed, his head bobbing up and down at the excitement all around him.

"What are you doing the weekend after Christmas?" Cooper said.

"I . . . ah . . ."

"You're really flattering to a guy's ego," he muttered.

"I really am doing something, but it just isn't coming to mind."

He glared at her. "Washing your hair, perhaps?"

Alyssa felt Coco come awake in her lap, bark softly once, then perk her head up and wag her tail as she stared at the parrot to the left of Cooper's shoulder.

"Your grandfather really likes those dogs, doesn't he?"

"His mother had Pekes. It's a family tradition."

"Pekes," agreed Lafitte, staring at the lap dog.

"Like parrots in mine," Cooper muttered.

"Your family keeps parrots?"

"No, Alyssa, this is a first for me. What about the weekend after Christmas?"

She hesitated. "Cooper, I'm really not trying to be difficult. It's just that—"

"You're scared."

"Scared?" She narrowed her eyes as she stared at him. How dare he think he could read her mind, tell her what she was thinking! *And how dare he be so close to the actual truth!*

The guy was scary, he could read her so well.

"Not scared exactly, but—"

"Scared. Let's not mince words. Scared that I'm going to hurt you. Scared that I'm going to disappear or walk away. Scared that I'm going to abandon you like your father did—"

Her temper fired. "What is this, intro to psychology? I don't have to sit here and listen to this—" She started to get out of her chair, but he managed to pin her with a look.

How did he *do* that?

"You're scared, Alyssa; I'm scared; we're all scared. Relationships are terrifying. But listen to me just a moment. I've been around the block a bit in my thirty-two years, and what we shared that night in Wilmette is not the norm. I've never felt anything like it in—"

*"Six thousand!"* Lafitte screamed at the top of his avian lungs. *"Six thousand it is!"*

*"Sold!"* shouted the auctioneer, slamming down his gavel as the spotlight highlighted them both again, surrounding their table in blinding white light. Mr. LePew made for the safe haven of Cooper's jacket, Coco barked, and Lafitte fluttered his wings madly as he walked up and down the length of his perch.

*"What?"* Cooper said, and Alyssa craned her neck toward the front of the stage in time to see one of the volunteers come walking toward them, an adorable, tiny, fluffy white puppy in his arms.

"Congratulations, sir, you have just won yourself a bichon frise."

"A bichon what?" Cooper said weakly. Alyssa started to laugh.

"How did this happen?" Cooper demanded, taking the puppy into his arms.

She really was an adorable little thing, Alyssa thought. The pup wriggled excitedly, then swiped at Coop's face with her little pink tongue.

"You'll also receive a leash and collar, two bowls, a complete set of grooming tools, her first haircut at Le Pooche Palace, a large bag of puppy chow, and a free vet's visit," the young man said. "Enjoy her, Mr. Sinclair; she's just a darling, and we all love her at the shelter."

"Then let me give her to you—"

The young man backed up, his hands in the air. "I couldn't do that, sir, not after you so generously donated six thousand dollars to the shelter."

Alyssa almost laughed out loud at the expression on Cooper's face. "Oh, Coop, Grandpapa will be so pleased!"

He took a deep breath. "Okay. A bird and a small dog. But that's my limit!" He glanced back at Lafitte, nervously pacing on his perch, his head cocked toward him. "But that's enough! Got it, my feathered friend?"

"That's enough, that's enough," Lafitte agreed. "Pieces of eight!"

"I want you to know something," Cooper said, turning in his chair and facing her as the auction continued around them. "I have *never* in my life gone to so much trouble to arrange a date with *anyone*. Now, how about the second Saturday in January?"

"It's just the sex, isn't it?" she said. As long as she was

trapped at this table with Cooper, she might as well get the truth out of him and finish things off once and for all. "It's all about the sex, and you just want a repeat performance!"

*"Sex!"* Lafitte agreed.

"Damn it," Cooper said to his bird, "would you put a lid on it!"

"Don't yell at Lafitte!" Alyssa said, and she watched as Cooper raked his fingers through his dark hair in frustration.

"What do you mean, it's all about the sex?"

"Remember our ride in the limo, after Mindy's wedding?"

He blinked.

"On the way to the country club?" Alyssa said. "You told me it was more than just sex, and you wanted to let Bambi know. And I'm assuming here that you meant more than just sex in the sense that it was incredibly terrific sex, not just ho-hum regular sex, right?"

"Huh?" he said.

"But then later, when Mindy was kissing Tom, you reconsidered and said, 'Don't go trying to pretty this up and make it all romantic. I know what it was, and even knowing what it was, it was pretty incredible.'"

He stared at her, clearly shocked. "What do you do, go around with one of those spy tape recorders concealed in your dress?"

"No, I just have an incredibly good memory. And if I recall, you also said, 'I have a healthy respect for love's limitations.' So, Mr. Sinclair, if you want to have some hot sex with me, that's one thing. But don't pretty it up and try to get me to believe that you fell in love with me and have to be with me because of one sweaty, misguided night we spent together before a wedding."

"Sweaty," Lafitte agreed.

Cooper looked like he wanted to strangle that parrot.

"I don't know what you're getting at, Alyssa, but I do know you couldn't possibly be saying you'd be open to a sexual relationship with no possibility of commitment. Women aren't like that."

"No. That's true. There would have to be a minimal amount of ground rules in order for me to feel . . . safe."

He paused for a long moment, then said, "So what you're saying is that there's a possibility of our just having sex again."

She nodded her head. "To be totally honest, I can't quite get that night out of my mind, and I'd like to have sex with you one more time to see if it was just the circumstances of the evening, or if you were really that good."

"Wow. Nothing like giving a guy a little performance anxiety."

She almost laughed out loud. "What do you say, Mr. Sinclair? Or aren't you up to the challenge?"

Those sparkling hazel eyes were going to be his downfall.

He knew it, and he didn't even care. The thought of getting Alyssa into his bed drove everything else out of his head. He didn't care where they were, or what was going on around them, he had to make sure she was saying what he thought she was saying.

*If this is a dream, don't wake me up.*

"You've got to be kidding, Alyssa. This is some sort of joke, right?"

"Nope." She leaned toward him and whispered in his

ear, "I've had a lot of trouble sleeping, remembering our night together. How about you?"

His imagination went into overdrive.

"When do you want to meet?" He wanted to get straight to the point. What he really wanted was a repeat performance with her, in his bed, in his arms, as soon as possible.

*"Seven thousand dollars, my man, and not a penny more!"* screamed Lafitte at the top of his lungs.

"Oh *no!*" He'd been so busy with Alyssa, thinking of all the things he wanted to do to her, with her, that he hadn't kept a lid on his bird.

*"Sold!"* the auctioneer bellowed, "for *seven thousand dollars* and not a penny more!" And the spotlight was on them once again. Cooper stared in horror at the stage, where a potbellied pig that had to weigh close to one hundred pounds was standing patiently on a leather leash held by Phillip Preston.

"Thank you, my boy!" he called out as he and the portly porker started down the stage steps toward their table. "I cannot *begin* to tell you what this means to me!"

"Mommy," said a little girl's voice from the table next to Cooper's, "that nasty man is buying up all the animals and there won't be any left for us! I don't *like* him!"

Cooper turned toward the child. "Would you like a pig? How about a parrot?"

"Certainly not!" said her affronted mother, gathering her little girl closer.

"But Mommy—" the child began.

"I said *no!*" said the flustered woman.

Alyssa started to stand as her grandfather approached their table, pig in tow, and Cooper knew she was getting ready to make her escape.

He thought fast and faced Alyssa. "We can't talk now. Coffee tomorrow, that little Italian place on Sacramento Street. I'll call you with the address." And then the pig's snout was in his face, the animal snorting happily, Lafitte screaming raucously, LePew hiding in his jacket, and the tiny white puppy still in his arms, wriggling and licking his face.

"Don't ask," Cooper said wearily to the concierge at his hotel. He knew how this had to look to the man behind the elegant, polished wood desk.

"A rough night, sir?" came the measured reply.

"In a manner of speaking. Please don't worry, I'll be leaving in a few days, and I'll certainly pay for any damages."

"We have an excellent pet-sitting program, sir. Please don't feel that your animal friends are of any concern to us. Many of our guests bring their companion animals with them when they stay here. The suite you're in is actually quite popular."

"That's good to know." He knew how it had to look, standing in the lobby of the elegant hotel with a gigantic pig on a leash by his side, a baby skunk clutching his shirtfront, the bichon puppy in his arms, and a wise guy parrot on his shoulder.

Doctor Dolittle and his animal friends.

"Will you need assistance with that large pig in the elevator?"

These guys were good, he had to hand them that.

"I'll see how Baco does. They assured me he was house-trained and quite used to both elevators and stairs. But could I have a few things sent up to the suite?"

"Certainly, sir."

"I'd like three of the largest litter boxes you can find, complete with litter, several copies of the daily paper, some bottled water, and a large fruit plate from room service."

"I'll get on it directly, sir. Anything else?"

"I'd like a movie tonight. Something suitable for a small child."

The concierge's eyebrow rose.

"For the pig. He loves television."

The concierge checked his DVD movie list.

"Here's a child's film and an excellent one. *Charlotte's Web.*" His brow wrinkled with concern, then he quietly cleared his throat. "Oh dear, obviously not. The beginning might not be quite suitable for your porcine friend; it might disturb him."

"I agree."

"Hmmm. There's nothing else really suitable for children."

"What else do you have?"

*"When Harry Met Sally?"*

"Too close to home."

*"Eat, Drink, Man, Woman?"*

"Nope. I'm stuffed."

"Ah, here's one. *Die Hard,* the original, with Bruce Willis and Alan Rickman. And based on a quite excellent novel by Roderick Thorp, if I do say so myself."

*Bruce. Explosions. Nonstop action.*

Cooper glanced down. "You like that, Baco? And of course, you understand that all the bloodshed is merely special effects."

Baco looked up at him adoringly, snorted happily, and leaned against him, all 120 pounds. He was like a very large dog with a snout and rough, wiry hair.

"*Die Hard* it is."

"Will that be all, sir?"

"I hope so." Cooper sighed. "But who knows, the night's still young."


Once he and his animal friends were settled in his suite, Cooper knew there was one phone call he had to get out of the way as soon as possible. Stretched out on his bed, he reached for the phone and called Jake.

His friend and business partner mumbled a sleepy hello.

"Hey Jake, I just wanted to let you know that I spent a little more money than I intended at the charity dinner tonight."

That woke him up.

"How much are we talking about?"

"Eighteen grand."

"Eighteen grand! Just what exactly did you get for that?"

As succinctly as possible, Cooper told him.

"I even got a bichon frise."

"A bitchin' what?"

"A bichon frise."

"God, I'm sorry to hear that. Is it something penicillin can take care of?"

"You idiot, it's a dog!"

After Jake finished laughing, Cooper said, "What do you think about opening an office out here?"

"Why?"

Cooper sighed. "I really like the coffee."

"It's that woman, isn't it?"

"Yeah."

"What about earthquakes?"

"Would you rather freeze to death out there?"

"Good point."

"I'm thinking we're about ready for a change," Cooper said.

"You just don't want to move all those animals back here. And speaking of animals, Riley's doing just fine."

"I'm glad."

"I can't believe you won a pig."

"I can't, either." Cooper glanced toward the big-screen television, where Bruce Willis got on an escalator with a huge stuffed bear for his children. The movie had just started, and as soon as he finished up this call with Jake, he'd microwave himself some popcorn and join Baco on the couch.

"Think about that office, okay?" he said.

"Will do. And Coop, if I don't talk to you, try to have a Merry Christmas. Stay out of any more trouble, okay?"

"Yeah."

Alyssa couldn't sleep, so she pulled on a sweater and a pair of warm sweatpants and let herself out into the backyard. At around two in the morning, the night sky twinkled with stars and there was a decidedly chilly nip in the December air.

She wondered what she'd been thinking when she proposed having sex with Cooper.

But she had to know. She had to do this to get on with her life. It felt as if she were stuck at that night in his den, as if she couldn't get past it.

*It couldn't have been that wonderful.*

They would have some coffee tomorrow, set up a time to have a date or do something before the inevitable happened.

And she knew it would. She couldn't seem to be any-where near Cooper Sinclair and not think about sex. There was just something about the man.

She walked through the immense backyard, past her grandfather's greenhouse and farther back into the prop-erty, where the Japanese-style gazebo her grandfather had commissioned sheltered the hot tub. She'd turned it on earlier and knew it had to be heated up by now. And even though it was cold outside, once she was in the bubbling water, she'd be warm enough.

She'd never felt what she felt for Cooper for any other man. And she'd had plenty of possibilities, what with her active social life and a grandfather who always kept his eyes open for a suitable life partner for her. But the mo-ment she'd seen Cooper . . . then started to talk with him . . .

She'd never met a man like Cooper, and in the social circles she ran in, probably wouldn't have if it hadn't been for Mindy's wedding and the outrageous request her friend had made. But that request had put her at the right place at the right time, and now if she was honest with herself, she had to admit that she and Cooper suited each other.

*Why beat around the bush? You were made for each other.*

But even knowing this didn't take away the fear.

Alyssa let herself into the gazebo, opening the latch that led inside. Though the tub was exposed to the open air, the wooden slats that had been built halfway up the side of the enclosure ensured complete privacy to anyone who wanted some time in the large hot tub.

She slipped off her clothing and slid inside, then reached for the button that started the hot water bubbling and churning. Leaning back, she closed her eyes and tried to relax, tried not to think about Cooper . . . and started to fantasize about having him right here, next to her, naked and in the tub with her.

*Maybe take it a step at a time. Don't look that far into the future. Stay in the present. Take this affair . . .*

She hesitated.

*Take this* love *affair one day at a time, moment to moment. You can at least try, can't you?*

But even as these thoughts raced around in her head, images of Cooper in the Jacuzzi with her kept interrupting her thought process.

*When can I see him again? Besides our coffee date . . .*

Her eyes opened, and she almost laughed out loud.

*Perfect!*

Her grandfather already had Christmas arranged, but he always gave a large and lavish New Year's Eve party. And she was sure that after Cooper had dropped such a bundle for one of her grandfather's favorite charities, he would have no trouble with her inviting him to the house on New Year's Eve.

What a way to start off the year!

Alan Rickman had just fallen from one of the top floors of the building when Cooper came awake. Baco's attention was still riveted to the screen, but both Pepe and the fluffy white puppy were curled up next to Cooper on one of the couches, asleep.

Baco took up the whole other couch.

A nice family tableau.

Lafitte, the cause of all this insanity, was sound asleep beneath the cover on his cage.

Stretching, Cooper lay quietly on the couch and thought about Alyssa.

He'd once had a rather insane notion that no woman was going to consume his thoughts. He would stay aloof, in control, always the captain of his ship.

And cold, unfeeling, and passionless.

This was strange new territory to him, but it felt right. It all came back to feeling so much more alive when he was around her. He didn't know why or how, but Fate had given him a chance at a different sort of life than the one he'd been pursuing.

It wasn't that he'd been unhappy with his life. It was that he'd had no idea what he was missing. From the moment he'd stormed into his family room, wondering what had been going on to make his guests howl like dogs at a full moon, nothing had been the same.

It had been wonderful.

Strange, how he'd dated women who hadn't even inspired him to pick up the phone for another get-together, while Alyssa had spurred him on to fly two thousand miles to the West Coast and find her. Pursue her. Claim her.

Oh yeah, he had it bad.

As far as he was concerned, they were perfect for each other. She was everything he'd ever wanted in a woman: a gorgeous physical presence, a wit so sharp he had to work to keep up with her, and a sexuality that absolutely knocked his socks off.

He was one content man. Well, as content as he could be with his future still in a rather precarious position. Cooper didn't think he would be able to rest until he knew that Alyssa was his. And he was willing to wage an all-out battle in order to get what he wanted, as soon as possible.

Primitive thinking? Yes. A tad chauvinistic? You bet.

But there was nothing to be done for it. He was a man in love, and had finally surrendered to the inevitable.

He got up off the couch. Lifting Pepe up, he placed the little skunk in the carrier Danielle had provided for him, then took the white puppy into the bathroom, where she sleepily peed on the newspapers he'd put there for her. Satisfied that she might last through most of the night, he headed back toward the large, king-sized bed that dominated one side of the spacious master bedroom.

Baco was staring at the screen, watching the credits.

"Okay, boy, time for bed."

The pig obligingly trotted into the bathroom, used the litter box, then came out and approached the side of the bed. Cooper, lying facedown with the puppy curled up on the pillow next to his head, turned his head slightly and eyed his new pet. Baco eyed the soft mattress as he snuffled.

"Not up on the bed. Got that?"

The pig sighed, then slowly lowered his immense weight to the carpeted floor.

The phone rang at about eleven the next morning, and Cooper felt as if a ten-ton weight was on his legs. He couldn't seem to move.

Glancing down, he realized that a ten-ton weight *was* on his legs. Sometime during the night, Baco had climbed up on the bed and was now lying across his legs. And Pepe had escaped his cage and was lying on top of the pig.

White Puppy—he had to give her a name!—was still snoozing on the pillow, and Lafitte was mercifully silent, the cover still on his large cage.

He picked up on the fifth ring.

"Cooper?" a feminine voice said.

Danielle. He didn't know why he thought it might be Alyssa. She didn't even know where he was staying.

"Hi, Danielle."

"Well, I want to tell you that you made quite an impression on Phillip Preston last night! He couldn't stop talking about how generous you were, all the way home in his Bentley. But Alyssa was strangely quiet."

"Hmmm," was all he said in reply to this. He wondered if Alyssa still meant to meet him for coffee today.

"But anyway, this is the reason I really called. I know you're new in town, and if you have nowhere to go on Christmas Eve, please come to my home. I'm having a group of people over, nothing really, we'll just eat dinner and drink wine and play some silly card games. And you're welcome to come to Christmas dinner the following day, as well. I just hate to think of anyone alone at Christmas. Oh, and please bring all those adorable animals with you."

He'd made a great friend in Danielle. Her generosity overwhelmed him, and for a moment, he couldn't reply.

"Cooper? Are you all right?"

With some difficulty, he pulled his legs out from under his pet pig. "I'm fine, Danielle, and I'd love to spend Christmas with you. But I have a coffee date with Alyssa this afternoon, and I thought I might ask you for a little advice as well as her phone number."

Danielle laughed, a husky sound that let Cooper know in her day she'd led quite a life. Probably still did.

"Certainly, my dear boy. And as for advice, I don't know that I need to give you any! I was watching you with Alyssa the other night, and I was enchanted with the way the two of you couldn't take your eyes off each other."

"Hmmm," Cooper said, considering this. *Nothing like an objective opinion.*

"Sparks were flying, as they say. You fascinate Alyssa as much as she fascinates you! How do you say it, the irresistible force meets the immovable object?"

"And which one would I be?"

"Oh, I think you are the force, while Alyssa may be a little immovable for a time, but not for long!"

"I have to admire your confidence."

"But of course! You see, while Phillip was busy with his auction, *I* had plenty of time to observe."

He had to laugh. Nothing got by this woman. "So you think I should just continue doing what I'm doing?"

"Exactly! Be that irresistible force."

"Good advice."

Danielle laughed, the sound a throaty chuckle. "Cooper, I live to serve!"

# Chapter Twelve

Cooper was sitting at an outside table at the little Italian café on Sacramento Street when Alyssa came walking around the corner, this time dressed in worn jeans, black boots, and a chunky fisherman-style sweater in cream-colored yarn. It looked hand-knit and expensive. She had a small crocheted purse that looked like a sack made of turquoise cotton yarn slung over her shoulder.

"Hey, Cooper." She smiled and he was smitten. But he tried not to show it.

"Hey, yourself." He stood up and pulled out a chair for her at the small, round, black iron table he'd been sitting at. As he stood, he tucked the white puppy more firmly against his side. She had been absolutely adorable so far, hadn't had an accident in the hotel room once, but he hadn't felt right about leaving her at the hotel.

Baco and Pepe had gotten along famously with the pet-sitter he'd left them with; they'd all started to share another room service fruit plate. And Lafitte was enjoying his perch by the screened window and the glorious view of the Golden Gate Bridge and the bay that it afforded him. But as he'd left, Cooper had sensed the little white puppy had been afraid, so he'd decided to take her with him.

"You brought the puppy!" Alyssa said. She lifted her arms up. "Mine. Mine. Have to hold her."

He laughed, then handed her his little dog.

"And her name is?" Alyssa said as she settled the frantically wagging puppy into her lap. A woman sitting near their table lowered her newspaper and smiled as she saw the little dog.

"White Dog. Cream Puff. The six thousand dollar dog. I don't know, I haven't really had a moment until now to even think about it. But I figure that, like most dogs, she'll tell me her name when it's time."

He couldn't look at Alyssa enough. His MO for today was to let her take the lead. She'd said she needed some basic ground rules in order to commit to a purely sexual affair, and he was curious to know what they were.

*One step at a time.* As Danielle had said, patiently be the irresistible force. But not too much force, or he might frighten her off.

He had to be like water on a rock, slowly wearing away Alyssa's resistance to a permanent relationship.

First the sex, then they would see about anything more permanent. But he couldn't afford to frighten her off at this stage of the relationship, so if it was sex she wanted—

"What are you having?" she said, glancing at his coffee.

He came back to the present with a start, his mind veer-

ing abruptly off its one-track groove. "Double espresso.
And I've already had a blueberry muffin."

"Hmmm. I'm going to go inside and look at the menu."
She got up and handed him the puppy. "Just for a minute,
and then I want this baby back."

Cooper liked this café. It was an unpretentious place,
with a menu that changed daily printed in colored chalk
on a medium-sized blackboard up by the front register.
But most of its business was in coffee and pastries. Just
like a Starbucks, but with atmosphere.

He sighed and leaned back in his chair, absently
stroking Little White Dog's soft, curly fur. She'd come
with a dainty collar and leash, in pink leather studded with
rhinestones. Not what he would have picked, but it suited
her.

"Cream Puff?"

No response, just total devotion and love shining out of
those dark, puppy eyes.

"The Six Thousand Dollar Pup?"

More adoration.

"White Dog?"

Nothing.

He laughed. "How about White Fang?" The name
came to him as he remembered an old Soupy Sales show
he'd seen on late-night cable television.

She barked.

"White?" he said hopefully. This little pup didn't even
have full-grown fangs.

No response. Just those eyes.

"Fang?" he said weakly.

She barked, then scrabbled her way up his chest to lick
his chin.

"Fang?" he repeated again.

She wriggled some more, barked twice, then sat back and waited for him to say it again.

"Fang it is."

The sun felt wonderful on his back, even through the black leather jacket. Another glorious San Francisco day. His guidebook said it could rain in November and December, but he hadn't seen any signs of rain clouds yet. Instead, that cool, brisk ocean breeze followed him wherever he walked in the city. Compared to Chicago in December, he was truly having another day in paradise.

"What are you doing for Christmas?" Alyssa said, seating herself back down at the table. She had a large white ceramic mug of some sort of coffee drink, and a lemon square on a small ceramic plate. She reached for the puppy, and he relinquished her.

"Having dinner with friends. You?" He'd already decided that he had to play a little hard to get. A man had his pride, after all.

She seemed taken aback at this. "I thought you didn't know anyone in the city."

"Well, not when I first arrived."

"Wow. You make friends quickly."

He wasn't sure if she considered this a good thing or a bad thing, and decided to change the subject.

"Do you still want me to come over for New Year's Eve?" he said, referring to a message she'd left at his hotel. Nothing like jumping right in. Cooper had no time for subtlety.

She didn't even flinch. "Yes."

The lady certainly knew what she wanted. He decided to run with it.

"And the ground rules?" he prompted, picking up his

espresso. Cooper had only been half kidding with Jake the other night; he'd never tasted coffee this good in Chicago.

"Exclusivity for the duration of the affair."

"You got it."

"Complete and total discretion."

"Of course."

"And I can stop it whenever I wish."

He leaned forward, sensing she needed this control and totally willing to give it to her. "As much as I may regret saying this at a later date, I want you to know that you can stop things from going any further at any stage of the game, just by saying the word *no.*"

"Thank you."

Actually, it was on the tip of his tongue to suggest they blow this joint and find a hotel room, but he didn't want to come off as a crude and rude pig. Though he had no pretensions about understanding the opposite sex, he'd done his homework.

He'd glanced through *Cosmo,* that contemporary source of dating advice. He'd sat through his share of chick flicks. He'd even picked up a copy of that dating bible, *The Rules,* and made it through the fifth chapter.

He let her take the lead because she seemed to need that reassurance, that control. After all, he'd pursued her with a vengeance, come all the way to the West Coast, found her phone number through a mutual friend, and met her at this café. Now the power was firmly in her hands, and Alyssa seemed to have no trouble at all with exercising it.

"How's your grandfather?"

She smiled, and he sensed she was very pleased he'd asked.

"So happy about the success of his charity dinner. Do

you know, he raised almost seventy-three thousand dollars for his animal shelter?"

*Indeed I do, because eighteen thousand came directly out of my pocket!*

"That's fantastic."

"His first big project with that money is to try to trap and spay and neuter a group of feral cats down by the fishermen's boats. Once they're fixed, he'll let them loose again, but he wants to try and keep the general population down."

"A wise idea. What are you up to today?"

"I thought I might get in some Christmas shopping."

"I thought women didn't wait until the last minute; only men did that."

"Did you wait?" She leaned forward, and he was struck by the fact that she was teasing him.

"The only last-minute presents I have are for the little friends I bought the other night." He frowned. "Though I have absolutely no idea what to get a potbellied pig."

"Come with me. We could find out together!"

The temptation was irresistible. And wouldn't it be wise to spend some time with her so that she'd get used to having him around—besides in the sack?

"That sounds like fun. But what should we do with Fang?"

The little bichon barked once, sharply, then wagged her tail. It was clear to Cooper that she really liked her name.

*"Fang?"* said Alyssa. "For a dog that size?"

"I think she's one of those little dogs that thinks she's a big dog."

She gave him a look.

"Hey, it's the name she likes. None of this wimpy Pookie or Cream Puff stuff. Fang is a good strong name, and I think it gives her confidence. Besides, she'll grow into it."

"I don't think this breed gets to be more than ten pounds—" Alyssa began.

"Shhh. Don't tell her that!"

She laughed. "Then Fang it is." She ruffled the fluffy white hair on the pup's head. "Why don't we take her with us?"

"Shopping?"

"I'll bet we could even take her into the stores if we hid her in my purse, she's so small." Alyssa picked up the pup and placed a kiss on the black button nose. She promptly received a quick swipe of a tiny pink tongue in return.

"You're on!"

Shopping with Alyssa was a lot of fun.

The shopping centers they went to were jam-packed with last-minute shoppers, but as both of them were in no real hurry, they didn't let their tempers fray or the crush of people get the better of them.

At one of the several bookstores they visited, he found a book of essays on animal rights, bought it for Alyssa's grandfather, and had it gift wrapped. But he had no idea what to get for her.

That changed when they strolled by a needlework shop.

"I've always wanted to learn how to do needlepoint," she said, staring at the gorgeous finished canvases in the large front window.

Thirty-five minutes later, they exited the store, and Cooper had learned yet another detail about Alyssa. While some women would have started small, with a five-by-five-inch canvas that only used the most elementary of stitches, Alyssa went into whatever she did with all her heart. The canvas she'd picked out was quite large and depicted a group of Pekingese pups.

"This will look stunning in my grandfather's den," she'd said, eyeing the canvas. "And I can buy yarn to match his three little guys."

He'd insisted on buying both canvas and yarn for her, along with a snappy carrying case for the entire affair.

"Then I have to give you your gift early, as well." She pulled a wrapped present out from one of her several shopping bags.

She'd slipped that one by him; he hadn't seen her purchase it.

"You want me to unwrap it now?"

"Of course!"

They sat on a bench in an outdoor area between the shops, and he fumbled slightly while trying to get the tape to come off. What could she have possibly gotten him?

Then he laughed when he saw the two book titles. *The Idiot's Guide to Potbellied Pigs,* and *The Complete Dummy's Guide to Parrots.*

"These will come in extremely handy." He tucked the books into his shopping bag. "Thank you very much."

"You're welcome." She was practically beaming, and he found he liked the fact that she found joy in giving presents.

As the day wore on, it got colder, and he insisted they stop first for cookies and hot chocolate, and then later, for dinner. The bichon puppy slept in Alyssa's purse as they ate at a Japanese restaurant, steaming bowls of miso soup and then teriyaki and sushi.

"You have an adventurous spirit," he said, and he realized this was the quality he probably admired about her the most. If she hadn't possessed such a spirit, he doubted they would have met in the unique way they had.

"You think so?" She leaned forward, elbows on the black lacquered tabletop, her chin resting on her folded hands, studying him. "Sometimes I think I'm way too cautious."

"I don't think so." But then he realized maybe she was referring to her heart. He had a feeling it would take quite a lot of courage for Alyssa to truly give over her heart. And he was surprised at how badly he wanted to be the man who received it.

He saw her to the ornate front gate of her grandfather's mansion.

"I had a wonderful time," she said, looking up at him.

Fog was just starting to roll in; the air was nippy and smelled of the sea. Warm lights were coming on in the surrounding houses. Christmas trees twinkled in front windows, and elaborate decorations made some of the neighboring houses look like fairy-tale creations.

"So did I. Thank you for the books. I'm sure Baco and Lafitte would thank you as well. You were right; I don't have a clue what I'm doing with the two of them."

She laughed, then scratched Fang's curly white head. Cooper had tucked the pup into the V neck of his wool sweater, and now she rested against his chest, safe and warm, her tongue lolling out of her mouth.

"That's quite a name you gave her," Alyssa said.

"I'm telling you, she'll grow into it. I have it on good authority that this breed gets really huge. Why, someone told me today that they max out at about ten, eleven pounds." He grinned. "She'll strike terror into the career criminals." He wondered if Alyssa expected him to kiss her, and decided it would be more effective if he didn't.

"She'll just lick them to death, then Baco can do them in."

"Or Lafitte can talk them to death. Or bankrupt them."

An awkward pause.

He decided not to go for the kiss, and he could have sworn she detected the exact moment he decided, the shift in his emotions.

"Well . . . Merry Christmas," he said. "And please give your grandfather my best."

"Thanks, Cooper. And thank you for all the needlepoint supplies."

"I expect to see a masterpiece."

He turned away before he was tempted to try for a kiss, and walked off into the fog. Half a block away, he wanted nothing more than to turn and take another look at her, but he fought the urge.

He liked the thought of becoming unpredictable, a man of mystery.


"I thought we did rather well," Cooper said that night to Fang. They were sharing a steak dinner on the king-sized bed in his hotel suite, though Fang seemed to be getting more of the steak than the rest of the dinner. Baco snored on the far side of the mattress, while Lafitte's attention was completely captured by a Spanish *novela* on television.

*"Ay! Caramba!"* the parrot shrieked, as one of the female characters began to wail and cry, then gesticulate with her hands.

*Strange,* thought Cooper, *I'm used to the noise.* Amazing what one could adapt to.

Danielle had stopped by his suite and picked up Mr. LePew, so now he was reduced to the animals he'd bought at the auction. But Cooper hadn't missed the expression on Baco's face when Danielle had started out the suite's door with the tiny skunk in its plastic carrier.

"If Baco gets too depressed—" Cooper began.

"I'll let you have him back, I promise. Now remember, Christmas Eve dinner is at six. I'm starting early so we have plenty of time for cards."

"Sounds good."

Cooper grabbed the remote and changed the channel, ignoring Lafitte's squawks. He channel-surfed until he found what he was looking for: that evening's showing of *It's a Wonderful Life*. Call him a sap, but it didn't seem like Christmas without Jimmy Stewart as George Bailey.

"You'll like this," he called over to Lafitte, who was pacing up and down his perch, muttering to himself. *Oh great, now I'm talking to a parrot.*

"I will?" said the bird, and Cooper had to laugh. African grays were so damn smart; sometimes it seemed like they were really talking to you.

He'd already booked one of the hotel's vans for tomorrow evening, and the driver had assured him that he had no problems transporting a pig, a parrot, and a puppy. So everything was set for Christmas to unfold. Not quite the way it usually did, but what the heck; nothing in his life had been normal since he'd met Alyssa.

Baco snorted softly, and Cooper handed him a thick-cut steak fry. "Only because it's Christmas, pal. Don't go getting any ideas." He couldn't believe how fond he'd become of the pig in just over twenty-four hours. He'd found out later after the sale, from the package of carefully typed documents that had come with each animal, that Baco wasn't technically a purebred potbellied pig. He was one of the victims of the breed's popularity. At his size, around 120 pounds, Baco obviously had some real farm pig in his family tree somewhere.

He'd been abandoned down by the beach, left to fend for himself. An old Italian woman had found him, cold and terrified, and brought him to the shelter. Baco was special, Phillip had explained to him, because no matter what bad things had happened to him, the pig had an outstanding attitude and a real optimism for life. He loved people, even though during his early life, people hadn't been too kind to him.

"And pigs are extremely smart," the older man had assured him.

*That's for damn sure; he's sleeping on the mattress instead of the floor.*

A soft snort sounded from the side of the bed. Cooper, his eyes glued to the black-and-white opening credits, automatically handed the pig another fry without looking at him. "Last one, Baco. Happy hour's over after this."

As the stars in the sky twinkled and Clarence the angel prepared to make his trip to Bedford Falls to save George Bailey, Baco began to snore contentedly, Fang curled up against Cooper's chest, and even Lafitte watched the classic black-and-white movie, enthralled.

She missed him.

Alyssa sat back on her heels amid piles of sparkling wrapping paper, French wired ribbons, gift tags, tape, and scissors, and wondered at how she could miss Cooper so much.

They'd had so much fun today, shopping. She certainly hadn't meant for him to pay for her needlepoint, but he'd stepped right in as she'd piled all her purchases up by the front counter, including probably three times the amount of Persian yarn she'd need to complete it.

Then hot cocoa, then dinner, then the long ride back to her home, and then—

She frowned.

He hadn't kissed her.

*Why?*

*Maybe because he's just as unsure about this whole thing as you are.*

That had to be it. She picked out another present, a hand-painted silk scarf in vivid shades of turquoise and green, with just enough iridescence to remind her of a peacock's feather. It had reminded her of their neighbor, Danielle Tallant, as soon as she'd seen it in the store display.

She wrapped it carefully, putting as much time, thought, and energy into the wrapping as she had in picking out the actual present. Danielle had been a friend of both her grandparents for as long as she could remember, and a good neighbor. She was fond of the woman and planned to drop this present off for her as soon as she finished wrapping it.

Within the hour, she was on Danielle's doorstep. After she rang the bell and the butler ushered her inside, she was escorted into the front parlor, where Danielle lay on her red velvet chaise lounge, Maurice, her Persian cat, cuddled in her arms.

"Alyssa! How lovely to see you!"

"I just wanted to drop this off for you."

"You darling child! I have presents for you and your grandfather as well. What are the two of you doing for Christmas?"

"It's just the two of us Christmas Eve, but he's having

the rest of the relatives over Christmas Day." Phillip Preston didn't really get along with his extended family; they thought him a rather odd and eccentric man. But that didn't stop him from keeping in contact with them, though he determinedly went his own way no matter what they said or did.

"Well, if you get lonely on Christmas Eve and want a little excitement, I'm having a group of people over for dinner and games. Cards, board games, that sort of thing."

"Oh." Actually, that did sound like fun.

"You could come over directly after dinner, if Phillip already has your meal all planned. I'll be serving cake and cookies, and my homemade eggnog, of course. It's my mother's recipe."

"I'll mention it to Grandpapa."

"I think you know everyone who'll be here. The Harrises, and the Devereuxes from down the block—oh, and that lovely young man from the auction the other night, Mr. Sinclair." She laughed delightedly. "I even told him he could bring all his animals with him. I wouldn't want them to spend Christmas Eve all alone."

*Cooper. Here. Christmas Eve.*

Alyssa thought swiftly. "I'll talk to my grandfather about tomorrow night, but I'm sure we'll come by for the games. Is there anything I can bring?"

"Just your sweet self."

"Good." Alyssa stood. "I have to run right back. I'm still wrapping presents."

"Aren't we all!"

Danielle watched her leave the room. She hadn't missed the way the girl's hazel eyes had lit up at the mention of Cooper. And of course she knew how Cooper felt about Alyssa. That had been the whole point in inviting him to the Christmas Eve festivities—and making sure Alyssa knew he was going to be here.

Love could always use a helping hand, if not a downright push.

"Sometimes," she said, stroking Maurice's soft fur as the Persian purred contentedly, "I amaze even myself."

## Chapter Thirteen

Dinner at Danielle's was a lively affair. Cooper found himself enjoying the evening immensely. She had a brief cocktail hour, then moved them all into her enormous formal dining room, lit with masses of stunning candles, where they feasted on standing rib roast with all the requisite side dishes and some very fine wines.

Then, after they'd had a chance to sit and relax for a bit, she herded them all into her large family room, where he could see several card tables, along with two or three board games set up, ready to play.

"And the television is here for Baco," she said. She seemed practically willing to give his pig the remote. And for a moment Cooper wondered if his pet was that smart.

Armed with dessert plates filled with bûche de Noël cake and both spicy gingerbread people and star-shaped sugar cookies, and carrying small glasses of amazingly rich homemade eggnog, all the guests took their places.

Baco stretched out in front of the wide-screen television to watch the Dr. Seuss cartoon, *How the Grinch Stole Christmas.* He'd found Pepe the minute he'd entered the house, and now the tiny skunk lay on top of the immense pig, much like he had at the hotel.

Lafitte held court on his portable perch in the far corner of the family room. His new favorite expression to shriek was, "Look Daddy, teacher says that every time a bell rings, an angel gets his wings!" But thankfully, he didn't do it more than once an hour.

And of course, Fang stayed in his lap.

Cooper liked to play cards, so he sat down at one of the tables and was soon in the midst of a rousing game of hearts. He and Danielle were neck and neck, each having won two games, when he glanced up and saw Alyssa and her grandfather in the family room doorway, and his spirits lifted even more.

This was a present he hadn't counted on.

She was wearing a cranberry-red sweater along with a long, plaid skirt that hit about mid-calf on those gorgeous legs, and dark brown leather boots. And to his eyes, she looked absolutely wonderful.

She caught his eye immediately and smiled such a tentative smile that he couldn't resist grinning back. And he glanced at Danielle, wondering if she'd set this whole thing up . . . but the woman was busily studying the cards she currently held.

"I don't know about this hand," she murmured.

Instinct told him she'd set this up for them.

"Thanks," he whispered. "I owe you one."

"Whatever are you talking about?"

"You know."

"Ah well, they say the Christmas holidays should be all

about romance!" She picked another card, then called, "Get over here, Phillip, and play cards with us! You, too, Alyssa!"

The Devereuxes professed they wanted to turn their attention to the Grinch and his antics, so within minutes the four of them were seated at the table, and Danielle, Phillip, Cooper, and Alyssa began a new game.

"You have to watch that one," Danielle said, indicating Cooper with a nod of her perfectly coifed head. "He doesn't cheat, but he's a formidable player!"

"I can imagine," Alyssa said, as Fang tried to teethe on the bottom of the cards she held. Of course, she'd insisted on having the puppy sit in her lap as soon as she'd sat down.

Cooper looked at Fang with new respect. True, she probably wouldn't amount to much as a watchdog, but if she enchanted Alyssa and therefore helped them to spend more time together, then Fang was another in a long line of inducements he could use to his advantage.

Three games later, Danielle asked him if "You and Alyssa could bring Phillip and me each another glass of eggnog. You young people have more energy."

Nothing like being a little obvious. But he was so happy, he didn't even care. And even though Alyssa had insisted she wanted to be able to set the pace sexually, he didn't think she'd mind a kiss. She seemed willing enough to go with him, as she handed Fang to Danielle.

To hell with being a man of mystery; he wanted her. And a kiss, even a couple of kisses, would be an effective way of setting that in motion.

They'd barely entered the dining room where the large table had been set up with all the desserts and the sparkling crystal punch bowl filled with eggnog when he pulled her the rest of the way inside and up against him. Cupping her face in his hands, he lowered his lips to hers and kissed her.

It was as if he'd been starving for her since that night in his den.

And if the way she was kissing him back was any indication, she was just as hungry.

He broke the kiss and glanced around the dining room, exasperated. Too open, not enough privacy for the way he wanted to kiss her. He couldn't really risk anyone coming into the dining room and seeing him practically all over Alyssa, even though both of them were enjoying it very much, thank you.

"There's a pantry," she whispered, and he smiled.

"I like your mind."

Danielle was no fool. She knew what she'd set in motion, and she had all her bases covered. With a discreet nod of her head, she indicated to her butler that he should bring them two more glasses of eggnog. Then she got up from the table and plucked down a huge, hardback book from one of the many bookshelves lining the family room walls.

"Phillip," she said. "I have a problem with one of my rosebushes, and I wondered if you could take a look at this gardening manual and give me a hand with it. I really need your opinion on this matter. I don't want to lose this particular plant."

She could almost see the moment when all thoughts of his granddaughter or the remaining card game flew out of his head. She and Phillip were both passionate gardeners, especially when it came to their beloved roses.

"Show me what the problem is," he said.

\*    \*    \*

Alyssa led Cooper into the darkened kitchen, past a huge butcher-block table and to the far back, where she opened a door and stepped inside, dragging him with her.

The moment she shut the door behind them, a soft light came on from up above, illuminating shelves filled with cans and boxes of various foodstuffs.

"I like this," he whispered. "I can see you."

And then no words were necessary as he pulled her into his arms and kissed her.

Now that they were alone, he threaded his fingers through her hair and gave her mouth the attention he'd wanted to lavish on it earlier. One kiss blended into the next, and as his hands moved down her body, shaping her waist and then sneaking beneath the bottom of her red sweater, he thought for sure she'd try to stop him.

Instead, her hands were busily moving beneath his dark blue sweater, then unbuttoning the shirt beneath, until he felt her palms flat against his chest. He broke their kiss, his breath hissing into his mouth at the sensual contact.

What this woman did to him was beyond belief. Having his chest touched had never been a big deal before. But having Alyssa touch his chest—

They stood face to face, foreheads touching, breathing hard. She stepped away from him and linked her fingers with his as she started to lead him toward a small table, oak, with a marble top, directly behind a freestanding shelf filled with food. The table was sheltered and out of sight of the main entrance and just large enough for—

"Here?" he whispered. He had to be sure.

She nodded.

"Now?"

She smiled and kept walking with him toward the table. It had obviously been put there for a utilitarian purpose, but its surface was just large enough that she could sit on it and he could—

"You're sure?" he whispered against her mouth as he began to kiss her. "You don't want to wait till New Year's—"

She reached for him through his slacks, and he gritted his teeth as her hands, with unerring accuracy, closed around his aroused length.

"Far be it for me to dissuade you," he whispered as he placed his hands around her waist and lifted her until she sat on the table's edge. Between kisses he said, "What exactly do you have on underneath that skirt?"

"Boots—and a thong."

"In this weather?"

"We only had to walk from one house to the other."

"Good point," he said, pushing her long skirt out of the way and hooking his fingers around the sides of her scanty undergarment. He pulled, and it came right off. Not wanting to leave any evidence that could incriminate them, he stuffed the silk garment into the side pocket of his slacks.

She was already working at those same slacks' fastenings, and before he could do anything else, she'd freed him. And there he was, primed and ready, unable to hide the incredible attraction he had for her.

"Okay," she whispered, leaning back on the table, propping her upper body up with her elbows. "I'm ready."

"You are? What about foreplay?"

"I've been thinking about you all afternoon; that's enough foreplay for me."

*What a woman.* If this was a dream, he didn't want to wake up.

He moved between her legs, positioned himself as close to her as possible, and in a moment of clarity reached inside his pocket and found the small foil packet. After protecting them both, he pushed back her long skirt and her silky slip and hooked her booted legs up over his shoulders.

And kissed her. Kissed her long and hard as he found that wet, hot heart of her and slowly began to push inside. She broke the kiss, gasping, her head going back, but he couldn't stop his progress and kept pushing, relentless now, until he was all the way inside her.

He couldn't seem to think coherently, he could only move. Pressed up on top of her, his hands slid to her waist, then down beneath her skirt to cup her buttocks. He held her still on the small table as he moved, the sexual motion driving, urgent, filled with a need that had been denied for far too long.

Through the haze, he thought to bring his hands around to where they were joined together so intimately, to stroke her quickly, lightly, to ensure that she reached her pleasure as soon as possible.

And then she moaned low in her throat, reached for him, reared up, and grabbed his shoulders. He felt her climax, felt the contractions that sent him over the edge, driving into her, pumping harder and harder until he felt his release, felt its inevitability, and then he was there as well, groaning into her hair, saying her name, and then—

Done. Spent. Gasping as he lay on top of her, trying not to crush her, and wondering if this time in the pantry had been as wonderful for her as on the floor of his den.

"I wonder . . ." he said, then took another deep, steadying breath. "I wonder what it would be like to have sex with you in a bed?"

She laughed, and he felt her flat stomach move ever so gently. She laughed from down in her belly, and he liked that.

"We'd better get back," she whispered. "My thong?"

He stepped away from her, breaking their sexual link, then reached into his pocket and retrieved it. She slid it back on while he disposed of the condom in a large black lidded trash can and zipped himself back up.

"You'd better hit the bathroom," he said. "Your hair's all over the place."

"Yours, too." She started to laugh. "Just come with me."

They found the downstairs bathroom, straightened themselves up, and then walked back into the dining room.

"What should we say took us so long?" she whispered.

"Hey, in my book, it didn't take us that long." He glanced at his watch. "That was accomplished in about, oh, fifteen, twenty minutes."

"You're kidding?" She grinned up at him. "Just think, my first quickie!"

*It boggles the mind. . . .*

"How about, we were getting the eggnog and you felt a little nauseated—"

She shook her head. "I have a stomach like a truck driver's, I never get sick from too much food."

"Okay. Then maybe we took our coats and went out for a minute to look at the Christmas lights."

"That my grandfather would believe."

As it turned out, they didn't even need an excuse, as

Phillip and Danielle were deep in a discussion about garden pests as they came back into the family room.

Baco's entertainment had segued into the movie *White Christmas,* and Bing Crosby and Danny Kaye were singing the song about sisters, while Lafitte was eyeing the feathers in their costumes with interest.

"At this point, Rosemary Clooney and her screen sister are already getting on that train to Vermont," Cooper said.

She turned toward him. "Do you like Christmas movies?"

"I'm a big sap. I like all of them."

"You're not a sap, you just have a generous heart. Look at all the animals you've given a home to."

At this point, if Phillip had been auctioning off a baby rhino, he would have made a bid for it. Things were definitely looking up.

"Do you still want me to come by for your New Year's Eve party?"

"Yeah."

He had to know. "So . . . uh . . . how did that measure up, I mean, in comparison to what we shared before the wedding?"

"Even better."

"Better?"

"Well, it was better because I knew what to expect, and I wasn't that afraid."

"You were afraid the first time?" He felt like a heel.

"Only of the unknown. But mostly I was excited."

He smiled. "What time do you want me over on New Year's?"

They sat down on one of the couches facing the wide-screen television.

"I was thinking you could come by sooner. Tomorrow

night, after all the guests leave. I mean, you'll be right here anyway, didn't you say you were having dinner tomorrow with Danielle and her friends?"

"She just didn't want me to be alone at Christmas."

"I know, she's a sweetie. Anyway, why don't you come over around midnight? I'll wait by the gate."

She liked adventure, that was for sure.

"I'll be there."

The van picked Cooper and his menagerie up that night at midnight, just as planned. And as friends and neighbors softly called out "Merry Christmas!" and headed for their respective homes, Alyssa came up behind him as he was helping Baco into the back of the van.

"I just wanted to tell you one more thing," she whispered.

"What?" He glanced at Danielle's front porch, where she and Phillip were still engaged in an animated conversation.

"You don't have to worry about any . . . protection."

"Really?"

"Really. I went to my gynecologist as soon as I knew I wasn't pregnant, and let's just say that I'm definitely safe."

"Hmmm." He didn't want to pry or ask her which method she'd chosen. "So you're okay if we don't—"

"I like it even better when you don't wear anything. Unless—" She hesitated. "Unless there's a reason you should?"

"No, there's not."

He could see the relief in her face, and he admired her for asking tough questions that had to be asked. Cooper took her hand and squeezed it, not wanting to risk a kiss with her grandfather watching them. But he couldn't resist asking once again.

"So," he said, trying to sound casual. "Did I pass the test?"

"With flying colors."

On the way home, Cooper knew he'd won a major battle, but the war wasn't over yet.

"Boys," he said to both Baco and Lafitte as they returned to the hotel suite, "I'm leaving you both with a pet-sitter tomorrow night. I don't care what it costs, but sometimes a man has to fly solo."

Baco grunted and headed toward the bathroom. Lafitte walked the length of his perch restlessly and muttered, "You're a fine one, Mr. Grinch. . . ."

He stared at the parrot. *No, impossible* . . .

He shook his head, then turned to Fang, perched on his bed.

"And you get to come with me, because if I ask Danielle to keep an eye on you for one evening, I don't think that's too much of an imposition, do you?"

Fang barked, then stood on her hind legs and waved her tiny front paws in the air.

"Great." He scooped her up in his arms and headed toward the spacious bathroom. "Now let's pee on those newspapers, because I have to get to bed and recoup my strength for tomorrow."

Danielle's Christmas Day dinner was a gourmet's delight, but Cooper couldn't have told you what he ate or drank within five minutes after leaving her house precisely at midnight. Actually, he couldn't have told you what he ate or drank as he was eating and drinking it. He was too busy thinking about Alyssa.

He hadn't felt too bad leaving Baco and Lafitte back at the hotel. They'd gotten their favorite sitter again, a young man named Eddie Palwick, who was in his twenties, wore all black, and had long, dark burgundy hair, three tattoos, and his lip pierced in several places. The guy was a walking piece of performance art.

Actually, Cooper had thought he looked something like a vampire.

But Eddie loved animals and was highly responsible; that was all that mattered.

"Order what you want from room service," he'd told him before he left for the day and—hopefully—most of the night. "But watch Baco if you get any fries, he's pretty tricky. If you leave the room without taking the necessary precautions, you're coming back to an empty plate!"

Danielle had stunned him by giving him Mr. LePew as a Christmas gift. She'd handed him the baby skunk after dinner was finished, complete with a red velvet ribbon around the little guy's neck.

"I saw the way he looked at Baco," she told him. "Sometimes animals just bond to each other. Pepe has missed him, and that poor pig has had enough upset in his life. They're firm friends and deserve to be together."

The bottle of very expensive French perfume he'd bought for her couldn't hold a candle to his very own skunk.

And little Fang was perfectly content. At this very moment the small puppy slept peacefully at the foot of Danielle's bed. She'd agreed to watch her this evening and keep her overnight, as well as his new pet skunk.

Now, at almost midnight after a very full Christmas

Day, Cooper walked up to the ornate iron gate in the fence that surrounded Phillip Preston's property. The evening had turned chilly and very foggy. The few Christmas lights that were still on gleamed through the fog, the wisps softening their bright holiday color. In the distance, a foghorn sounded.

It was too cold to have sex outside, but somehow he didn't think Phillip would take kindly to Alyssa sneaking him into her bedroom. He wasn't even really sure if he'd be comfortable there.

As Cooper waited by the gate, he restlessly stuck his hand inside his jacket pocket. The small velvet box reassured him, the ring inside it one he'd taken great care in choosing. He knew Alyssa would like it, and she might even wear it, if she would only come to trust him.

In time, he had to believe she would.

He didn't mind her taking control of their sexual relationship, as long as within a certain amount of time they could start to make decisions as a couple.

"Hey, Cooper!"

He heard her voice float out of the fog, then she was at the entrance, key in hand, unlocking the ornate gate and ushering him inside.

"Did you have a good Christmas?" he said.

"It was wonderful. I got to avoid all the relatives by saying I had a very important gift to deliver." She took his hand and began to lead him back into the extensive yard.

"And did you?"

"Yes. A bay pony to an eight-year-old girl and her family. They'd almost given up on Santa, and we couldn't have that." Briefly she told him about how she'd made all the arrangements for the pony to be delivered to a nearby stable, and a full year's worth of boarding fees, riding lessons, vet bills, farier bills, and food to be included.

"What happens at the end of the year?" he asked as they passed the back of the silent mansion.

"I'll throw in another year's expenses. The important thing is that she realizes it's really important to have your dreams. If she likes this pony as much as I think she's going to, I'll just sponsor her riding. It's done all the time."

Every time he thought he couldn't possibly like her more than he already did, she surprised him.

"And yours?" she said.

"Wonderful. I'm now the proud owner of my own pet skunk!"

"Mr. LePew?"

"The one and only. Danielle couldn't bear for Pepe and Baco to be separated."

"I thought it was really cute the way they watch television together."

"Where are we going?" he said, wondering if she was planning to have her way with him in the middle of the garden. Though he was no sexual prude, Cooper preferred being nice and warm as opposed to freezing his naked ass off.

"Right here." She led him toward a Japanese-style gazebo, and he could hear the faint bubbling sounds of a Jacuzzi.

Nice and warm. Hot. This would do nicely.

"This is great," he said as they entered the small structure and Alyssa latched the half door behind them.

"Total privacy," she whispered.

"There's no chance that your grandfather—"

"He was in bed by nine tonight. Our relatives simply exhaust him."

"Why does he even have them over?"

"Because family is important to him. And realistically, it's only a couple of times a year." She stood on her tiptoes and gave him a swift kiss on the lips. "Now get undressed, Cooper. We have a long night ahead of us."

He liked the way she thought.

# *Chapter Fourteen*

Both of them shed their clothing with record speed, and within minutes were in the hot tub, surrounded by the steaming, bubbly water.

"Now *this* is what I call a Merry Christmas," Cooper said.

Alyssa laughed, then submerged herself in the water and came up, slicking her hair back from her face. This was the first time since the night they'd met that they were actually naked with each other. Though it had only been about two weeks' time since the bachelor party, it seemed that she'd known Cooper a lot longer. So much had happened.

"Do we have to get right down to it," Cooper said, "or is it all right with you if we have a little conversation first?"

"Oh my God, am I really that bossy?"

He started to laugh. "No, I just love to tease you."

"We could talk first, if that makes you feel more comfortable."

"It does," he said. "If we don't talk a little first, well, then afterward, when I'm all alone . . . I just feel so . . . cheap. Degraded. Sordid. A soiled dove, as it were."

Laughing, she splashed water at him, he splashed back, and soon they were engaged in an all-out water fight. When he grabbed her ankle, then her arm, and lifted her up into his arms, Alyssa finally admitted defeat.

"You're a lot stronger than I am," she said.

He let go of her instantly, and she knew he'd misunderstood.

"I would never do anything to—"

"No, I like that strength. I really do. You . . . you fascinate me, Cooper."

"I do, huh?" She could tell he really liked hearing this.

"You are truly unlike any man I've ever met."

"What you're trying to say, as nicely as you can, is that I'm totally outside of your usual social circle."

"No, that's not what I meant."

"Then tell me."

"Most of the men I meet are so . . . *boring*. They've been raised with their parents' money, work for their fathers, and have absolutely no initiative of their own. No dreams, nothing to accomplish. You, on the other hand, from everything I've heard about you from Mindy, made it on your own."

"You asked her about me?"

"She told me all this way before I crashed the bachelor party. I'd heard all about you years before I met you, but I never thought much about it until I really met you, in the flesh. Does that make sense?"

"Sure."

She frowned. "Cooper, you aren't ever going to tell Tom that it was me at that party, are you? I would feel awful if anything I did that night ever came back to harm Mindy's marriage in any way."

"Cross my heart," he said, crossing his index finger over his muscular, hairy chest. "I wouldn't want to do anything to hurt Tom, either. And I think it really would hurt him if he found out that Mindy still didn't trust him the night before their wedding."

She had to make him understand. "It wasn't Tom, Cooper. It was that jerk before him, the one she found in bed with his old girlfriend. But Tom was the one who was paying for that other guy's behavior."

"I think that's true for all of us, Alyssa. The things that happen in our past have to color where we are now. Whether we can trust, or love, or even let go and have a good time."

He was looking a little too close to comfort for her.

"Did Tom have any issues with trust?" she said, consciously changing the subject.

"Nope. He comes from a shockingly boring and very nice family, one I've known for years. No scandals there. The only problem that Tom may have in the future is that, as the youngest boy in a family of six, he's been spoiled a little. But I think Mindy can whip him into shape. But would he cheat on her? Never."

"That's good to know. So my horrible secret is safe with you?"

"Yep." She watched as he stretched those muscular arms along the edge of the Jacuzzi. "I wouldn't have told anyone that you spent the night with me, anyway. I didn't, you know."

"You didn't?" She hadn't been sure, but it had crossed her mind. She'd wondered if he'd bragged to the other men at the wedding that he'd managed to get it on with one of the hired dancers at the bachelor party.

"No. The only person I told was . . . you. And you were part of it. And you guessed what happened before I actually told you, because you were there."

She started to laugh, remembering their ride to the country club in the limousine. "Women's intuition."

"That, and a ringside seat!" He peered at her through the slight steam rising up off the surface of the bubbling water. "Truth. Did you think I was some sort of jerk?"

"No, actually I thought you were awfully sweet, trying to work things out in your head. It was only when you were . . . when you—" She stopped.

"When I what?"

"When you became so cynical about love. Then I wondered what had happened to you to make you feel that way."

"I don't feel that way anymore," he said, and the look in his eyes caused her to glance away.

"I'm sorry, Alyssa, I don't want to push you. You set the rules for this, and I'll respect them."

She glanced back at him. "I just don't like getting out of my comfort zone emotionally."

"Fair enough."

"What made you so cynical?"

He tilted his head back, and she guessed he had to be thinking about when it had all begun.

"When I was in military school, there weren't a lot of girls around. Tom and I were only around them in the summer, when we came home for vacation. And it seemed to me that a lot of them were only interested in the image. What a guy could give them. How he'd make them look.

What kind of clothes he wore, what kind of sports car he drove, that sort of thing."

She nodded her head.

"I never really had a problem getting dates. But then business intervened. Jake and I hooked up right out of college, and everything changed. He's the computer genius, while I had the degree in business and all the marketing savvy. We worked our butts off, and within three years, we'd made it about as big as anyone ever had."

"Wow. That must have been a great feeling, to have done it all by yourselves."

"My dad was pretty astounded, but after he got over his surprise, he was really happy for both of us. I bought my parents a new house, treated them to a cruise in the Caribbean, invested wisely, that sort of thing. But then I noticed that the women were really attracted to me now. And it was all about the money."

"That must have hurt you," she said.

He seemed surprised that she got it. "Yeah, that's exactly it. Because I knew that most of the women I dated could have been sitting next to a toad instead of me and they would have been just as excited with the toad as long as he'd had access to my bank account. So I just stopped dating and threw myself into my work."

"All work and no play," she said softly, remembering her phone conversation with Jake.

"That about sums it up."

"But I know exactly what you mean," she said. "My grandfather's sheltered me a great deal, and I know it, and there were times in my teens I even used to resent it. But one time, in private school, I started to go out with this boy, and he introduced me to a friend of his who he told me really liked me. It didn't take me too long to understand that it was my grandfather's money he liked."

"He's worried about you," Cooper said, thinking about Phillip Preston.

"I know."

"He doesn't want anything bad to happen to you."

She nodded her head.

"He wants to protect you."

"But don't you see, if I'm protected too much, it's like, it's like . . ."

"Being up on that pedestal?"

She stared at him from across the Jacuzzi.

He got it. He got her. He'd really been listening.

"Yes," she whispered.

"And that's why you have to have control," he said quietly. "And I love you so much I don't even care."

*I love you.* He'd said the words she'd known were coming, but he'd said them much sooner than she'd thought he would.

"I love you, too," she whispered. She had to tell him the truth, even if she was scared to death of it. It wasn't the way she'd imagined it, this moment when they'd finally admitted they loved each other, but real life was seldom like a fantasy.

She swallowed, feeling extremely vulnerable. As a dancer, it was no big deal to run around almost naked onstage. She'd sunbathed nude at some of the most exclusive and private beaches in Europe.

But here, in front of this man, laying her heart out on the line, she felt incredibly, emotionally, totally naked.

"Where do we go from here?" she finally asked him, trying to regain some sense of control.

He seemed uncomfortable. "I'm kind of nervous admitting this, because I'm scared if I tell you, you'll figure out a way to never see me again. Run away."

"Marriage?" She had to have it all out on the table.

After a long hesitation, he said, "Yes," his tone quiet and resigned.

"Why?"

"Because . . . I've never met anyone quite like you. I've never felt about anyone the way I feel about you. Oh, and by the way, I have no problem signing a prenup, I have absolutely no interest in your money—"

"Cooper, it's not about the money, and you know it." She felt her entire body go incredibly still, as if the outcome of this conversation between them had her future in its hands.

"It's about you," he said softly.

"Yeah."

"You're scared I'm going to try to crush you, like your father did to your mother. That, or put you back up on that damn pedestal."

"Yeah."

"I wouldn't want you dancing privately for any other guy. I'd never cheat on you, either. But I wouldn't stop you from doing any of your other dancing, and I wouldn't want you to change at all."

"Just so you're aware of this, my entire family thinks I'm strange."

"Even your grandfather?"

"Well, they think he's strange, too."

"So you two strange ones live together and see the rest of your uptight family only when you have to. And even then, you manage to slip out and deliver ponies rather than sit in a room and make polite conversation with them. Am I getting the picture?"

She could feel her lips curving into a smile. "Yeah. We're the odd ones."

"I've got news for you, Alyssa. Your grandfather doesn't think you're odd. He understands you only too well, and that's why he's scared to death for you."

"What do you mean?"

"He knows what it's like to live in a world where most of the people in it are walking dead. Where nobody is passionate about anything, and someone who does have genuine passions is seen as strange, or crazy, or someone to make fun of. He knows what it's like to have a heart as big as yours and how easily it can be hurt."

"Cooper—"

He held out his hand. "Hear me out. Please."

She nodded her head.

"And he knows how much you love your friends, how you'd do anything to make them happy. Alyssa, I can't think of one other woman who would've crashed that bachelor party and stripped down to her underwear in front of total strangers just so her best friend in the world could walk down the aisle the following day feeling totally at peace."

"But I had to—"

"No, you *didn't* have to. You *wanted* to. You wanted to give your friend the best gift anyone could give a bride the morning of her wedding. Peace of mind. The assurance that she was doing the right thing. Am I right?"

She hesitated. "Yes, but—"

"You can't see it because you're not any other way. There's no pretense, no bullshit to you. You're just the way you are, and that morning when I woke up on the floor of my den and you weren't there was one of the worst of my entire life."

"But that was Bambi—"

"No, that was *you*."

The silence, so total, seemed to reverberate around them, the only sound the bubbling of the water. Alyssa sank down lower in the steaming water.

"Are you cold?" he said.

"A little."

"Do you want to go inside?"

She started to laugh. "I'm beginning to feel like a prune."

He smiled. "Are there any towels around here?"

"Next to the sauna."

He cocked an eyebrow as he looked down at her. "A sauna? Near here?"

"Right off the indoor pool."

"Lady, I like the way you think."


*So this is how the really rich and famous live,* Cooper thought.

They'd jumped out of the Jacuzzi, pulled on their clothes, carried their shoes, and raced toward the back of the mansion. Alyssa had silently let them in the back door to what seemed to be an area devoted to physical fitness, then led him to an enclosed room that proved to be an actual sauna.

Now they sat on the wooden benches, undressed once again, a towel wrapped around his waist, another around her slender torso. And he felt wonderfully warm, while their clothing hung up to dry directly outside.

He liked the way she felt against him, leaning back against his chest, sitting between his legs. He had his arms around her, but lightly. Lightly. Cooper had a feeling that he'd pushed Alyssa enough for one night.

A safer topic was in order.

"Were you lonely, living with your grandfather?" he said.

"Sometimes. I used to really wish for a brother or a sister, but I knew that wasn't going to happen. Then I went away to boarding school and met Mindy."

Now he had an idea of how much that friendship meant to her.

"She's a terrific woman."

"Yeah, she is. She even shared her family with me. My grandfather let me spend a summer with them one year, and I couldn't believe how much fun it was to sit around the dinner table with all her brothers." She started to laugh.

"What?"

"The first time I ate dinner there, this big plate of fried chicken was being passed around the table, and Mindy whispered to me, "Better take what you want when it comes your way, or you won't get a second chance!""

He laughed, the laughter a quiet rumble as it made its way up his chest.

"Ah yes, we men are beasts."

"Not all of you. You know, her father used to do a lot of the cooking, and when he made bacon and eggs for breakfast, the frying pan he used was enormous!"

"Speaking of bacon, I'm going to keep Baco."

"You are!"

Briefly, he told her the story of how the pig was found on the beach, cold and confused, and the various hardships and traumas the animal had been through.

"No one would want him now," Cooper said. "When someone wants a potbellied pig, they're talking about a pig that tops out at about forty pounds. Not this guy."

"I'm glad he's staying with you." She sighed, and he felt her lean back against his chest. "Cooper?"

"What?"

"Can we just stay this way tonight? I mean, can we just talk?"

For some reason, his eyes stung. "Sure, honey."

He slipped out the ornate iron gate a few hours later and took a cab right back to the hotel. He didn't want to go to Danielle's looking as if he'd spent the night with Alyssa, so he let himself into the suite and decided he'd take a long, hot shower and get a few hours of sleep before he went to pick up his skunk and his puppy.

Eddie was crashed out on the couch. There had been a dinner tray in the hallway, so Cooper knew the young man had eaten. Baco was sprawled out, snoring, across the entire king-sized bed, while Lafitte had been put in his cage and covered.

He tried not to wake Eddie as he came in the door, but the pet-sitter came instantly awake.

"Hey, thanks for staying so late." Even though it had been their original agreement, it had been Christmas, after all.

"No problem." Eddie glanced at the parrot's cage. "We watched Michael Caine in that Muppet Christmas movie, and Lafitte has a new expression."

"Let me guess. 'God bless us, every one!'"

"You got it. Oh, and you were right about Baco and French fries. I had to really watch him."

"He's clever when he wants to be." Cooper pulled a few extra bills out of his wallet and handed the cash to Eddie, tipping him generously.

"Wow, thanks!"

"Merry Christmas, Eddie."

"Yeah, whatever," came the reply.

Something wasn't right. "Do you have any family to spend the holidays with?"

The young man hesitated, then said, "My mother's new boyfriend and I don't get along."

Cooper thought fast, knowing Alyssa would go along with his plan. "Can I hire you in advance for New Year's Eve? You'd watch the animals, but it would be more like a party, up in the Nob Hill area."

Eddie's eyes brightened. "Sounds cool. Sure. Call me the day before and give me all the details."

He saw the young man out the door, then shut it behind him and turned, surveying his suite.

Forget the shower, he already felt like a prune. Grabbing a bottle of water, he twisted off the cap and took a long, healthy swallow. The sauna had sweated off at least a few pounds of fluid. He took another long drink, then screwed the top back on and set the bottle down on the end table by the bed.

He was pleased with the way the evening had gone. He'd learned a lot more about Alyssa and could understand why she did what she did—as much as any man could ever understand any woman.

It wasn't his style to go this slowly, to pace himself. He and Jake had always worked flat out, working all night and into the next day, hot on the next project and eager to see it done.

You couldn't approach a woman the same way. You had to give her time. Cooper thought about Danielle and silently thanked Jake for hooking him up with the older woman. Without her take on things, he could have messed up badly, and that was the last thing he wanted to do where Alyssa was concerned.

Baco grunted softly, almost a whine, and his legs worked in his sleep as if he were running.

"On that beach again, eh boy?" Cooper said softly. How well he knew about personal demons and how they could ride you. It had taken him years to come to terms with suddenly making more money than his father had made in his lifetime. He'd lost a few friendships that, in retrospect, hadn't been that solid to begin with, and he'd had his heart thoroughly broken before he'd figured out that almost all the women he'd been dating wanted him for his money.

Until he'd met Alyssa.

*Ah, well. Live and learn.*

Baco snorted again in his sleep, and Cooper sat down on the edge of the bed.

"Okay boy, shove over." Putting both his hands beneath the enormous pig, Cooper gently eased the sleeping animal across the bed so that he could at least have a small corner of it. He unlaced his shoes, slipped off his belt, threw his wallet, keys, and the ring box on the end table, and was asleep within seconds of his head hitting the pillow.

If someone had told her, Alyssa thought as she got ready for bed that night, that she would invite Cooper Sinclair over for a night of being naked in a Jacuzzi and then later near-naked in a sauna and that nothing would happen, she wouldn't have believed them.

But they'd been naked, been close together, and nothing had happened. Nothing sexual. But on an emotional level, a lot had transpired.

She was beginning to really trust him. Oh, she'd trusted him when she'd decided to spend the night with him. She'd known he was the sort of man who wouldn't hurt her. But at the time, most of her mind had been on helping Mindy.

Cooper had been a devastating distraction.

Once they'd spent the night together in his den, she'd really believed that the whole incident was going to be relegated to a very happy memory. A one-night stand. A night when she'd taken a dare and plunged headlong into her life, finally lost her virginity, and begun to have a clue as to what it meant to be a sexual woman.

A night when she'd felt so alive.

But then Cooper had confounded the odds and come out to the West Coast. She hadn't seen that coming. And she hadn't been prepared for the way she'd felt when she'd seen him again at the charity auction.

When feeling had rushed over her at that first moment of recognition, she hadn't been prepared for the fierce delight she'd experienced at seeing him again. And until she'd felt that emotion, Alyssa hadn't realized how much she'd wanted to see Cooper. How much she'd missed him.

Once she'd gotten beyond the initial attraction and started to get to know him on their Christmas shopping expedition, she'd found that she really liked him. Even before that, she'd loved the way he'd given his disparate group of animals a kind and loving home, especially Baco. Something about the large pig touched her.

And the joy Cooper had so effortlessly given her grandfather, the way Cooper had supported his favorite charity.

Now, after the evening they'd just spent together,

*Chapter Fifteen*

The following day, Cooper decided that if love was indeed a battlefield, he needed to make a couple of preemptive strikes. He had to stake a claim, make his intentions clear, and show Alyssa that he had no intentions of going anywhere. He was here in San Francisco for as long a time as she needed to feel comfortable with their relationship.

Thus, first thing in the morning, he called a Realtor.

"I want to buy a house," he said.

And he wasn't kidding. He called Eddie and had him pet-sit that day, as he drove all over the city with a very competent real estate agent the concierge recommended. His name was Marty, he was totally bald and built like a linebacker, but he knew his stuff.

"A pig, huh? Can he do stairs?"

"He can. But I'd like to have a large downstairs area with a family room, so that he has the option of never having to go upstairs if he doesn't want to." Cooper knew that most people didn't consider a hundred-pound pig a pet, but the city of San Francisco allowed potbellied pigs to be kept as pets. And Baco wouldn't cause any trouble. Most likely he'd charm the pants off all their neighbors.

After just three days, he found the house he was looking for. And as is usual in house-hunting expeditions, it was nothing at all like what he would have thought he'd buy.

He hadn't wanted anything pretentious or huge. He'd wanted something that would feel like a home. So the minute Cooper saw the jaunty little Victorian in Pacific Heights, with its bay window, sunshine-yellow paint job, and ornate trim, he knew this was the one. It just felt right, and he knew Alyssa would like it. He could see Lafitte's perch set up right in front of that bay window and the parrot enjoying the view of pedestrians walking by.

And most important, Pacific Heights was just a quick hop, skip, and a jump from Nob Hill and Alyssa's home. So he'd have a cozy base camp for as long as this "war" lasted.

"I don't even have to step inside," he said to Marty as they stood on the small front lawn. This house had just come on the market; there wasn't even a sign out front yet.

"But let's go in, just in case," the Realtor suggested.

Inside, what they found was a flawlessly maintained interior. The owner, an elderly woman who had inherited the house from her mother, had passed away recently. Both her children lived on the East Coast and were selling the property, complete with all the furniture, immediately. They wanted the money the sale could bring, not the house itself.

There was even a respectably sized backyard with a deck and a large, sunny lawn. Cooper narrowed his eyes, imagining Baco stretched out in the sunshine, his ears twitching.

"Their loss," Marty had muttered as he glanced around the Victorian.

"I'll take it," Cooper said, whipping out his checkbook.

"How were you thinking of financing this?" the Realtor asked.

"I thought I'd just write a check."

He appreciated the fact that Marty remained calm, but he supposed that, as a real estate agent working in the Bay Area, he'd seen it all.

"How soon can I move in?"

"With no mortgage to negotiate and the kids anxious to sell . . . and it's already passed both home and termite inspections . . ." Marty stared at the backyard, but Cooper knew he wasn't really seeing it.

"I tell you what, Mr. Sinclair, I'll see what I can do to speed things along."

The second preemptive strike was an actual date. So far, since Mindy's wedding, Cooper thought, he and Alyssa hadn't really gone out on a date.

They'd met at a charity event, gone shopping for Christmas presents one afternoon and then out to dinner, spent the holiday together, and talked—naked—in a Jacuzzi and a sauna. This would be the first time he'd ask her out on an official date, and Cooper really wanted it to be special.

It couldn't be just any first date. He had to do some planning, think up something that would delight her. Cooper knew he had to be imaginative, it had to be something fun. Somehow he had to create an evening where Alyssa didn't feel pressured.

When he found out about the outdoor skating rink at The Embarcadero that was set up each Christmas, he decided that this would fit the bill.

"Ice-skating!" Alyssa had said over the phone, and he'd loved hearing the delight in her voice. "I haven't been skating since I was a little girl."

"Think you still know how?" he teased.

"It's just like riding a bike."

They'd arrived at the outdoor rink, and Cooper had surprised Alyssa again with a new pair of ice skates.

"I figured this was the perfect post-Christmas date, and a pretty fun present," he said as she opened the package, exclaimed in delight, and began to lace up her skates.

He'd grown up with blustery Illinois winters and had also played his share of ice hockey as a boy, so skating was utterly familiar territory for him. He was fast on his feet on ice.

They glided out on to the ice amid all the other skaters and circled the large rink a few times, hand in hand.

"Cocoa afterward?" Alyssa said as she glanced up at him, and he loved seeing the bright color in her cheeks, the sparkle in her hazel eyes. She looked absolutely adorable in a fluffy white sweater and hat and light brown pants.

"Whatever you want," he said.

"This is *wonderful,* Cooper," she said, squeezing his hand as they skated along. "I don't know what it is about ice-skating, but I've always thought it was so romantic. The only thing missing is the snow. You know, just a really gentle little fall. A few strategic flakes, like in the movies."

"You like snow?"

"I *love* snow. It's the only thing that I miss living here. And there have even been a few winters when we got some, but they're few and far between. And we always went skiing at least twice every winter, so I certainly got my share of snow."

"Huh." He'd never thought about the concept of missing snow. In Illinois, it was as relentless as death and taxes. But he smiled to himself, thinking of what was yet to come.

The rink was somewhat crowded, and they had to avoid young children, especially the boys, as they darted in and out among the other skaters. There seemed to be some sort of improvised hockey game going on, and Alyssa got tremendous amusement out of watching the two teams battle it out while trying not to trip up the people who were skating at a more sedate pace.

She sighed in disappointment when an announcement blared, stating that the rink would be closing earlier than usual because of a private party.

"I wish we could've skated a little longer," she admitted as they glided over to the side of the rink. "I hope I don't sound like I'm complaining—"

"Your wish," Cooper said, laughing, "is my command. Is there anything else that the lady wishes?"

"You're so silly." Alyssa glanced up into the sky, up above the tall city buildings. "Okay, smart guy, while you're at it, how about some snow?"

"You," he said, tapping her pink nose, "read minds."

"What are you talking about?" she said as she sat down on a bench close to the rink and started to unlace her skates.

"Not so fast," Cooper said. "Aren't you at all curious as to who this private party is?"

She stared at him for a long moment, and he knew the exact moment when comprehension dawned in those beautiful eyes.

"You?" she breathed.

"The one and only. And not just me. *Us.*" He loved doing things for her, making her smile. The look she was giving him at this exact moment could only be described as incandescent.

"Cooper! I can't believe it!"

Her enthusiasm charmed him; she reminded him of Audrey Hepburn in *Roman Holiday,* a sheltered and beautiful princess taking delight in quite ordinary things. Like a simple night of skating beneath the stars. And cocoa afterward.

Well, he was going to shake up the order a little.

"First, our cocoa," he said, indicating a small pushcart being positioned near the edge of the rink. "Let's go over and see what they have to offer. Get warmed up."

"This is amazing," she muttered as he reached for her gloved hand and pulled her to her feet.

They sat on the edge of the rink, right on the ice, and drank their gourmet cocoa.

"Magical," she whispered, looking up into the sky. Then, once she finished, she handed her empty cup to the vendor and turned to Cooper.

"Let's skate!"

He watched as she took off out over the ice, practically flying. Her daring took his breath away, and he knew he wanted to see her dance, to see one of her troupe's recitals. He had a feeling that Alyssa onstage would be just as full of life as she'd been on the dance floor at

Mindy's wedding and out here on the ice, at night, the sky a deep, deep blue against the crystal whiteness of the ice.

He skated slowly along the outside perimeter of the rink, watching as she sped up, jumped, turned gracefully in the air and landed smoothly, looking for all the world like a long-legged filly running full out on the track and enjoying her own speed. Or an Olympic hopeful, full of energy.

Cooper glanced over at the vendor and gave the man the prearranged signal, all the while anticipating what Alyssa would do when she realized what else he had planned for them.

She skated up to him, sliding to a sharp stop, breathless. "This is so wonderful, Cooper! The whole rink! Imagine what those little boys could've done with their hockey game!"

"A frightening thought," he said, laughing, then took her hand in his and they started to skate.

The first few snowflakes clung to her hair, but she must have noticed them because she stopped dead, almost tipping them both over, and looked straight up into the sky.

"Oh my God, it's snowing!"

"In a manner of speaking," he whispered into her ear, then pointed. Alyssa looked in the direction he was pointing, then started to laugh.

A large snow machine stood on the far side of the rink, shooting snow into the sky, so it fell naturally down onto them, a light sprinkling of snowflakes.

Just like in the movies.

"This is so—I can't believe you—" Her voice sounded dangerously close to breaking, filled with emotion.

They skated in silence for a while, through the glittering snow, taking their time, totally enjoying themselves as they made their way through this magical night.

"How did you think this up?" she finally asked, more composed as they continued to skate along.

Cooper tapped the side of his head, above his ear.

"There are many master plans inside this formidable brain," he said, and she laughed.

They skated to the middle of the rink and came to a stop, standing close together, a distance from either the cocoa vendor or the other man operating the snow machine.

"Cooper," Alyssa said softly, into his ear. "I don't have the words."

"That's okay."

"How long can we stay?"

"As long as you want." He thought back to his days on ice, all the crazy stunts he and his friends had pulled. And a sudden inspiration came to him; something he knew Alyssa would love.

"Let's dance," he said.

"On ice?"

"Sure. People do it all the time."

She hesitated.

"Hey, we already know we're good on a dance floor," he said, feeling cocky now that his idea had paid off.

"When we're not arguing," she reminded him.

"We have nothing to argue about now, and only the night to enjoy." He moved a short distance away from her and executed a slight bow. "Would you do me the honor, Alyssa? May I have this dance?"

"Yes."

And he took her in his arms and they danced, skimming over the ice amid the shimmering snow. They danced until they couldn't dance anymore, until they finally skated over to the side of the rink.

He kissed her several times as they took off their skates, and they ordered cocoas for the road after Cooper generously tipped both men for staying out a little later than he'd planned.

The totally blissful expression on Alyssa's face was something he could never put a price to. Cooper decided that, as far as first dates went, this one had been a success.

It was such a successful date that Cooper decided he didn't want it to end.

"And now, for the pièce de résistance," he said as they pulled away in the car he'd rented. "Dinner at my place."

He saw the slight hesitation and added, "It's not like we're going to be alone."

She started to laugh, and he could tell that even though she might be a little nervous around him, she'd love seeing all the animals.

"That's true."

"Come on, Alyssa. It'll be fun. And you have my word, I won't lay a hand on you, unless you say the word."

He had one hand on the wheel and the other on the seat between them. He felt the slight weight of her hand as she placed it on top of his, and the simple gesture moved him.

"I'd like to have dinner with you, Cooper."

An enormous pig was an extremely effective chaperone.

As usual, Baco was sound asleep on the king-sized bed when Cooper walked in, and for a moment he was frustrated by his lack of success when it came to disciplining his animal kingdom. But all was forgiven when Alyssa burst into peals of laughter as she saw the huge pig sound asleep on the bed, with Pepe lying on his stomach.

"Now *that's* a romantic image," Cooper said, and this made Alyssa laugh even harder. The little skunk rose and fell as Baco breathed, and even Cooper had to admit that it was funny.

They sat at the dining table in the penthouse's living room, overlooking the city, the lights of San Francisco spread out at their feet in a magnificent view. The Golden Gate Bridge twinkled in the distance, and they could see lights from the boats leaving the bay.

"Order anything you want," Cooper said, indicating the large room-service menu. "Anything at all."

Alyssa sat across from him, Fang in her lap.

"This is a lot better than a restaurant," she said, scratching the bichon puppy's tiny head. Fang, totally blissed out, leaned against her stomach. "I've missed these guys," she said. "Even when I've seen them the night before, I really miss them."

And Cooper thought, as he watched her while pretending to study his menu, that stranger things happened in the world all the time. This was like being part of an animal-style Brady Bunch.

Though the only animals Alyssa had around her were her grandfather's three Pekes, he knew she loved animals. And if a pig, a parrot, a skunk, a puppy, and a golden retriever gave him any advantage with her, he'd gladly take it.

They ordered dinner, and Cooper was impressed with the speed with which their choices arrived, along with the wine he'd chosen.

He let her guide the conversation, and she talked about many things. Her grandfather's garden, especially his prized roses. The vacation Danielle was planning to take to Paris to see some old friends. Her dance troupe and her work at various animal shelters around the city.

And she listened as he told her stories about how he and Jake had started the business, the years where everything had been new and exciting and they'd been flying by the seat of their pants.

There were also a number of comfortable silences, and Cooper liked the fact that neither of them felt a need to rush in and fill them. He only hoped that Alyssa was as comfortable with him as he was with her.

"How are things going with that Christmas pony?" he asked, and was glad to see her surprised response. He could tell it mattered to her that he'd remembered.

"Hannah loves Cider. She races to the stable every day, and would spend all her time there if her mother would let her."

"That," Cooper said as he speared another bite of a really excellent crab and shrimp omelet, "was a truly outstanding thing to do. You and your grandfather are really very generous people."

"You think so?" she said, and he sensed that his opinion of her and her grandfather was important to her.

"I know so. Look at how much money your grandfather raises every year for his various charities. That's a very unselfish thing to do."

"You gave him a great deal of help this year."

"Thanks to Lafitte, here."

"You're welcome," said the parrot, eyeing their dinner from his perch by the window.

"Hmmm." She took another bite of her fettuccine Alfredo, and he could tell she was considering what he'd said.

He didn't rush to fill the silence, simply waited.

"That's strange to hear you say that, because some of my grandfather's brothers and sisters—my great-aunts and uncles—think he's an extremely selfish man."

Cooper couldn't repress a smile. "Let me guess. Does it have something to do with the fact that they don't all have access to his money?"

"Cooper!" she said, pretending to be shocked, but then she laughed, and he knew he'd scored a direct hit.

"And let me take another wild guess. Your grandfather's wise enough not to start something like lending them money, something that will be a never-ending source of irritation."

Alyssa put her fork down, reached for her glass of wine. "It's strange. My grandfather was the oldest of seven, and when both his parents passed away, he became something of a surrogate father to his younger brothers and sisters. And, aside from one of my great-uncles who lives up in Alaska and is very self-sufficient, and a great-aunt who married and lives on Martha's Vineyard, the rest are . . . the rest just want . . ."

"The rest just want your grandfather to make things easy for them."

"Yes. And, while each of them had money given to them when they came of age, several of them squandered it. When the money ran out, they came running to my grandfather to ask him for more. He shocked them when he said no. I guess they all thought he'd take care of them forever."

"A wise man, your grandfather. It would've never ended."

"He once told me that he thought that getting their inheritance so young spoiled some of his siblings, that the money was the worst thing that could've happened to them. It just took away their ambition."

"I can see how that would happen."

"He was very careful when I was growing up, so that the same thing didn't happen to me."

And that, thought Cooper, explained why Alyssa was not the typical little rich girl. Phillip Preston had been a wise and loving grandparent.

"Money can make some people a little crazy," he said. "Jake and I found that out the hard way when our company first started making big money."

"Was it hard for you?"

"For a time. I went around with my guard up for a couple of years until I finally realized that there were people out there who would like me for who I was and not for what I could do for them."

"I know exactly what you mean." She hesitated. "I didn't know you had money when I met you. I mean, your home is beautiful, and I knew you had to be somewhat successful, but not to the extent that you are."

"I know you didn't." He grinned, then said, "And I sure didn't think that Bambi had any money."

The minute the words were out of his mouth and he saw the quick change of expression in her hazel eyes, he regretted what he'd said.

"Alyssa, I'm sorry. I didn't mean to hurt your feelings."

"It's stupid."

"It's not stupid if I hurt you."

She looked down at her plate for a moment, the food clearly forgotten.

"Tell me," he said, keeping his voice soft. Persuasive.

"It's just . . . sometimes I think that the woman you really like is . . . is Bambi. I know it's insane, to be jealous of myself, but sometimes I wish . . . I wish I could be a lot more like her."

*This is dangerous ground.* Cooper thought quickly.

"You *are* like her. You'd have to be. No, I'm saying this badly, hold on. What I mean is, there's a part of you that's exactly Bambi, because you would've come off totally phony if that weren't the case. You had me completely fooled; I didn't think you were anything other than what you pretended to be that night." He hesitated. "Does that make sense?"

"Kind of." She picked up her fork, played with her pasta. "I've thought about that night a lot. It was a strange way to meet, neither of us really knowing the other."

"But it worked," he said.

"What do you mean?"

"What I mean is, we got past that first meeting, and here we are having dinner together. And Alyssa, you have no reason to be worried. I really like you. I have from the moment I met you."

She looked at him, her eyes still worried.

"I still can't get over how loyal you are to Mindy, how far you were willing to go to ensure her happiness."

"Cooper," she replied, "sleeping with you had nothing to do with Mindy."

"I know that. I just meant that the way you got into my house and ended up dancing on my coffee table—all of that came about because of loyalty to a friend. Alyssa, that's rare in this world, and a quality to be treasured."

Their conversation was interrupted when dessert arrived, and Cooper deliberately steered the rest of their conversation toward more humorous subjects. But as he walked Alyssa to her door that night, to that ornate iron gate that let her into her grandfather's property, Cooper wondered how she could possibly think that her real self held any less appeal to him than Bambi had.

New Year's Eve approached, and after their dinner date, Cooper held back a little. He decided on a very light approach as far as Alyssa was concerned. He called her but didn't push her. He didn't tell her about the house; he wanted to do that in person.

In the meantime, he tried to make her laugh. Shared amusing moments of his day, especially the animals' antics. In return, he began to get a feel for her life: much more quiet and sheltered than his, but he discovered a woman full of compassion, always ready to help solve any problem she came across. And totally committed to her dance troupe.

Every so often, for confidence, he'd take the small velvet box out of his jacket pocket and study the engagement ring; a flawless, two-carat diamond set in a platinum band.

He'd propose when the time was right. And hope to God she'd accept.

Alyssa rehearsed for her troupe's January dance recital until she was exhausted, and even then, her thoughts still continued to bother her. She couldn't sleep. She looked forward to Cooper's telephone calls and dreaded them at the same time. Why couldn't she just be a normal woman and enjoy the fact that a really terrific man wanted to have a committed relationship with her? Why did she have to be so totally terrified?

Though she hadn't done a lot of therapy, she knew where her fears came from. Sometimes, when you'd been through so much at such a young age, it was as if your heart and your body just shut down and said, *I can't take any more.* And she knew she must have made that decision, however unconsciously, at the age of six. She couldn't even remember her mother's funeral, though almost every member of her extended family had told her about it in great detail.

When she was a very little girl, she'd sat alone on the mansion stairs or retreated back into the garden and wondered why her father had never wanted to see her or be with her. And for a long time, she'd thought there was something very wrong with her.

She loved her grandfather deeply, but even he and her grandmother, with all their love, care, and concern, hadn't been able to put her fears to rest. She'd been told she'd had horrible nightmares for six months after her mother died. She'd even regressed and wet her bed a couple of times, but her grandparents had never made her feel ashamed.

Now, so many years later, she thought she'd been able to put those fears to rest: her fears of not being good enough, of being abandoned and left behind by someone she'd loved so very much. It had happened so long ago, almost twenty years ago, so why was the past rushing up to meet her and making her so terribly afraid of Cooper and what he represented? Alyssa hadn't even suspected how powerful those fears were until Cooper Sinclair had arrived on the scene.

*But something must have seemed right about him,* she thought as she lay out in a hammock in a far corner of the garden. It was one of her favorite places to think, and she'd come here to do just that.

*You wouldn't have just jumped into bed with anyone.*

Something *had* been right about Cooper. Right for her. Even meeting him the way she had, at the party, she'd instinctively known he was a strong man. And she'd once read an article, probably in *Cosmo*, that said that women made up their minds if they were going to sleep with a man within minutes of meeting him.

Maybe what had seemed like such a crazy, snap judgment, such an insane decision, hadn't been so crazy after all. Maybe it had been her body's wise way of forcing her out of an emotional deep freeze.

She'd had conflicted feelings about Mindy's wedding from the moment her best friend had called her and told her Tom had proposed. Your best friend couldn't get married without you wondering whether you wanted to get married, too. That wedding had put a real spotlight on all her fears, on her most private feelings about real intimacy with a man and losing control.

She'd lost control with Cooper that first night. She'd put herself in his hands, literally, and he'd given her pleasure such as she'd never experienced before in her life. She'd trusted him, and he'd repaid that trust. He hadn't talked with his buddies and made something that had been so important to her into something cheap and laughable. Even when he'd thought she was an exotic dancer and used to exposing her body to groups of men, he'd treated her with kindness and respect.

Alyssa was beginning to see that Cooper was one man in a million.

Angrily, she brushed the quick tears out of her eyes. She always seemed to be on the verge of crying these days, and it didn't take a rocket scientist to understand why.

"Alyssa?"

She heard her grandfather's voice and scrubbed her cheeks free of the few tears that had fallen. Hoping her eyes didn't look too red or her voice didn't sound choked up like she'd been crying, she called out, "Over here!"

"I thought I might find you here," her grandfather said, walking toward her, a thick envelope in his hands. "The mail just arrived, and I thought you might want to take a look at this."

At that exact moment, it was as if she saw him, clearly, for the first time in many months. He was having trouble walking, and using his rosewood cane. He approached her slowly, with a little difficulty, and she knew with a sudden instinctual clarity that he wasn't going to be in her life forever. And he had been so much a part of her life she didn't know how she would go on without him.

And she realized that even if someone loved you and wanted to be with you, the natural rhythms of life, of change and renewal, determined there would be times when you would face great loss.

"It's from your friend Mindy, and I thought—"

She threw herself into his arms, being careful of his fragility, and hugged the old man tightly.

"I'm so sorry," she whispered.

"Sorry? For what?" He sounded totally incredulous.

She held on even tighter. "For being such a disappointment to you."

"Disappointment? Never!" He held on to her, his embrace warm and familiar, then stepped back in order to look at her face. "What nonsense are you talking about?"

"I should be married by now, with babies—"

"No, Alyssa, that's not true. I haven't gotten to this age without learning a few things, and one of them is that everything comes to us as it should, and in its right time."

She couldn't meet his eyes, so she sat down in the hammock and put her head in her hands. "My life is such a mess."

Her grandfather walked over to a small wooden chair and lowered himself down into it, the envelope still in his hand.

"Can you tell me about it?" he said. "Do you want to?"

She remained silent, wondering what to say.

"Perhaps this might help you," he said, and handed her the envelope. As he started to rise, she whispered, "Don't go. Please."

He remained where he was.

She opened the thick envelope. Mindy had sent this envelope Express Mail, and from the size and shape of it, Alyssa had some idea of its contents.

Wedding pictures.

The hastily scribbled note that accompanied the numerous photographs sounded just like her best friend: "I meant to buy a little album and arrange them all for you, but I was so excited by how well they came out that I wanted you to see them right away!"

Alyssa slowly thumbed through the pictures, handing each one to her grandfather as she finished looking at it. The entire wedding party. Tom and Mindy, over and over again, dancing, cutting the cake, standing at the altar and looking at each other with so much love in their eyes.

And then one picture, the last in the pile, of her and Cooper. They were both smiling at the camera, but she remembered the exact moment. He'd been looking at her just before the photographer had taken the shot, those blue eyes narrowed with speculation, wondering where it was that he'd seen her before.

"It must have been a beautiful wedding," her grandfather remarked.

Those wise old eyes didn't miss much. She felt so much more behind those words, but he waited patiently for her reply.

"It was."

"Was that where you met your young man?"

*Your young man.* She had to smile. How simple and clear her grandfather's world was. If you loved someone, you married them. You had children. You raised a family and did the best you knew how.

"Yes."

"Alyssa."

She raised her eyes to his. He was gently tapping the stack of photos in his fingers, lining up their edges, before he handed them back to her.

"I want you to know that you have never, ever, been a disappointment to me. Do you believe me?"

She couldn't quite believe that, so she remained silent.

"Perhaps I've pushed you a little too hard in one particular direction, but please believe me when I say I only wanted you to be happy."

"I know that," she whispered.

"And I also want you to know that I like this young man of yours. Very much."

"Thank you." She thought of Cooper and how pleased he would be to hear this.

"And I have to admit that I . . . well, I did a little investigating."

"What?" She couldn't believe it, her grandfather acting like Detective Columbo.

"I checked your young man out, and he came through with flying colors. Ambitious, tough, but fair. He made his own way in the world, and did quite a fine job of it. But he's a kind man, as well."

"I know. Mindy told me."

"He's a fine young man," her grandfather said. He reached for his cane, then slowly rose out of his seat. "But the final choice is totally up to you."

She nodded her head.

"And I hope you know that I will love you no matter what you do, and that has always and will always be the case." He glowered down at her and she almost laughed, his expression was so fierce.

"I know." She handed the envelope to her grandfather. "Would you take these back to the house?"

"Of course. Will you be in for lunch?" He hesitated. "Maybe we could go out to that little Chinese place you like."

How like her grandfather, to think of specific ways to cheer her up. When she'd been little and skinned her knee while roller-skating, he'd kissed the boo-boo and taken her out for ice cream. Now he was going to attempt to do the same with Chinese food.

But it did sound good. And she couldn't sit back in this hammock and hide from the world forever. Moping around never solved a thing.

"I'd like that." She stood up, then linked her arm through his. "Let's walk back to the house and head out for some lunch. That dim sum place, right?"

"Exactly."

Jake was reading the newspaper at his desk in his Chicago penthouse apartment when he heard the slight whine. Lowering the paper, he saw Riley, Cooper's golden retriever, with his favorite toy, a plush stuffed carrot Cooper had bought him last Christmas.

He sighed. "You want to go for a walk, Riley?"

No response. The large dog simply lay down next to his feet and let out a long, mournful sigh.

This was bad, when even the mention of a walk couldn't get Riley on his feet.

"You miss Cooper, too, don't you?"

Riley whined.

"I know, it's hard being here on the sidelines, not knowing what's going on, wondering if—I mean, *when* Cooper's going to come back."

Riley sat up, stuffed carrot in mouth, and leaned toward Jake, putting his head in his lap. Jake began to pet the silky head, stroking the velvety ears.

"Hey, we might have to open a San Francisco office if he really gets serious about this girl. And from the way he talks about her, he's already head over heels. You'll have to learn to chase seagulls, Riley. And I might have to learn to surf."

The dog merely looked up at him, his large brown eyes mournful.

"This," Jake said, "is getting both of us nowhere. And you know, it's not like a ton of work is accomplished right after the New Year, not the way this office parties. So, what do you say that you and I plan a little road trip and head out West to see what your demented dad's up to?"

Riley's ears moved, ever so slightly, and Jake knew he had him.

"Riley," he said, smiling down at the dog. "Car. How would you like to go for the longest car ride of your life?" If there was one thing he knew, it was that Riley, like most dogs, loved to take rides in the car. "We can take my convertible. Or maybe the Jeep. Yeah, the Jeep might be safer this time of year."

Riley began to prance around the office and bark.

"That's the spirit! No more of this sitting around on our asses doing nothing, it's getting both of us nowhere. We're heading out West and figuring out just what's going on with Coop! And if he's having any trouble convincing Bambi Alyssa to give him a chance, well, we'll just have to help him out!"

"This place is awesome!" whispered Eddie as he led Baco into the formal foyer, with its black-and-white marble floor. "What a place for a New Year's party!"

Cooper was thinking much the same thing. Phillip had assured him that tonight's party was rather informal, but he'd still dressed with care. Lafitte perched on his shoulder, taking in everything, while Fang stood by his side in her pink leash and collar, her tail wagging from side to side, and Pepe remained beneath his jacket.

He'd come to the conclusion that he was a complete and total pushover with his animals. He'd bought a king-sized bed with orthopedic support for Baco that would be delivered once they moved into their new home, and quite possibly the largest parrot cage in the civilized world for Lafitte. Mr. LePew didn't ask for much, thank God. And Cooper knew that all Fang had to do was gaze at him with her dark puppy-dog eyes, and he was willing to lay the world at her furry feet.

"Me and Baco and Pepe were thinking we'd watch Dick Clark's *Rockin' New Year's Eve*," Eddie said. "We'll camp out by the television."

"Sounds like a plan. I may drop Lafitte off with you later." Cooper saw Phillip coming toward them, a very pleased expression on his face. Quickly introducing Eddie to the older man, Cooper scanned the room for any sign of Alyssa.

"She's still upstairs, getting dressed," Phillip said.

It was uncanny, Cooper thought, the way the old man seemed to read him so well.

"Sometimes she can get herself all worked up, wondering what to wear," Phillip said.

"I'm sure anything she wears will be fine."

"My sentiments exactly," Phillip replied. He turned to Eddie. "What would you like to drink, young man? And would you mind my asking, doesn't it hurt to have those piercings in your lip?"

The two of them and Baco started in the direction of the huge family room. Cooper had to grin at the sight, the young man with his Goth appearance, and Phillip, who looked as if he'd stepped off the screen of a Hollywood movie from the forties, impeccable in gray flannel slacks and a dark green pullover sweater.

"God bless us, every one!" Lafitte muttered beneath his breath.

Then Fang began to yip as she caught sight of Alyssa. Cooper glanced up and saw her coming down the stairs, and as always, she took his breath away.

Dressed in a silvery, sparkly, short-sleeved dress, she'd worn her hair down around her shoulders. Strappy silver sandals completed her outfit, and Cooper thought she looked good enough to eat. He wanted to haul her into his arms and kiss her until neither of them could think straight, but he saw the cautious light in her hazel eyes and thought better of it.

"Cooper." She came walking toward them, and he found he even liked watching the way her body moved.

She was a dancer, with lithe, fluid lines to her body, and she moved with grace.

"How are you?" he said, leaning forward and kissing her cheek.

"Good. You?"

"Tired. It's hard work, relocating an office."

"I should think so. Drink?"

She found them both flutes of champagne, and a slice of apple for Lafitte.

"Thanks," the parrot said as she handed him the apple.

She glanced at Cooper, clearly amazed.

"I don't even wonder about it anymore, this bird's so damn smart."

The party was mainly concentrated on the first floor of the mansion, in the family room, the formal dining and living rooms, and the immense library. And as Cooper walked through the ground floor of Alyssa's home with her, he marveled at the fact that even though this house could have been stark and cold and overwhelming, someone had taken the time to turn it into a home.

"My grandmother, mostly," Alyssa said. "Once she passed away, my grandfather kept it exactly the way she left it."

"I can understand that."

They wandered back into the family room, where Cooper deposited Lafitte and Fang with Eddie. He and Baco and Pepe were watching a documentary on the making of a Rose Parade float.

"He really does like television," Alyssa said, indicating the large pig.

"They're supposed to be smarter than dogs," Cooper said. "At least, that's what your grandfather told me." He felt as if there was a silent glass wall up between them, and that Alyssa was letting him get just so close and no closer. She seemed so fragile tonight, and he wondered what had happened to the closeness they'd once felt.

It was frustrating, because he had no idea how to bridge the space between them.

*Time,* he thought as they sat down on one of the large couches in the family room. *Give her time. Just get her used to being with you, spending time with you. She'll come to trust you.*

Later that evening, Fang came running over and jumped into Alyssa's lap. Eddie had taken off her pink leash, and now the puppy wriggled all over at the prospect of seeing her friend again. Cooper could see the delight she took in the little dog.

"You have a knack," she told him, "of selecting the most extraordinary animal companions."

"Oh, I like to think they're all extraordinary, given the chance. These guys were just a little down on their luck."

"But to have gone from a man who had absolutely no animals—"

"I did have a dog. I mean, I *have* a dog. A golden retriever named Riley. Jake's looking after him for now."

"But he wasn't at your house."

"He was with Jake at the office that night. Riley tends to get a little nervous with a lot of strangers around, so I didn't want to stress him out any more than I had to."

"Not like this crew," Alyssa said, and Cooper glanced in the direction of Eddie and his menagerie.

Baco was sprawled by the television, but his attention was on the large tray of chips and dips on a low coffee table. Cooper had a feeling that the pig knew he would be banished in disgrace if he tried to sneak any of the goodies. Baco was smart; he was biding his time.

Lafitte was perched on Eddie's shoulder, and the young man was feeding him grapes, his absolutely favorite fruit. Pepe slept at Baco's side, oblivious to the talking and laughing, the shuffling of cards, the clinking of glasses, the general merrymaking.

"Nah, they're pretty indestructible." He thought fast. "Would you like to take a quick walk outside? I could use some fresh air."

"Could I take Fang?"

He knew she was employing the bichon frise puppy as a shield. If they had the pup with them, not too much hanky-panky could take place. What she didn't seem to understand was that he wouldn't want anything to take place that she wasn't totally comfortable with.

"Sure."

They got up from the couch and headed toward the French doors that opened out into the garden. As they slipped outside, Cooper glanced over toward where Phillip and Danielle were playing cards. The older man had been watching the two of them and now gave Cooper what he thought looked like an encouraging smile.

Cooper nodded his head, then followed Alyssa into the dark garden. And as he did, he wondered what the New Year held for both of them.

# Chapter Sixteen

Once outside in the garden, he noticed she didn't go anywhere near the Japanese gazebo or the Jacuzzi. They walked in silence for a while, stopping to let Fang sniff and explore. Then Cooper heard the words he'd been dreading.

"I just don't know if this is fair to you," she said.

He could have just run right over her, denied her any of her feelings, told her to let him be the judge of that, but he decided to listen. He had to understand exactly what it was she was going through, or they didn't have a chance.

"Tell me what you mean," he said.

"Cooper, I look at you and I see a man who could have any woman he wanted."

He resisted the urge to tell her that was so untrue. He'd dated a lot, met so many women both at work and on the few vacations Jake had managed to drag him on. He'd seen so much of the world that he was sure all he ever wanted for the rest of his life was the woman who stood right in front of him.

But she couldn't see her own value.

It was no fault of her grandfather's. He suspected it had more to do with what had happened when she was small. Some wounds took a long time, if not a lifetime, to heal.

"Go on." He wasn't going to tell her she was wrong. He wanted to know what she was feeling.

"I just keep thinking about what would happen if we did—"

"Get married," he said for her. This was bad; she couldn't even say the words.

"Yes."

"Well," he said, "just for the record, I think we'd have a great time."

She didn't even smile. This was worse than he'd thought.

"Alyssa, there isn't another woman in the city who would put up with Baco. Or that smart-mouthed bird, Lafitte. I feel like a divorced woman with children. I'm a package deal, and you know the whole package."

"But I would let you down."

Now they were getting to the heart of it.

"How would that be possible?"

"On those days when I might not be at my best—"

"Real life," he supplied gently.

"You might not like what you saw."

"I'm sure your worst is a lot less frightening than a lot of women's best. And I'm not always at my best. Jake's accused me of being a total workaholic, though you wouldn't know it from the past month."

"How can you be so optimistic?"

"Because you've got to be, when you're considering

marriage. The divorce rate is over fifty percent, and those are crappy odds, no matter how you slice them. But all I know is that those odds don't know you and they don't know me, and they certainly don't know how much I love you."

She looked up at him, and he studied every feature on her face by the light of the moon. He couldn't lose her now, not when he'd traveled so far, both physically and emotionally, to find her.

"This will work, Alyssa." He decided to amend that statement. "We'll make it work."

"I'm not your normal woman."

"Thank God for that."

"I can't even cook."

"We can eat out a lot."

"There are things about the real world that I don't know, that I'm not very good at."

"We'll learn together."

"You have an answer for everything, don't you?"

"When it comes to you, yes."

They stood in silence, then heard bells start to ring, and the soft *pop-pop* of firecrackers. The New Year had officially begun.

"Come here," he said, gently guiding her closer to his embrace.

"Oh, Cooper," she whispered.

He covered her lips with his as Fang snuggled up against their legs, totally content. He kissed her with every ounce of emotion he could dredge up out of his soul. He had to get her to understand what she meant to him, how he'd been a—what was that expression from that movie he'd seen?—a "dead man walking." He'd been existing, but he hadn't been living.

Life had started to get exciting the minute Alyssa as Bambi had thrown him her black satin bra. Then he'd pursued her all the way out to the West Coast and found out that the woman who had danced for him, the woman who had refused to back down to him, the woman who had practically singed off his body hair with her erotic sensuality, was a much more complex human being than he'd realized.

He wasn't backing off now.

Their lips parted, and he stepped away.

"Happy New Year, Alyssa."

"You, too, Cooper."

"You know what they say," he said, enfolding her in his arms, "they say that whatever you're doing or however you feel on New Year's Eve, you're fated to do or feel that way for the rest of the year."

She was snuggled so close to him that he knew she could feel every contour of his body, and that body was currently shamelessly revealing his emotional and erotic state.

She didn't try to move away from him, just rested her cheek on his chest.

"Does this mean you're in for an extremely uncomfortable year?"

He started to laugh. "I choose to view it as I'll be in a state of intense and enjoyable sexual excitement throughout most of this year." He kissed the top of her head, then whispered, "I haven't ever enjoyed a New Year's Eve this much."

"Me, either."

For one insane moment he was tempted to pull the ring out of his pocket and go the whole nine yards, down on bended knee, the whole proposal. But he had a feeling he'd frighten her more than anything else.

"Will I see you this next year?" he said.

"If you want to."

"You know I do."

"You'll get tired of me, and all this . . . emotional baggage."

"Nope. Not a chance. I'll let you have your emotional baggage if you don't mind my animal baggage."

She laughed at that, and he started them walking back toward the lights of the mansion. Music, popping champagne corks and excited voices could be heard floating out on the midnight sky.

She stumbled as they made their way up on to the terrace, and Cooper caught her before she fell. And he realized she was tired; she probably hadn't been sleeping much. This whole thing was eating away at her.

They'd never have a chance as a couple unless she resolved this whole issue. The question was, did she want to?

"I think you should go straight to bed," he said firmly. "Without me, I mean. Let's get you in the front door and up the stairs. I'll tell your grandfather you retired early."

"Thank you, Cooper."

That she agreed with him so readily told him just how emotionally exhausted she was.

They went in the front door and she crossed the black-and-white marble floor, then started up the stairs. Cooper waited, standing at the foot of those stairs, Fang in his arms. He watched her until she went all the way upstairs, watched her until he couldn't see her anymore.

Only then did he let down his guard. His shoulders

sagged, his posture crumpled, and he sat down on the bottom steps with Fang in his arms.

"Ah, she doesn't want me, Fang. It's hopeless."

"She wants you very much, and this is far from hopeless."

He glanced quickly around and saw Phillip Preston come out of the shadows, a concerned expression on his lined face.

"Come into my private study, my boy, and let me get you a glass of very good cognac."

Too discouraged to offer an excuse, Cooper followed him down another hallway, away from the crowds of guests.

"She's terrified of her feelings," Phillip said, pouring two glasses of cognac into balloon snifters. "She's scared of losing you, yet everything she's doing is more than likely pushing you away."

He thought about this. Not yet, but with time he would probably get discouraged. What man wouldn't?

"I blame myself," Phillip said suddenly.

"No," Cooper said.

"I do." He offered Cooper one of the glasses of cognac, then indicated that he should join him by the fireplace. A warm and inviting fire crackled in the grate, and Cooper had the distinct feeling that this conversation with Phillip was one that the older man had wanted to have with him for some time.

"Her mother . . . well, there were no halfway measures for Elizabeth. She loved with all her heart. She was so very young and inexperienced. I often wonder what would have happened if she had hooked up with a genuinely decent man, but it wasn't to be."

"What happened to the guy?"

"He lives on the East Coast, quite happily. And he doesn't have a clue that he abandoned his daughter. My daughter and granddaughter were an inconvenience in his life, nothing more. What's that expression? A blip on the radar screen of his life."

Cooper couldn't fathom this.

"Good. You look stunned. As I was." Phillip took a sip of his cognac, then said, "I like you very much, Cooper, and I want to help you in any way I can. And I want you to know you can call on me any time, day or night."

Cooper thought about this. He was sure Phillip didn't mean help in the financial sense.

"Help me to understand her," he finally said.

"This is the key," said Phillip. "No matter how hard she tries to push you away, you must not back away. You can't give up. I think she's really close to breaking through, close to understanding how not allowing her heart to feel is the worst thing anyone can do with their life."

"What would feeling do to her?"

"If she fully acknowledged her feelings for you, Cooper, she would have to go back and feel all of those emotions she's repressed from almost twenty years ago and even earlier. Do you know that she continued to ask me why her father never called or came to see her until she was sixteen?"

"What happened then?"

"The private school she attended here in the city for her last two years of high school had a father-daughter event, a big picnic on a Sunday afternoon out in Marin. It was all she could talk about. I thought she assumed that I would attend, but she'd tracked her father down on her computer, with the help of some agency she'd found on-line. She called him at his office and kept trying to get him to speak with her. To acknowledge her. But he kept telling her he didn't know what she was talking about, he had no daughter."

Cooper put his cognac down on the table in front of his chair. "Right about now, I could strangle the man."

"My feelings exactly. That was the moment that broke her. I found her in her bedroom, sobbing. Her heart had been broken, Cooper. My granddaughter is a dreamer, and I believe she'd concocted some teenage fantasy in her head about what would happen when she finally talked to her father, that they would somehow create this magical relationship and everything would end happily. You and I know that isn't always so."

"So does she, now," Cooper said.

"Yes, but here's where we're different. You and I both know that the world can be a challenging and sometimes miserable place, but we keep putting ourselves out there. She stopped."

*No, she didn't,* thought Cooper. *She put herself out on the line that night at the bachelor party. She jumped into an affair with me feetfirst, not even looking to see if there was water in the proverbial pool. She threw off her clothes and told me to get with the program, to try to keep up.*

*Why?*

He'd never met anyone as alive as Alyssa, yet at the same time he knew that what Phillip was telling him was true. She was pulling away from him quite deliberately. And the only thought that Cooper could come up with was that Alyssa was just like her mother and experienced her feelings in a most passionate way. He could understand Phillip's desire to protect her, to protect her from what her mother had suffered.

And he also knew that he would never hurt her, if she only trusted him enough to give their relationship a chance. How funny that they'd both stepped into this relationship backward, being so terribly physically intimate right from the start, but having to work their way to true, lasting emotional intimacy and trust.

Both men stared at the fire for a long moment; then Phillip said softly, "I had a feeling that Mindy's wedding would bring up some of these issues for her again. And then when she came back, she seemed . . . changed. Of course, then I met you, and she told me she'd met you at the wedding, and it all fell into place."

Cooper suddenly felt shame. This man had invited him into his home, trusted him with his beloved granddaughter, while he—

"I know you'll understand this," said Phillip. "Do you agree with me that we make the most important decisions of our lives with our hearts?"

Cooper thought about this for a second, then nodded.

"I'm glad you agree. And I've also noticed that, in life, if someone doesn't feel it's safe to express herself, she generally won't. If a person anticipates hurt, they stay silent. Or go into hiding."

Cooper nodded, wondering where the conversation was going.

"I think that my granddaughter has lost a part of her heart. Oh, not literally. But when a parent is abusive and cold, like her father was, or helpless, like my daughter was, the outcome for a child isn't a good one."

"I agree."

"A person's heart is their guidance system, and what I'm trying to tell you is that Alyssa's has been damaged.

So she's not quite sure how to fly, if you know what I mean."

"I do."

"A person can become disheartened by grief or loss. That's the true meaning of that word, when you lose heart." Phillip stared into the fire for a long moment, but Cooper knew better than to interrupt the older man.

He had his memories, and had suffered his share of losses.

"But," said Phillip quietly, "the heart has also always been regarded as the seat of courage, the place where our courage comes from. And one of the most courageous choices that any individual can make in this day and age is to love. I hope, with all my heart, that you'll help my granddaughter make that choice."

Cooper nodded his head. There was nothing left to say. Phillip had said it so well.

"There's one more thing I have to tell you, Cooper. It will help you understand her. It will help you fight for her."

"Go on."

"We had an agreement. It's something that, in retrospect, I'm not proud of. When she graduated from high school, I told her that if the only man she was ever intimate with was her husband, then I would gift her with one million dollars on the day she married."

Now he *really* felt like a heel. Had Alyssa tossed one million dollars to the wind just to be with him?

"I know that may sound shocking to you, but you have to understand my point of view. I'm an older man, not of this generation. I find the casualness that some people enter sexual relationships with—well, I can't understand it. I wanted to protect her, and unfortunately, I think I did exactly the opposite. It was a mistake. I know that now. I think I just put another row of thorns around the castle, if you know what I mean."

"I do."

"You may think of Alyssa and me as rather odd people, Cooper. I know my own family does."

"No, I don't. I think you loved her when you made that bet with her, and I know you still do. And when we love someone, we just do the best we can."

"Fight for her, Cooper. She needs your courage. Fight for her even beyond when you think it's over. She needs you more than she'll ever admit to herself." The older man's voice trembled, and Cooper saw him make a conscious, focused effort to steady himself. "I'm terrified that this may be her last chance. *You* may be her last chance. She has so much to give to the right man, and I feel that man is you."

Phillip took a deep breath, and Cooper could see the anguish in his eyes as he spoke. "I don't want to see her become an old woman, wealthy, frightened . . . and alone."

Cooper used the hotel's van service once again to transport his menagerie, and Eddie, back to the hotel.

"That was an awesome party, Mr. Sinclair! Thanks for inviting me!"

He tipped Eddie generously, then called the young man a cab.

"It's on me," he told Eddie. "Just get home safely, all right?"

"Sure thing."

He couldn't sleep once Eddie had left, so he lay back

on his side of the king-sized bed and reached for the day's copy of the *Chronicle*.

When he got to the society page, one of the items in a column caught his eye. He read it once, then twice. Then he picked up the phone and called Phillip, even though the clock on his bedside table told him it was almost three in the morning.

*You can call on me any time, day or night. . . .*

"Cooper?" the older man said when he answered on the second ring.

"How did you know it was me?"

"Who else would it be?"

*Good point.*

"This charity extravaganza you're helping to host. Is Alyssa going to be participating in the auction?"

"Why, yes, she is! Cooper, that's a wonderful idea!"

"Don't let her know I'm coming."

"Not a word."

"I'm going to keep calling her, but I'll only come over if she wants me to. This dinner is on the ninth, so it's not that far away."

"Give her some time to miss you," Phillip said. "I'll keep a careful eye on her for you."

"All right. One more question. These costumes, how elaborate do they get?"

"Oh, people go all out."

Briefly, Cooper described to Phillip what he wanted to do.

"My boy, if you can pull that off, you'll bring down the house!"

He didn't have much time to put his plan into effect, little more than a week.

The first thing he did was call Marty, the Realtor.

"How soon can I move into that house?"

"I have some great news for you, Mr. Sinclair. As I told you before, the house has already passed all its inspections, both the general inspection and the one for termites. And everything was done through a trust, so there was no probate. The only thing that would take time is we need to clear title. But I talked to the woman's two children, and they both said they wouldn't mind renting the house to you for a few weeks until escrow closes. And then it's all yours."

*Perfect.*

"You really did pull some strings for me, Marty, and I appreciate it. And please, call me Cooper."

"When did you want to move in?"

"Would tomorrow be too soon?"

He didn't have much to move, if you didn't count a hundred plus pounds of pig and a parrot, a bichon puppy and a small skunk. The house came entirely furnished, and as Cooper surveyed his new home the evening of the day he moved in, he felt completely satisfied.

The doilies on the easy chairs were a bit much, but once he had all his stuff shipped out, he would find good homes for all of the elderly woman's furniture he chose not to keep. But actually, there were some exquisite pieces, and they suited the sunny yellow Victorian.

His next step was to plan his costume.

If you were going to create a brand-new persona, then San Francisco was the place.

Cooper had spent the first part of his day making an elaborate list. He'd called Eddie for another day of pet-sitting, as he didn't want to leave Baco alone in a strange house. The pig was sensitive and might get upset at too much change in too short a time.

Then off he went to shop until he found everything on his list.

He arrived back at his home with about half of it when his cell phone rang. Fishing around in his jacket pocket, he took it.

"Cooper here."

"It's Danielle. Phillip tells me you have to have a costume for the charity ball on the ninth. Did he tell you I'm an excellent seamstress?"

"No. And actually, that talent could come in very handy right about now!"

She laughed. "Oh, I do love a good intrigue!"

On January ninth, the night of the charity auction, Cooper tried on his entire outfit, then stood in front of the full-length mirror upstairs in his new master bedroom.

*Not bad.*

He descended the stairs and swept into the living room to find Baco and Eddie sprawled out on Baco's new king-sized bed. Eddie was playing Pink Floyd's *Dark Side of the Moon* on the CD player, and Baco was blissed out.

"He gets it," Eddie said as he saw Cooper enter. "Man, they weren't kidding when they said that pigs are so smart. This is a radically smart dude!"

Baco merely grunted softly in time to the music.

"You look fantastic, Mr. Sinclair."

"Cooper. Call me Cooper. Mr. Sinclair makes me feel like your father."

"Cooper. That is one great outfit. Can I borrow your cloak sometime?"

"Sure." He raked his fingers through his hair. "I hope to God this works."

"She won't be able to resist you! Man, do you look great! It's like you stepped back in time or something!"

"Or something," Cooper agreed nervously. "Where's Lafitte?"

"Right here!" said the parrot. He'd been perched on an antique dresser and was now busily chewing away on the polished wood trim with his beak.

"Lafitte! What are you doing over there?" Cooper yelled.

Eddie glanced back. "How'd he get over there? I had him on his perch! God, I'm really sorry, Cooper—"

"No, it's all right, he's done the same thing to me. I leave him on his perch, and then I find him on that dresser. Maybe I need to get his wings clipped again or something."

"No, he still can't fly."

"Then how the hell—never mind, we're going to be late." He held out his arm for the parrot, and Lafitte obligingly climbed on. "Don't wait up for me, I have no idea what time I'll be back."

"Cool. Baco and I will chill. Pepe's right here, and Fang's on her pillow."

"Great." Now that he was on the verge of doing either one of the most incredibly foolish or romantically brave things of his entire life, Cooper closed his eyes and counted to ten, trying to calm himself.

Outside, a taxi honked.

"Your ride's here!" Eddie called out. "Let the party begin!"

# Chapter Seventeen

*The million dollar stud.*

Cooper stared out the taxicab window as it careened around a corner and down one of San Francisco's famous hills. Christmas lights still twinkled in storefront windows, while the rain-swept streets reflected back both headlights and taillights of the traffic around them. Even in this rainy weather, and with this much traffic, his driver was making great time.

That's what he'd been, essentially: a million dollar stud. Alyssa had thrown it all away, one million dollars, in order to hit the hay with him. And while it had been great for him, he wondered how she'd felt once she'd realized she'd lost the bet.

She obviously hadn't told her grandfather yet. Knowing Alyssa, he guessed that honor would demand she refuse the check on her wedding day.

While he supposed he should have felt totally flattered,

instead he felt awful. True, a million dollars wasn't what it used to be, but still . . . and it really wasn't even about the million, it was about losing a bet, a crazy sort of deal she'd made with her grandfather.

An archaic deal, to be sure, but he could understand exactly why the old man had done it. A woman as beautiful and desirable as Alyssa, and all the wealth she stood to inherit—Phillip had wanted to make sure, very sure, she chose the right man. He'd wanted her to have something in the way, something that would make her think, perhaps even pause before she took that great leap that could have either such wonderful or disastrous consequences.

This particular charity function, for the San Francisco Orchid Society, was taking place at the St. Francis, one of the grand hotels of San Francisco and a Union Square landmark. As the taxi pulled up in front of the hotel, Cooper saw sheiks walking through the main entrance with milkmaids, and Norman warriors striding alongside Saxon princesses.

At least he wouldn't feel too out of place in his getup. Because on top of tonight's auction being about raising money for a good cause by bidding for dates with some of San Francisco's most eligible bachelorettes, the men and women who attended had been asked to don costumes to maintain the wonderful fantasy element of this gathering.

He glanced over at Lafitte as the taxi rolled to a stop. This was it. Now or never.

"Okay, boy, it's time to pull out all the stops."

Lafitte eyed him with those beady parrot eyes, then said quite calmly, "Dead men tell no tales."

*My sentiments, exactly.*

\*     \*     \*

Alyssa stood backstage and wondered why she simply hadn't called in sick. She didn't feel good. She felt like she had a slight fever, or maybe she was coming down with a cold.

No. That wasn't true. She was sick, all right. Heartsick. She missed Cooper so terribly. The last week had been miserable. Oh, he'd called regularly, almost every other day. But each time when he asked her if she wanted to see him, she'd felt it was only right to say no. She was damaged goods and had nothing to offer him. At least that had been her reasoning at the time.

Now she wasn't so sure. Now she was beginning to think that she was filled with fear.

The last thing she wanted to do was go out to dinner with a man she hardly knew. But it was emotionally safer than being with Cooper. She could handle a dinner date with a stranger. No intimacy there. But Cooper? He wanted it all: marriage, a family, a whole lot of pets, happiness, and they lived happily ever after. . . .

She had to be crazy not to want the same thing, but sometimes when your perfect dream came right up to you and looked you in the eye, you just became a gutless wonder.

Maybe she could call him after the evening was over. Maybe she could ask him if she could come over and they could talk. Because wishing she could see him, missing him so much, that had to count for something. She knew she could live her life alone, and on her own terms. She'd been doing that for years. But once she'd had a taste of how sweet things could be with a partner, there was no going back.

Alyssa knew she'd do anything to make things work with Cooper, even if it meant going into therapy for the rest of her life and reopening wounds she'd fought so hard to keep closed. She'd do whatever it took because she loved him, and she'd discovered that fact as she'd moved through her days. They were a lot less bright without Cooper Sinclair. And Baco. And that crazy Lafitte. And Pepe and Fang.

She wanted it all, even though she was still scared to death. And here she was, hiding out in her comfort zone, thinking she was safe, when the truth was that she wasn't safe at all, and she wasn't at all comfortable with the choices she'd made.

Alyssa glanced at the watch on her wrist. It wasn't really in keeping with her costume as a Barbary Coast dance hall girl, but she'd wanted to leave as soon as was decently possible, so she'd made sure to wear a timepiece.

As soon as she could, she'd give Cooper a call. She had to start changing her life, make the attempt. But how long could she expect a man like Cooper to stick around while she fumbled her way toward love?

Eddie heard the front doorbell's sharp peal through the music in his headphones.

"This was one of Lennon's best, dude," he said, propping his headphones up against Baco's ears. "I'm telling you, this song will take you to a whole different place."

Impatient banging on the front door commenced, and Eddie hurried to the front hall, then opened the door, keeping the heavy chain in place.

"Cooper Sinclair's residence. Who are you?" he said, taking in the man standing on the front porch. He was wearing faded jeans, a black T-shirt, a black leather jacket, and black boots. He had longish, dark brown hair, a scruffy start of a beard, and a large, gentle-looking golden retriever on a leather leash.

"Jake. His partner."

"Coop didn't say anything about a partner coming by tonight," Eddie said, suspicious.

"I'm not just coming by. I just drove two thousand miles in the last three days. Cooper doesn't know." Jake hunched down in his leather jacket. "Say, could I come in? It's raining out here. Not to mention freezing."

"You're on a covered porch, you have a jacket on, and I'm still not sure you're legit." Eddie thought for a moment, then said, "What's his pig's name?"

"Baco."

"The bird?"

"Lafitte, after the pirate."

"The dog?"

"You mean that white fou-fou thing he claims is a dog?"

"Hey, watch it, you don't want to hurt Fa—what's her name?"

"Fang. And yeah, she'll grow into it."

"Man, you're good. How about the skunk?"

"Pepe LePew, like the cartoon character. Now will you let me in the door? I'm freezing my ass off!"

"Sure thing." Eddie paused before he unhooked the latch. "Just so you're warned in case you're thinking about pulling anything funny, I want you to know that that pig in the living room? He's attack trained."

"Run this by me again," Jake said, "'cause I'm having a little trouble believing it. My business partner, my uptight, stuffy, all-work-and-no-play friend, is dressed in a costume and prepared to spend even more of our company's money buying a date with this woman he loves?"

"That is it, in a nutshell," said Eddie, jabbing his finger in the air for emphasis, then reaching for another piece of pepperoni pizza. They'd ordered in a large pie when Jake had explained he hadn't stopped for dinner and had driven straight through the last two hundred miles.

"This is great!" Jake said. "Just where is this party? Because I think I'm going to crash it. Maybe I can even take pictures."

Baco eyed the pizza mournfully.

"None for you, big boy," Jake said. "It would be tantamount to cannibalism."

"Whoa," said Eddie. "I hadn't even thought of that." He considered this for a moment. "I feel bad for him. We should have ordered half of it plain cheese."

"Next time," Jake said, swallowing the last bite of his slice and wiping his hands with a paper napkin. "Now, you're sure you'll be okay with Riley if I head down to this charity thing and see what's going on?"

"He's a cool dog," said Eddie. "And it's kinda nice, now Fang has someone to play with."

Jake snorted. "She's like a chew toy to Riley."

"Oh, no. He likes her, I can tell. And I wouldn't drive down if I were you, I'd call a cab. The parking situation will be a mess."

"Good thinking. Know a good company?"

"I'm dialing as we speak," Eddie said, grabbing his cell phone.

Cooper almost fell asleep in the midst of a long and very boring talk about the San Francisco Orchid Society's origins, its numerous past presidents, and other bits of business that didn't interest him in the least. But when his head hit the table with a loud *thunk* and Lafitte squawked, that woke him back up—not to mention several other guests seated at the same table.

Thank God Baco finally had his own bed. He loved his pet dearly, but the pig snored, and it had kept him up several nights.

No, that wasn't true. It hadn't been only Baco's snoring. He'd been worried about Alyssa, especially after his talk with Phillip. Now that he knew what he was truly up against, he could feel the smallest amount of doubt starting to creep in.

"Big fat windbag!" Lafitte shrieked at the top of his lungs. While several people laughed in the darkened audience, just as many glared.

"Calm down, boy," he murmured. "This can't go on forever."

"Easy for you to say," muttered the parrot. "Look, Daddy, teacher says that every time a bell rings—"

"Can it," Cooper said.

Lafitte stopped in mid-sentence.

Just as he had given up hope for a reprieve, the woman behind the podium, a busty, elderly lady who reminded Cooper of Margaret Dumont in all those Marx Brothers movies, said, "And now on to the part of the evening I know you'll all enjoy, our auction! Some of the loveliest women in San Francisco are going to walk across this stage tonight, and all of you have a chance to bid on an evening with any one of them."

"Hot damn!" Lafitte cried out, and this time most people laughed.

"Just let me do the bidding," Cooper said through clenched teeth. He wondered why the elderly gentleman next to him was giving him such a strange look, until he realized he'd just been caught talking to a parrot.

\*     \*     \*

The first three girls were gorgeous, but none of them were Alyssa, so Cooper sat back and let the bidding commence without him. The average price for a date seemed to be in the vicinity of about three grand.

*So this won't be all that hard. The bidding, at least.*

But number four—there she was.

Her outfit was, in his eyes, the best so far, some sort of Western saloon girl or dance hall girl. She walked onto the stage and was introduced, and Cooper heard the auctioneer say she was dressed as an authentic dance hall girl from the days of San Francisco's infamous Barbary Coast.

"Let the bidding commence!" the Margaret Dumont look-alike called out.

And Cooper opened it, shouting, "One thousand dollars!"

Jake got out of the taxi and walked toward the stately hotel. And as he approached the main entrance, he realized he wasn't exactly dressed for a fancy event.

But thinking fast was what had put both him and Coop ahead of the rest of the pack, so when a doorman said, "And who might you be, sir?" he was all ready with his reply.

"Marlon Brando," he said, never breaking his stride. "In *The Wild One.*"

The only thing Cooper hadn't counted on was that there might have been a bozo in the audience who wanted a date with Alyssa, too.

Not a Bozo in the literal sense, of course. There wasn't a clown costume in sight. The man was dressed as a sheik and showed no signs of slowing down the bidding.

"Four thousand five hundred!" he shouted, glaring at Cooper.

The auctioneer barely had a chance to ask for the next bid before Cooper shouted, "Five! Five thousand!"

"You tell him!" screamed Lafitte.

"Five thousand, five thousand, do we hear—"

"Five-five," Omar Sharif called out.

"Great," muttered Coop. "Jake's gonna kill me."

"Only if you don't win," his partner said, sliding into the chair beside him.

"What are you doing here?"

"Six thousand!" Jake called out, then turned back toward him. "Don't lose your concentration. God, I wish I had a camera!"

"Just shut up!"

The sheik bid six-five.

Cooper bid seven.

The sheik considered his next move.

The audience watched, breathless.

"My, we seem to have a bidding war going on," Mrs. Dumont said into the mike.

"No shit, Sherlock!" screamed Lafitte.

"I thought he was supposed to say pirate things," Jake said, clearly amused. He'd gotten a rum and coke from the open bar and was enjoying himself immensely.

"That was the general idea," Cooper said.

Then all of a sudden, Alyssa shaded her eyes and stared out into the audience. "Cooper?" she called out tentatively. "Is that you?"

The audience was loving it.

And Cooper decided, at that exact instant, that he had to go for broke. There were no halfway measures in this race; he had to lay it all out on the line. Alyssa had been totally let down by the two people who were most important to

her. So Cooper decided that if he did something truly spectacular—or stupid, depending on how you looked at it—he
could convince her that she wouldn't be endangering her
heart if she hooked up with him.

Even though he was sure he would feel like a total ass in
the morning, and he might fail disastrously, he had to seize
the moment and make it his own.

Loving her, he had no other choice.

When the spotlight descended over his table, he clam-
bered up on top of it, whipped out his sword and brandished
it in the air. And women in the audience actually screamed.

"Aye, 'tis I, Captain Sinclair of the high seas, captain of
the ship"—he thought swiftly—"*The Doomsday!*"

And finally, *finally,* Lafitte came through.

"Pieces of eight!" the parrot squawked. "Pieces of eight!
*Arrghhh,* matey, ye'd better *walk* that *plank!*"

The crowd roared.

Jake blew his drink through his nose and began to cough
furiously.

The sheik looked stunned.

Alyssa ran to the edge of the stage and stared at Cooper
as if she couldn't believe what she was seeing.

And Lafitte glanced over in the direction of the sheik
and screamed, "Well, what are you waiting for?"

"Seven-five!" Lawrence of Arabia called out.

"Whose side are you on?" Cooper said to Lafitte.

"Keelhaul the bastards!" the parrot shrieked.

"Eight!" said Cooper aka Captain Sinclair.

*"Eight thousand dollars!"* said Mrs. Dumont, fanning
herself with her program. She looked as if she were about
to faint, and the auctioneer didn't look too happy at the
prospect of catching her.

"I'm out," the sheik called toward the stage.

And Cooper felt a glow of triumph until he heard, "Eight-five."

From *Jake*.

"What the *hell* do you think you're doing?" he whispered furiously.

"Go with it," Jake whispered back. "I want to make sure you get this woman. You've been doing a piss-poor job at work, hey, you haven't even been showing up, and I want this whole thing settled once and for all."

"Eight-five? From *you?*"

"Keep raising the stakes," Jake said. "Hell, we'll take it out of petty cash. But give me a little time here."

Cooper waited as long as he could before he called out, "Nine!"

"Can I borrow your cape for a moment?" Jake asked the young man who was dressed as The Phantom of the Opera.

"Sure," he said. He was clearly enjoying the show.

"And how about your sword and hat?" Jake said, to another pirate. "It's all for a great cause, and I swear, I'll have them back to you in under fifteen minutes."

"You got it, bud," said the pirate, and handed him his plumed pirate hat and the sword from its scabbard.

"Nine-five!" Jake called out as he shed his leather jacket and fastened the cape around his neck, then jammed on the pirate hat and picked up the sword.

"Ten!" Cooper called out as Jake came running down between the round tables to meet him, then swirled his black cape with a flourish.

"How *dare* ye insult Black Jake of Jamaica, captain of the *Intrepid,* with that monstrous bid! I shall have to challenge ye to a duel!"

*   *   *

At that moment, Cooper understood what Jake had planned. And he remembered the summer they'd been bored making money and decided to take fencing lessons. And though they had swords, not fencing foils, they could certainly improvise.

"Challenge me to a duel, will you?" squawked Lafitte.

"Hey. That's my line." Cooper turned to Jake and flung his red satin cape back off his shoulders, showing off his snowy white pirate shirt.

"Hold my bird, would you?" he asked the elderly man who had given him a strange look earlier. Before the man could voice his consent, Cooper eased Lafitte onto the man's shoulder, then turned back to Jake.

"Challenge me to a duel, will you?" he roared. "Well, you scurvy dog, we'll see about that!"

Alyssa screamed and darted back as Cooper flung himself up onto the stage, followed by a just as rambunctious Black Jake of Jamaica. And the two of them went at it, swords clashing, steel ringing. As the patrons of this charity prided themselves on authentic costuming, both swords were up to the duel.

And both swordsmen seemed to know what they were doing.

"Watch the head, dear God, not the head!" Lafitte screamed out from the nearby table. "Black Jake, you dog! I'll send you down to Davy Jones's locker myself!"

The crowd was on its feet, roaring its approval, giving both men a standing ovation.

They darted in, face-to-face.

"*Say* something about her," Jake whispered, then gasped for breath. "Women love that sort of thing!"

"Right," Cooper wheezed.

They darted apart, and Cooper, totally in the character of Captain Sinclair, brandished his sword and called out, "You'll be having no part of that lovely wench! She's mine!"

"Oh ho!" said Black Jake. "And here I thought what a lovely little piece she'd be, all soft and pretty and ready to warm my bed on a long sea voyage!"

Women in the audience sighed, and it was reported the next day in the paper's society column that one woman actually passed out.

"Say anything you like, but she's mine!" snarled Captain Sinclair.

"You'll have to kill me first!" shouted Black Jake.

"God bless us, every one!" screamed Lafitte.

They darted in, close together once again as they locked swords.

"On three, go in and make it look good. Remember how we did it for that benefit? I'll die," Jake muttered.

"Got it."

Then the audience screamed as Captain Sinclair "stabbed" Black Jake with his sword, and Jake stumbled, then staggered, then stumbled, then staggered.

The crowd roared.

Lafitte called out, "Crikey, let's set sail!"

Alyssa watched the entire fight hidden behind the podium with the auctioneer.

Mrs. Dumont almost did faint, but the auctioneer flung a glass of ice water in her face.

And finally, as Jake died, in an elaborate death scene that had him falling down and expiring, half onstage and half hanging off, the plumed hat covering his face and his cloak fluttering madly because of a nearby fan.

"Ten thousand dollars!" Cooper roared, pointing his sword at the auctioneer. "To the only woman who will ever have my heart!"

Women sighed.

Men were astounded.

And a lone parrot screamed, "And not a penny more!"

The entire audience cheered madly, the deafening sound almost rocking the dignified ballroom.

She'd watched the entire fight from behind the podium with a completely flabbergasted auctioneer. And as she'd seen Cooper and Black Jake careen around the stage, swords flashing, she'd felt the strangest feeling in her chest, as if her heart were literally expanding. It wasn't breaking; it felt as if it were swelling, filling with emotion, coming back to her.

She flashed back to a moment in time in her grandparents' garden when she'd been five years old. She'd found a baby bird that had fallen out of its nest and brought it back to her grandmother. In those days, she'd spent all her time with her grandparents, as her mother spent most of her time locked in her bedroom, sleeping or sitting in her chair by the window, waiting for a phone call that never came.

"What's going to happen to this bird now that its mother doesn't want it?" she'd asked her grandfather as her grandmother had made an incubator out of a shoe box lined with soft cloth and a lightbulb overhead.

"We shall take care of her," said her grandfather. "We'll take care of her until she's ready to fly by herself."

And they had, feeding the baby bird and keeping her warm, stroking her downy feathers and letting her know she was safe. And one day she and her grandparents had taken the little bird out into the garden and watched as it flew away and soared up into one of the trees with the other birds.

She'd cried that morning as her bird had flown away, then said to her grandmother, "Why does it hurt so much here?" as she pressed her hand to her heart.

"Why, honey, that's because your heart is growing, and when your heart grows, sometimes it hurts a little before it feels better."

"Like the Grinch?" she'd said, remembering the book they'd read together last Christmas.

"Like the Grinch," her grandfather had said, taking her hand.

Now she felt that same feeling. She glanced around her, and for one second she almost felt her grandmother's gentle hand on her shoulder.

*Time to fly, little one.*

It was time.

Cooper glanced up and dropped his sword as Alyssa flew across the stage and flung herself into his arms.

"My *hero!*" she said, and he heard the audience start clapping again. They all thought it was part of the elaborate performance, part of the fight he and Jake had staged.

But he knew better, and that crazily romantic side of his personality he hadn't even known existed until this woman danced into his life made his heart start to speed up.

"Let's blow this joint," he whispered in her ear as he hoisted her up into his arms.

"Okay," she said, and he loved the feel of her, so warm and trusting in his arms. He could hold on to her forever.

He planned on doing exactly that.

\*     \*     \*

Black Jake came back to life, bowing and charming the audience. He grinned, then watched as Cooper set Alyssa down, swiftly wrote a check, gave it to the Margaret Dumont look-alike, then lifted Alyssa back into his arms and carried her out of the hotel's large ballroom past astonished costumed guests. Some were still clapping. Some merely looked dazed.

"All's well that ends well," Jake said. He went through the audience and gave back the various pieces of his improvised costume, found his leather jacket, retrieved Lafitte from the still-stunned older gentleman, and ran after the happy couple.

He found them in the lobby, talking.

"I've got your bird, and I'm going to head on back to your place," Jake said. Now that Cooper finally had Alyssa, Jake certainly didn't want to ruin the moment. And he saw the appreciative look in Cooper's eyes.

"You know this man?" Alyssa said.

Cooper started to laugh. "Alyssa, meet my friend and business partner, Jake McConahay."

She took the hand he offered, smiling at him the entire time. "I remember you."

"We're not always this bad," Jake said, smiling back. God, she was a stunner. He could completely understand why Cooper's work ethic had gone straight to hell. "Just when Cooper wants something very badly. And boy, does he want you."

And with that, he headed toward the main entrance, and a taxi, Lafitte shrieking on his shoulder.

# *Chapter Eighteen*

They went to a tiny café that was open all night, ordered coffee, and sat in a back booth. And this being San Francisco, no one even questioned why they were dressed as a pirate and a dance hall girl.

"That was just wonderful, what you did," Alyssa said.

He basked in her praise.

"So, where do you want to go on our date?" he said.

"We don't have to go out," she said.

"Oh, I can still afford a decent meal," he said.

"That's not what I meant."

It took him a minute to get exactly what she meant.

"Alyssa, what are you saying? Do you mean that—"

"I can't stand being without you, Cooper. I thought I could, but I'm not that strong. And I think I learned something in the last week."

"And what was that?"

"There are worse things than failing. Or being hurt."

He smiled. How he loved this woman. "And what might they be?"

"Never trying at all."

He knew the time was right. Now or never. And he thanked his lucky stars that he'd never stopped hoping, and never stopped carrying the ring.

In complete pirate regalia, with everyone's eyes on them, he got down on his knees on the linoleum floor of the café, fumbled in his pocket, and pulled out the ring box, then said, "Alyssa, would you do me the honor of becoming my wife?"

With tears in her eyes, and to his utter relief, she said yes.

And everything was different that night, when they returned to his bedroom in the charming little Victorian. She'd loved it at first sight, the moment she stepped out of the taxi and into the light rain that had started to fall.

Then they'd snuck in together like a teenage couple trying to pull something over on one set of parents. They'd laughed at the sight of Eddie and Baco passed out on the huge king-sized bed in the front parlor, and Jake curled up beneath a crocheted afghan on a velvet love seat, his booted feet hanging off the side and Riley curled up on the wooden floor beside him.

"Your dog?" Alyssa whispered. "Is that why Jake drove out, to deliver him?"

"I think he wanted to know when the hell I planned on coming back to work."

Riley raised his head, that plumed tail thumped the floor, and Jake rolled to his side, pulling the afghan with him and muttering, "Baby, just go back to sleep, okay?"

"Baby?" Alyssa murmured.

"An all-purpose endearment that works for Jake," Cooper said. "It's okay, Riley, you can go back to sleep."

The retriever sighed and lowered his head to his paws.

Cooper swept Alyssa into his arms and carried her up the stairs as she tried to muffle her giggles.

He made one quick phone call to her grandfather.

"I just wanted to make sure he didn't wait up or get worried," he explained to Alyssa as he came back to the bed. "I told him it was so late when we left the coffee shop that I'm letting you sleep in my guest bedroom."

She considered this. "Did he buy it?"

"He's not that stupid."

Then he was fumbling with the fastenings of her costume and swearing at all the intricate lacings on her bodice.

She slapped his hands away, laughing. "Let me do it, it's just going to take more time if you snarl up the ties."

"Okay with me," he said, and lay back on the bed, his hands behind his head. "In fact . . ." He snapped on the bedside radio and played with the dial until he found a song that brought back memories for both of them: Chris Isaak's "Baby Did a Bad, Bad Thing."

Their eyes locked, and she began to dance.

And both of them remembered.

She stripped down to her underwear, then unfastened her bra and threw it at him, laughing when he grabbed it, then her, and the two of them tumbled into the huge bed.

"We're going to wake everyone up."

"I don't care," he said, and he covered her mouth in a soul-scorching kiss. When he finally came up for air, he whispered, "Jake's no innocent, and I suspect neither is

Eddie. However, I do worry about destroying Baco's innocence and Lafitte learning any new words."

She pinched his buttock until he yelped, then she kissed him and made him forget all about the pain.

And it was different, so different, to make love with this man and know he would be sleeping with her for the rest of their lives. That they would wake up together each morning and have all the time in the world to get to know each other; to care about each other.

She thought she might die of arousal alone as he caressed her breasts. Alyssa gave a muffled squeak as he rolled over so she was astride him, then that squeak changed to a groan of sensual satisfaction as he filled her and began the sensuous rhythm that would bring both of them such total satisfaction.

He was hers; he loved her. He loved her so much he'd risked making a complete idiot of himself in front of hundreds of people. It had totally thrilled her to see him put everything he was and everything he had on the line.

And he'd deserved nothing less from her.

"What are you thinking about?" he whispered as he kissed the side of her neck. "What are you smiling about?"

"You . . . as Captain Sinclair."

He started to laugh then, and grabbed her hips, pushing in deeper.

"Arrrgh, you're a fine wench!"

She was laughing so hard he had to roll over so they were on their sides. When she finally caught her breath, she looked up into his eyes and saw that he was gazing at her as if he'd never seen her before.

"I'm the lucky one," he whispered.

"No, me," she whispered back. "How many women get to marry their own pirate king?"

"That's true. Though how many men get to cavort with a fine Barbary Coast wench? What were you, a barmaid or something?"

Laughing, she leaned forward and whispered something into his ear. His eyes widened.

"A pros—"

"Ah-ah-ah!" she said, touching his lips with her finger. "I thought you liked this wild side of me."

"Oh, I do," he said as he rolled over on top of her and pushed her deeper into the mattress, as he kicked some of the bedclothes off his feet and repositioned the two of them. "I like you a lot. In fact, I think I'm going to like you all night. . . ."

Much, much later that evening, when they were both curled up and on the verge of falling asleep, Cooper asked her, "Just how long an engagement do you want to have?"

"Oh, that's clever, ask me when I'm exhausted and my guard's down."

He laughed. How well this woman knew him.

"How long?" he persisted. He wanted to know. The last thing he wanted was a drawn-out engagement. He didn't want to give Alyssa a chance to change her mind.

Another duel would probably kill him.

"Not long," she whispered sweetly, snuggling down into the sheets and pulling a corner of the blanket over her naked shoulder.

He waited almost a minute, then said, "How long is not long?"

"Oh, maybe about a week."

Her answer thrilled him down to his toes. "Good. You're a woman after my own heart."

The following morning, she woke up to an empty bed and felt a quick flash of fear. Then she heard voices and laughter coming from downstairs and realized Cooper had probably just gone downstairs to get some breakfast. After all, it was almost—she glanced at the clock on the bedside table—eleven o'clock.

And she hadn't slept this well since . . . since she'd first met Cooper in Illinois.

She was wondering if she should just dress herself in her dance hall girl costume when she noticed the note next to her pillow.

*Take your time, take a shower, and here are some clothes for you to wear.*

> *Your Humble Servant,*
> *the notorious Captain Sinclair*

She smiled. Humble, Cooper was not.

An arrow on a crudely drawn treasure map pointed to a pair of her favorite jeans, a peach hand-knit sweater, underwear, and her running shoes, all stacked neatly on a nearby chair.

Wondering exactly how Cooper had managed to sneak some of her clothing over to his new home, she decided to shower, get dressed, and start her new life as an engaged-to-be-married woman.

\*    \*    \*

Twenty minutes later as she came down the stairs, she heard hoots of hysterical laughter coming from the kitchen.

As she started inside the large, old-fashioned kitchen, Fang came shooting around the corner, a fluffy white bullet, followed by an enormous golden retriever in hot pursuit, and following *him* were all three of her grandfather's Pekes, yapping madly.

"Good morning!" several male voices chorused from the kitchen.

She couldn't believe her eyes.

Cooper was at the large stove, and it looked as if he were making pancakes, scrambled eggs, and bacon. Jake was handing her grandfather a cup of tea, and Eddie was making more toast.

The round kitchen table was piled high with food, glasses of orange juice, and a box of muffins and croissants from a local bakery. Baco stared at all of it, a desperate plea in his porcine eyes. Lafitte perched on her grandfather's shoulder, and Phillip Preston looked like he was having the time of his life.

"I heard all about your exploits at the charity ball last night," he said to Alyssa as she came into the room. "Five different friends called me this morning, it was all they could talk about! It's all anyone's talking about this morning, what your young man did in the name of love."

Smiling, feeling as if her heart would burst her rib cage and fly free, she slid into the seat next to him and showed him her engagement ring.

"Very nice," he said. "This is wonderful." His voice cracked on the last word, and she gave him a hug.

"What were you all laughing about?" she asked, as Cooper came back to the table with another plate of pancakes, Jake topped off everyone's coffee and handed her a fresh mug, and Eddie set down a plate of buttered toast. With all the food assembled, everyone sat down.

"We figured out how Lafitte was getting around the room, off his perch and onto that antique dresser," said Eddie.

"He was tearing up the wood trim with his beak," Cooper explained, "and I couldn't figure out how he was getting there, because his wings are clipped."

"But when I fed them all this morning," Eddie explained, "we figured out what was going on because Jake was still asleep."

"What?" she said, lost.

"I was snoozing underneath that afghan on the love seat," Jake explained, "exhausted after the workout I got last night as Black Jake of Jamaica, when I heard this voice, this soft little voice, say, 'Here, piggy-piggy-piggy.'"

He did such a deadly accurate imitation of Lafitte that Alyssa had to laugh.

"It gets better," said her grandfather.

"What's Baco's favorite food?" Cooper said.

"French fries?" Alyssa said.

"After that," said Cooper.

"I'm not sure."

"Grapes," said Eddie. "And I'd just given Lafitte a big bunch of them for breakfast, so Jake watched, and he saw that Lafitte was dropping grapes on the floor and calling for Baco."

"And when the pig taxi arrived and started snorting up the grapes off the floor," Jake said, "Lafitte hopped on his back."

"And as Baco trotted toward the kitchen to see what

else he could get to eat," Cooper said, "when he passed the dresser, Lafitte hopped on up and began to chew on the wood."

She glanced over at the parrot, who was strangely quiet. "Lafitte, is this true?"

The parrot just muttered beneath his breath, then fluttered his wings and said, "One for all and all for one, mates! Shiver me timbers!"

They all laughed at that, then Alyssa said, "Pass me those pancakes. I'm starving."

As she began to fill her plate, her grandfather asked with studied casualness, "And when do the two of you think you might be getting married?"

"I thought I'd leave all the planning to Alyssa," Cooper said.

"I thought," said Alyssa as she smeared butter on her three pancakes, "that we might go for about ten days from now."

A stunned silence greeted this announcement as she'd known it would.

She glanced around the table, taking in all of it, the bright sunshine streaming in the kitchen windows, and her grandfather and Jake, and Eddie and Baco and Lafitte—and especially Cooper, her Cooper, her crazy pirate king.

As four dogs came clattering through the kitchen again, all of them chasing after Fang, and as she noticed Pepe curled up on one of the seats in an empty chair, Alyssa realized she finally had the big, raucous, funny family she'd always secretly wanted.

That night, Alyssa sighed with contentment.

She and Cooper had made love twice, and now his

hand rested on her hip. Alyssa was lying on her stomach, and his fingertip lightly traced the red rose tattooed on her right buttock.

"I knew it was on the right. A man doesn't forget a detail like that."

She started to laugh, and he stopped.

"What? What was so funny?"

"I know you want to leave all the wedding plans to me, but there's one thing you could do for me before the wedding that I would really love."

"Anything."

Smiling, she turned around and whispered in his ear.

Eddie recommended the tattoo parlor.

"I'm going to tell Jake I was drunk," Cooper muttered as he gazed at the wall of elaborate designs.

"Just pick one out, but don't tell me," she said. "But before I go and have a long cup of coffee while you get it done, let's take a look around."

"Can I help you?" said a heavyset man who looked like a biker. He had long black hair pulled back in a low ponytail and amazingly muscular arms covered with intricately designed tattoos.

"I'm in the market for a tattoo," Cooper said.

"Ever had one done before?"

"Nope. I'm a virgin."

"Got any idea where you want it?"

Cooper glanced at Alyssa. "My right buttock."

"Good choice. Now, did the two of you want to pick out a design together?"

"We thought we'd look at a few."

"What do you recommend?" Alyssa said.

"Well, this one of a Viking ship is really a work of art—"

Cooper hesitated. "That's quite a crowd on that ship."

"Oh, you were thinking of something not as elaborate? How about this one, it's a depiction of Stonehenge. It's very popular with our Pagan customers, and especially nice during the Winter Solstice—"

"Ah, that's still a little big. I was thinking of something smaller."

"How about this one, Cooper?" Alyssa pointed to a rendition of the Battleship USS *Constitution*.

"Hah-hah. Clever girl. No, I was thinking of something along the lines of, well, she has a small rose on her butt—"

The clerk considered this. "Yes, I see what you mean. Well, I think you should both look around as much as you want, and I'll be right here behind the counter if you should need me. A tattoo is a very personal form of body art, and you'll know the one you want when you see it."

Cooper looked for about twenty minutes before he saw exactly what he wanted.

"Alyssa, go get some coffee at that place down the street. Take your time, and I'll come get you when I'm done."

"Am I going to like what you pick?"

"I'm sure you will."

"When can I see it?"

"Oh, I think we should wait for our wedding night." He wiggled his eyebrows. "Some things should remain sacred."

As she walked out the door, Cooper asked the clerk, "Can you do one design almost on top of another?"

"Show me which ones you want, and then I'll tell you if we can combine them."

Cooper did exactly that, and the clerk broke into a grin. "Very nice, if I do say so myself."

Cooper hated himself for being a wimp, but he had to ask. "How much does this really hurt?"

"It's not too bad, but there's a bar right next door if you want to get a stiff drink first."

"I think I may just do that."

Alyssa found the coffeehouse about a block down from the tattoo parlor, and after ordering a small latte and an almond biscotti, she found a round table right by the window and settled herself down to wait.

Dusk had fallen over her favorite city, filling it with that beautiful blue light, made all the more brilliant because of the warm golden lights glowing in windows and storefronts. She watched people strolling with their dogs, hurrying along with their young children, and smiled as she saw an elderly couple walking slowly, their arms around each other, totally engrossed in being together.

*That will be me and Cooper,* she thought as she took a sip of her coffee. *I know it.*

How extraordinary, that her life should change so completely in the space of a month. Her whole courtship with Cooper had been a whirlwind.

Mindy had married in December, and she was getting married to Cooper in January. She'd already called a meeting with her dance troupe, and there had been a very joyous and totally unanimous vote to delay the dance recital so that she and Cooper could enjoy a nice long honeymoon. Anywhere they wanted to go, for as long as they wanted.

She dunked the biscotti into her latte, swirled it around, lifted it out, and bit into the fragrant Italian cookie, then closed her eyes in pleasure. And as she closed her eyes, a very vivid and erotic image came to mind.

Bambi.

The short dark bobbed hair, the long, sooty eyelashes and killer eyeliner. Bambi's bad-girl lingerie, her short, tight skirt and sexy top. That name, those black, thigh-high, high-heeled boots, and those dance moves, swaying seductively on top of that coffee table while all those men had watched her.

And the final touch, that enabling touch, that sparkling purple Mardi Gras mask. Sometimes Alyssa missed that mask, and she wished she'd had the nerve to take it with her when she'd left Cooper's home that morning before Mindy's wedding. It was almost as if she'd completed a rite of passage, and the mask symbolized what she'd done.

Alyssa still couldn't quite believe that she'd gone along with Mindy's outrageous plan that night before her wedding. Crashing that bachelor party seemed so long ago, but it wasn't. And Alyssa wondered at the synchronicity of it all, that she should have met Cooper as Bambi. That the mask she'd worn had enabled her to throw caution to the wind and be a whole lot braver than she'd ever been before. That she'd had the courage to decide to lose her virginity that night with a man she'd felt an incredible sexual attraction for.

Now, looking back on the whole incident, she realized that Bambi had been like a life force inside her. She'd wanted to live, really live, and Bambi had obliged.

Alyssa knew that the night she'd spent with Cooper had ultimately convinced her that playing it safe in matters of the heart led to a life that was a living death, without vibrant color and laughter and feeling.

She had a sense that the big guy upstairs had been watching out for her, because if she'd met Cooper at the wedding, as herself, she would have felt the attraction toward him but would have shut herself down, muted herself, played nice and safe.

Nice and safe got a woman nowhere.

But where had Bambi come from?

Alyssa thought about this as she sipped her coffee and stared out the coffeehouse window at the swiftly darkening sky. And as she thought, she realized that the part of her that was a dancer had always reached for freedom. Even if her heart had been constricted and cautious, and she'd played it safe during most of her waking hours, when she'd been dancing, she'd been totally free. She'd been herself in a way she wasn't when she was still and not moving.

And with Cooper—when he'd met her, she'd been dancing. When she'd met him, she'd had a mask on so she'd been able to play a part and be a whole lot braver than she usually was off the dance floor.

She also had the intuitive feeling that Bambi had done the same to Cooper. Certainly she'd rocked his world; as Bambi, she'd gotten him really mad, then really turned on. Something had caught fire between them that night, and it probably couldn't have happened any other way.

But, as Bambi, she'd also gotten him off the all-work-and-no-play businessman's track. The man who had come scowling into the family room that night to break up the party was not the same man who'd rented an entire ice-skating rink complete with a snow machine. Cooper the sensible businessman had shocked everyone who knew him when he'd lit out for the West Coast in search of an exotic dancer who had made him . . . who had made him feel. Who had awoken both of them to deeper emotions than they'd ever felt before.

Bambi—or rather, her time as Bambi—had really affected both of them. The more Alyssa thought about it, the more she realized how much she owed Bambi. She smiled.

*Like the rest of my life.*

She'd almost finished her coffee when she realized Bambi had always been a part of her, one of the very best parts of her. In this last month it was as if she'd finally integrated that part of her personality into her life, with Cooper's help. She'd claimed it, and it had served her well.

Bambi had been the part of her that wanted to have fun. The child in her that didn't want to worry all the time, that wanted to—needed to—jump into her life and grab it and taste it and live it and not always be wondering when the emotional pain would finally descend. That old proverbial other shoe. She'd always been waiting for it to drop.

Bambi would have thought of that shoe as half of a glorious pair of outrageously expensive Manolo Blahniks. Or high-heeled, thigh-high boots. She wouldn't have wasted any of her time on this earth thinking about possible disasters. Bambi would have been too busy living. Loving.

*No more. No more denying that incredible life force.* As of tonight, she was taking a major page out of Bambi's book. She was going to live life to the absolute fullest, embrace it totally, and try to let go of all the fears she'd carried close to her heart for so long.

_No, not try. This is it. Life is not a dress rehearsal. I'm letting them go._

She could feel it happening as she thought the words. And her eyes stung, just a little, as she raised the last of her cup of coffee to the darkened street outside the window and whispered the words.

"Thanks so much, Bambi. I'm not letting you go. I'm taking your spirit with me, wherever I go."

## *Epilogue*

They were married ten days later, on a glorious, cool January San Francisco day. The sun was shining, fluffy white clouds scudded by in the brilliant blue, windy sky, and theirs was the only wedding high society had ever seen with a pig in attendance.

Cooper told Alyssa to do whatever she wanted with their wedding, and thus they were married outside in her grandfather's rose garden. The bride was barefoot and wore a bias-cut georgette dress with a charmeuse tieback that made her look like a Grecian goddess. Cooper wore the Armani suit he'd bought for The Dance for Animals. A totally shocked Mindy flew out from Chicago with Tom to be Alyssa's matron of honor, and a grinning Jake, complete with pirate hat, was Cooper's best man. Cooper's parents, stunned, flew in as well.

Phillip Preston walked Alyssa down the grassy aisle, with folding lawn chairs on either side. Eddie was the official "pig wrangler" for the day. Riley, Fang, Pepe, and the Pekes all sported brand-new bows, and Lafitte even managed to restrain himself during the ceremony as he perched on Danielle's shoulder.

And afterward, there was a killer reception at the mansion, with a band that played far into the night, tons of the most glorious food, and a spectacular wedding cake glazed with dark chocolate and covered with milk chocolate mosaic tiles.

But no one could stop talking about the pig.

"And you still get the million dollars, Alyssa, because the bet we had was that you would only be intimate with your husband," her grandfather said, his hazel eyes twinkling.

"I don't need it now," she said as she looked up at Cooper. "I think I have something worth a lot more than a million."

"My darling, it was a ridiculous bet, and I couldn't agree with you more."

That night, Cooper and Alyssa shared a suite at the St. Francis hotel. The following morning, they were taking a limo to San Francisco Airport and flying to Tahiti, where a two-week sail of the islands awaited them. She'd wanted him to pick their honeymoon destination and hadn't known that Cooper loved to sail.

"Captain Sinclair, eh?" she teased him.

But tonight, as Cooper unlocked the door to their suite and carried her inside, the only thing on Alyssa's mind was her husband's right buttock.

He'd been surprisingly modest about her seeing him naked since *l'affaire de tattoo,* but now that they were married, Alyssa knew she could demand her marital viewing rights.

"Before I strip down for you," he said, "there's something I want to give you." And he handed her a present, beautifully wrapped. It felt like a rectangular box, and as she took it from him, she said, "but you've already given me so much."

"Never enough," he replied. "Open it."

She did, and was delighted to find her original purple Mardi Gras mask from the bachelor party in December. He'd had it mounted in a Plexiglas box so it could be hung on a wall, the last vestiges of her night as Bambi, the exotic dancer.

"I love it!" she said. And Alyssa knew that every time she looked at that mask, she'd remember her first wild night with Cooper.

But he couldn't distract her any longer. "Okay, now strip!"

She sat back on the large, king-sized bed as he slowly began to take off his suit.

"Somehow," Cooper said, "it's just not as much fun when I do it."

"Speak for yourself," Alyssa said. "And don't stall, or I'll make you dance naked to music."

"Promises, promises," he muttered, and she laughed.

When he was finally naked, he walked toward her, still not revealing the tattoo he'd selected.

"Your turn," he said, and helped her shed her clothing with record speed. And then he was kissing her, and she forgot all about his tattoo.

Just before she fell asleep, she mumbled a sleepy, "Wait a minute. . . ."

He laughed softly.

"Turn over, you sneak."

He did as she told him to, and when she saw what was tattooed on his right buttock, she dissolved into gales of laughter. And he smiled, knowing he'd pleased her.

On Cooper's right buttock, as clear as day, was a small cartoon deer wearing a purple Mardi Gras mask.

"Bambi with a mask," he whispered as he kissed her, and she found herself suddenly not sleepy at all.

**Elda Minger** is the award-winning and best-selling author of dozens of romance novels, both series and historical. *The Fling*, her breakout single title, was published in September 2002. She lives in Los Angeles with her family, both two- and four-footed, and is currently at work on her next romantic comedy.

# The Fling

# Elda Minger

*Why let a perfectly good honeymoon
go to waste?*

After being left at the altar, Patti decides to treat
herself and her cousin Kate to sun and fun in
Hawaii—and maybe a good fling
instead of Mr. Right.

*Let the games begin!*

The girls begin to turn the tables on every man
they meet. One of them, however, winds up finding
the last thing in the world she was
looking for—a man worth keeping.

0-515-13372-8